A Lady to Treasure

MARIANNE RATCLIFFE

First published in 2023 by Bellows Press

A CIP Catalogue of this book is available from
the British Library

ISBN: 978 1 739 71016 3

Cover design by
Candescent

Typeset by
Typo•glyphix
www.typoglyphix.co.uk

Printed and bound in England

To Richard and Sylvia

Content Warning:
Chapter sixteen contains a
brief description of an
attempted sexual assault.

Chapter One

New York, July 1812

Where mathematical calculations were concerned, Louisa Silverton was never wrong. Yet, such was her alarm at the tale told by the company ledgers, she reviewed them a second time to be certain there was no mistake.

'Papa, can this be true? You have neglected to insure our fleet?'

'Do not concern yourself, Louisa. A successful man is one willing to take risks.'

'But we still owe thousands on each vessel. With British ships in our waters, I would rather mortgage our home than make such a dangerous wager.'

'A step I have already taken, to release funds to carry us through the next few months. Do not frown at me, child. I shall not change my mind.'

Louisa knew better than to argue. She was quite used to her suggestions going unheeded, her advice scorned as being overly cautious. As a child, she'd been nurtured not by love, but by numbers. Her father kept a good house but he was often absent and always busy. Louisa's neglected mother, who was subject to low moods, remained most days in her chamber, no matter how fervently her daughter pounded against the door with clenched fists. A more fortunate child might have found a friend among the servants, but Mr Silverton kept his domestics in constant fear of dismissal as a guard against complacency (or worse, a demand for higher wages) and it was rare for any to stay longer than a twelvemonth. There was no tutor or governess. Louisa's father was self-taught and wholeheartedly convinced of the merits of that method of education. Left to amuse herself with what was to hand, Louisa's first toy was an abacus and her earliest reading matter business receipts, from which she learnt to add and subtract. By the age of eight, she was performing calculations that would have troubled boys and girls twice her age. On scraps of paper, she invented vast fortunes, modelling her profits and losses using increasingly arcane calculations. No friend could have been truer than her numbers, for they did not lie and never shunned her company.

At fourteen, Louisa took up a book of company accounts and discovered several errors. Her father, observing his daughter might be useful, had her look over all his ledgers. It was like rain falling on parched ground. Such an array of numbers and calculations! Mr Silverton was a man of bold strategies and his moods could be traced to the value of his portfolio. Being as impressionable as most young girls, Louisa's feelings began to align with her father's. An increase in the value of their holdings would bring her a thrill of delight; a decrease would leave her vexed and anxious.

'Is there a means to increase our available capital?' she wondered aloud. To her surprise, her father seized upon her question with some enthusiasm.

'Indeed there is. It would rely entirely on you, Louisa, but I have confidence in your powers to accomplish it.'

Louisa felt a flush of excitement. Was she finally to be entrusted with a position of true responsibility within the company? A seat on the board, perhaps? Her father came up behind her and squeezed her shoulder in an unusually paternal gesture.

'Now that you are of age, what say you to getting married?'

Louisa twisted round to look at him.

'Married?'

It was an unexpected suggestion. Marriage was a topic they had avoided ever since her mother had run off with the handsome but penniless surgeon who attended her during her low moods. Louisa had been nine at the time. Her father had been more baffled than distressed, unable to comprehend how any woman could take such a financially irresponsible step. The whole affair had confused and upset Louisa, leaving her with a deep distrust of romantic love.

'Our need is pressing,' her father explained. 'Some of our investors have been frightened by all this talk of war into clamouring for the return of their money. If you cannot secure a wealthy husband, I may have to sell our shareholdings in the new canal venture at a significant loss.'

Louisa was every bit as distressed as her father at the idea of selling the canal investment. If it came to fruition, it would double their fortune. Who were these fickle investors, to put them to such inconvenience? But she was not yet quite convinced by her father's plan.

'Is it not more usual for the woman to bring a dowry?'

'I have not built my fortune by copying others. We need a like-minded fellow, one who recognises the value of combining assets. A man to whom I can bequeath the company when I am too old to run it myself. I have secured you a berth on the next ship to England. It is a country filled with men eager to seize the opportunities provided by our fast-growing economy. You will stay with your mother's relatives, Mr and Mrs Lowther, who have often invited you to visit.'

'Have they?' Until that moment, Louisa had been unaware she had any living relatives on her mother's side.

'I am confident they will wish to assist you. We must make haste. If we cannot assuage our investors, we must retrench, and I've no intention of going backwards. I hope you know your duty?'

'Of course.' It was not a role she would have chosen, for it did not align with her natural abilities. From her limited experience of the opposite sex, she'd observed that, unlike numbers, they didn't always add up. However, she knew the vital importance of liquidity and was gratified to be given an opportunity to prove her worth to her father. Should she succeed, he could no longer dismiss her ideas so readily.

'Reveal nothing of our current difficulties, Louisa. It is vital to play as if we have a strong hand. I trust that you will not let foolish notions of romance interfere with making a profitable transaction?'

'I will not,' Louisa asserted firmly. On that score at least, she was entirely confident.

Chapter Two

Northamptonshire, England, September 1812

The Lowthers lived at Athelton Hall, a red-brick Jacobean mansion whose roofline was crammed with sharply pitched gables and narrow chimneys. Having heard much talk of the manners and eccentricities of the English gentry during her long voyage, Louisa descended from her carriage with some trepidation. She did not want to make a fool of herself. Her Aunt Lowther, a large-boned woman whose cream muslin dress was spattered with remnants of soup and gravy, greeted her with such effusiveness that Louisa's chest and hat boxes had been carried away and the horses safely deposited in the stables by the time she was done. Louisa was grateful for the warmth of her aunt's welcome, although her cousin Eleanor's gentler manners did more to put her at ease. Unlike her mother, Eleanor paused for breath, permitting Louisa to speak, even if she was too exhausted after her journey to do more than express her gratitude for the invitation.

Eager to learn and observe, Louisa was soon amazed by the amount of time her English relatives spent simply amusing themselves. With a steward to manage the estate on his behalf, her uncle was at leisure to read his newspapers, or stroll around his beloved kitchen gardens. He treated Louisa with polite formality but said little except 'good morning' and 'good night', and Louisa soon learned that his 'how d'you do?' was not intended to stimulate any response. Her aunt, however, more than made up for her husband's taciturnity, and was as enthusiastic an advocate for Louisa finding a husband as Mr Silverton could wish for.

'We must have a ball, to show you off,' she said, the day after Louisa's arrival. 'I have agreed it with your uncle. I only wish we had a larger room. Perhaps it may be mild enough to use the terrace, although the summer is behind us. A closed ballroom can be frightfully stuffy. But I am putting the cart before the horse, for first you must visit all the important families in the neighbourhood. Eleanor, my dear, where should we begin? I suppose we must wait for Lady Melgrove to visit us?'

'We should start with the Davenports,' said Eleanor. 'It has been weeks since I have seen Sarah. She is so busy with the estate, she seldom visits anymore, and I am rarely well enough to travel myself.'

Eleanor suffered from a severe curvature of the spine that caused her left shoulder to be higher than her right and her back to be hunched. Her condition often gave her painful spasms, which would leave her greatly fatigued.

'Quite so, my dear. We have been great friends of the family ever since the first Lady Kenilborough came to the neighbourhood. The viscount has no son, alas, although in your case,

Louisa, it will not matter, for the estate is horribly encumbered. They were obliged to sell their house in town and now they live like paupers in the south wing of Kenilborough Hall. I heard they might be forced to let it out. What a shame that would be.'

'Sarah would never leave Kenilborough,' said Eleanor with a smile. 'She would be like those gallant captains who go down with their ships.'

'I hope so, my dear. I really do. But Lord Kenilborough's stepson will keep losing at cards.'

'If anyone can save them, it is Sarah,' said Eleanor with a wistful smile. Mrs Lowther placed a hand over her daughter's and gave her a compassionate look. Louisa was intrigued by this exchange, as well as the extraordinary level of hero-worship displayed by her cousin, who otherwise seemed a very sensible young lady. She was eager to meet its object.

'Poor Ann Davenport will be nineteen soon and they have never yet held a ball,' said Louisa's aunt with a sad shake of her head.

'But they shall come to Louisa's,' Eleanor said with delight. 'Louisa, what happiness you bring by being here.'

'I am glad to give anyone pleasure,' said Louisa, baffled but also secretly delighted by such unusual and undeserved praise. Her spirits were in want of lifting, for she could not help feeling anxious at being thrust into society. Although she had often been called pretty and her thick mahogany hair was universally admired, Louisa suspected her frame was too plump for true elegance. Added to that, she had attended so few parties, and never a ball, her father scorning such frivolities. Yet she was now expected to be witty and charming, accomplishments that had never been valued in the Silverton household. For the first time, she began to question her father's scheme. They had not considered how ill-equipped she was for society. However, with so much resting on her shoulders, she was determined to try her best.

The next day, Eleanor was in too much discomfort to travel. She begged Louisa to tell Sarah Davenport how much she longed to see her. 'But do not press her to visit, if she is too busy,' Eleanor said. Louisa promised to relay the message.

After an hour and a half driving along country lanes lined with trees whose green leaves were just beginning to fade to yellow and amber, the carriage wheels turned onto a gravelled track scarred with potholes. Louisa and her aunt were jolted quite violently as they passed beneath an avenue of mature lime trees. A cacophony of grunts and squeals broke across the sound of groaning wheels as they passed a large pig enclosure. Aunt Lowther pinched her nose between her finger and thumb as a strong scent of manure wafted through the open windows of the carriage. Louisa was unperturbed; the stench was no worse than that of the New York docks, where she had often helped take stock as her father's ships off-loaded their cargos.

Once they had left the avenue, the air cleared and a single-arch bridge of lichen-encrusted limestone carried them over a stream where a labourer stood in nankeen breeches, watching over a line of fishing rods. The basket by his bare feet was half-full of glistening, white-bellied trout.

'There it is,' said Louisa's aunt. 'What you see first is the east wing, which used to form the main approach. It is shut now, alas, along with the north wing, although you can still walk in the cloisters. The west wing is a complete ruin, but you cannot blame the present viscount for that, for it burned down more than a century ago.'

A grey limestone mansion in the severe Italian style rose grandly before them, atop a slight elevation. Two stories high and topped by a balustrade, it had four bays either side of a vast Venetian window, which sat above a carriage porch. Their driver eschewed this grand entrance and turned onto a narrow driveway that ran along the south wing of the house, whose sharp edges were softened by climbing shrubs and blankets of ivy. The southern facade was centred around an original Tudor tower. An oriel window bulged outwards above a round archway that was too low for the carriage to pass through. Beyond it, Louisa glimpsed a paved courtyard.

'Such a shame,' Aunt Lowther said in what she clearly intended to be a whisper, seemingly unaware that she had one of those voices that carried no matter how much she might attempt to disguise it, 'that we must come in through this little door, when the ceiling of the main entranceway was painted by Sir James Thornhill. It is remarkably fine — I wish you could see it.'

'But this is charming,' exclaimed Louisa, as a liveried footman led them through an ancient oak doorway and into a square hallway with an uneven brick floor. She imagined the thousands of footsteps that must have worn it down over the centuries, servants and lords alike.

'Eleanor would agree. She played here with Sarah when they were children. Lord Kenilborough is quite fond of it too, I believe. He and Sarah both keep offices here.'

They were led into a newer part of the house, where airy chambers were brightened by light from tall, multi-paned windows. Paintings of serious-looking men in court dress or gleaming armour looked down from heavy gilt frames. Here and there, patches of discolouration on the walls served as ghosts of other pictures, now removed.

'Now, Louisa, you are not to take it amiss if Lady Kenilborough appears cool in her manners,' said Mrs Lowther. 'We have not been good friends since she discovered I had made an unfortunate comparison between her and her husband's first wife. I do not know how she could have found out, for I am sure I did not venture my opinion to anyone besides Reverend Longbridge and his wife, and Mrs Chester and her daughters. I suppose I might have also said something to the milliner. But certainly, no more than that. I never meant to offend but I do not think Lady Kenilborough has ever forgot.'

They were shown into a morning room that was undeniably grand, although the silk coverings of the chairs and sofas were faded and the Turkish rug worn down to the threads in the areas of most frequent use. The lady who looked up from a game of solitaire on their entrance appeared in sharp relief against her tired surroundings. Her cerulean silk dress gleamed and her lace cap was dazzlingly white. She wore an antique ruby and diamond choker around her neck, despite it being only morning. Although her bosom was generous, she wore no tucker or chemisette to protect her modesty.

'I hope you are well, Lady Kenilborough,' said Mrs Lowther politely.

Lady Kenilborough nodded but did not cease playing her game, which Louisa thought extremely rude. Her aunt did not seem offended and took a seat without waiting to be asked, indicating with a tilt of her head that Louisa should do likewise.

'This is my niece from New York, Louisa Silverton,' said her aunt, by way of introduction. Lady Kenilborough paused her game long enough to look Louisa over.

'A colonial?'

'We prefer to call ourselves free citizens of New York,' said Louisa.

'I was not aware you had a sister, Mrs Lowther.'

'A half-sister, who I never met,' said Mrs Lowther. Not even her garrulous tongue could be persuaded to expound further on that unfortunate topic.

Their hostess took up a bell from a small table at her side and rang it with a vigorous motion.

'We have so few servants, I feel quite unattended,' Lady Kenilborough remarked as they waited. After some delay, a maid arrived to receive her orders.

'Fetch Ann and Sarah,' Lady Kenilborough commanded. 'We have visitors.' The maid curtseyed and departed with great promptness.

'It is impossible to maintain a decent appearance under such circumstances.' Her ladyship shuffled her cards. 'Those malicious gossips who make unkind comparisons with previous incumbents cannot understand the difficulties of my situation.'

A pretty young woman entered the room. Although her primrose cambric dress was so faded it was almost cream, its lines were elegant and showed off a pleasing figure. She hurried to greet them.

'Mrs Lowther, how lovely to see you. Is not Eleanor come too?'

'She suffers her usual complaint. But here is my niece, Louisa, who has come from New York to get a husband.'

The young woman turned to Louisa and held out her hand with a welcoming smile.

'I am Ann. Very pleased to meet you.'

'Where is your sister?' Lady Kenilborough asked.

'In the orchard. I do not think she will join us.'

'I insist she come at once.' Another furious ringing of the bell brought the return of the same maid, who was instructed to inform the Honourable Sarah Davenport that her mother required her presence in the large morning room. Lady Kenilborough then dealt herself another hand of solitaire. An awkward silence settled upon the group. Ann smiled encouragingly at Louisa, but Louisa didn't know what she was supposed to say. Fortunately, Aunt Lowther was not the sort to permit a silence to continue.

'How is your son, Lady Kenilborough?' she asked brightly. 'I hope he is in good health?'

'I cannot say so. Forced into the army against his will, the poor boy. That the stepson of a viscount must earn his own keep is a monstrous injustice.'

The maid returned and hovered uncertainly by the door.

'Whatever it is, out with it,' snapped Lady Kenilborough.

'Beg pardon, your ladyship. Miss Sarah says she must get the apples in before it rains and kindly asks Mrs Lowther and her niece not to take it amiss if she don't come in.'

'I know you will forgive her, dear Mrs Lowther,' said Ann, leaning forward in her chair. 'You know how fond she is of you. Only our close friendship would presume so much upon your indulgence.'

'Oh, do not mind us, my dear. I know Sarah means no offence.'

'Not for the world,' said Ann with great earnestness. 'Miss Silverton, I am afraid you must make do with our poor company.'

'I am happy to accept your assurance that no offence is intended,' said Louisa, although she did feel somewhat slighted. 'However, I have a message from Eleanor for Miss Sarah. How am I to deliver it?'

'I shall take you to her, if you do not mind a walk?' offered Ann. Louisa was ready to accept before Lady Kenilborough intervened.

'No, Ann. You must not leave me alone with Mrs Lowther. We have so little in common.'

Ann blushed and seemed uncertain what to do.

'Perhaps I could seek out the Honourable Miss Sarah myself?' Louisa suggested. 'Might a servant show me the way? Eleanor was insistent regarding the message and I would hate to fail her.'

It was agreed. Ann remained with her stepmother and the maid took Louisa out through the kitchen gardens and into a walled orchard, gesturing vaguely towards the back wall before returning to the house. There was no path, although a line of beaten-down grass between two rows of apple trees indicated where others had passed. Louisa followed it, ducking beneath narrow boughs that drooped under the weight of ripe fruit. The dewy grass plucked at the hem of her cotton dress which was quite sodden by the time she reached a handcart full of ripe apples. This was manned by a young boy and girl, both barefoot and wearing smocks with frayed seams. A half-filled reed basket lay by their feet and apples rained down from the tree above. The children found this a great game, giggling as they caught the apples and placed them in the basket.

Louisa peered up into the branches. A pair of legs encased in close-fitting buckskin pantaloons, tucked into riding boots with a brown roll top, balanced on one of the branches. The soles of the boots had been patched in several places and the leather above was cracked and grey. They were a woman's legs, she realised in surprise. Although slender and firm, they were too shapely to be those of a man. Distracted by such a shocking sight, Louisa did not notice a stray red orb flying towards her. It struck her on her forehead, just beneath the hairline.

'Ow!' she yelped in shock, clasping her hand to her brow. The torrent of apples ceased abruptly, and the owner of the boots swung herself down in one easy motion, landing on the ground with a heavy thud. Above the pantaloons, the woman wore a linen shirt with sleeves rolled up above the elbows, her front covered by a rumpled apron. She had brown hair, a few shades lighter than Louisa's, pulled into a simple knot from which several strands had sprung free. Her face, although not delicate enough to be called pretty, was striking, with a firm, square jaw and arrestingly blue eyes.

'Good heavens, I didn't see you there. Are you hurt?'

'The Honourable Sarah Davenport, I presume?' said Louisa, still holding her hand to her forehead.

'That title is not generally spoken, but I shall not hold it against you. Miss Davenport will do fine, or Sarah if you prefer.'

'But Lady Kenilborough⊠'

'My stepmother constantly reminds anyone within hearing of my rank, in the vain hope that one day I shall start to behave like a lady.'

Louisa removed her hand from her forehead. There was a tiny smear of red on her fingertips. She swayed and found herself gathered up swiftly and deposited on the lip of the handcart. The Honourable Miss Sarah whipped out a white handkerchief and dabbed at Louisa's forehead, peering first at the handkerchief and then at the wound.

'It's only a graze. Stopped bleeding already. Pip, fetch some water.'

The boy disappeared round the back of the cart and reappeared with a ladle filled with cool water. Louisa accepted it gratefully. She was thirsty after her walk and drank the whole lot down, unable to drag her eyes away from Sarah. She had never seen a woman so attired, yet somehow it suited her. It reminded Louisa of the time that short sleeves had suddenly become fashionable. It had seemed peculiar at first, yet undeniably alluring.

'Whom have I the honour of addressing?' asked Sarah.

Louisa introduced herself.

'Aha! The rich American cousin. Come to marry an Englishman.'

'I guess my reputation precedes me.'

'Mrs Lowther is a terrible gossip. No, not terrible, for she is extremely good at it. I expect she's already told you a thing or two about me. Am I what you expected?'

The corner of her mouth twitched in amusement and Louisa realised she had been staring. She felt obliged to defend herself.

'I was warned that the English aristocracy were eccentric, but I did not expect to find the daughter of a viscount climbing trees.'

'No, I expect you didn't. But the apples are ripe and our gardeners are busy elsewhere. Fortunately, I was able to enlist the help of Sergeants Pip and Lucy. Excellent assistants and, more importantly, happy to be paid in apples.'

The children giggled and shuffled to attention, giving an enthusiastic but untidy salute, one which Sarah returned briskly.

'At ease. Miss Silverton, are you recovered enough to walk?'

Louisa rose and stepped away from the cart. 'Certainly,' she said, although she could still feel a dull ache on her forehead where the apple had hit her.

Sarah slung the full basket onto the cart and grasped each handle, the muscles on her forearms cording as she lifted the heavy load.

'Back to the shed. Lead on, troops.' Pip and Lucy skipped ahead of the cart, swinging their arms with delight.

'Have you not a land agent to help with all this?' Louisa asked as she fell into step beside Sarah, who was moving briskly despite her burden.

'The last man my father trusted with the job was a black-guard. When I realised how extensively the estate had been mismanaged, I had the villain dismissed and took over responsibility myself.'

'But surely there is no need for you to do manual labour?'

'I happen to enjoy climbing trees. And apples fetch a shilling a basket.'

'Two shillings, surely?'

Sarah glanced sideways at her, whilst continuing to propel the laden cart through the grass. 'In London perhaps, but not at our local market.'

'Then why not ship to the city? You cannot be more than two days from London.'

The path of beaten-down grass rose slightly as they approached the kitchen gardens. Sarah eased the cart through the open gate. Louisa could not imagine herself managing half such a load, but Sarah seemed barely out of breath. Louisa looked back at the orchard, quickly counting the rows and multiplying that with the number of trees per row. 'You have two hundred trees and let us say your yield is three baskets per tree. For ten wagon loads, with a carrier's charge of six shillings and another ten per cent for handling, you'd be five pounds better off if you shipped to town.'

'You have a remarkable head for numbers, Miss Silverton. But five pounds won't save us.' Sarah swung the cart round and eased it backwards towards a large shed.

'How can someone with such a vast estate claim poverty?' Louisa exclaimed. 'Forgive me, I don't mean to be impolite.'

'The estate pays out well enough.' Sarah lowered the cart to the ground. 'But my stepmother and her son can spend it. And we have substantial debts. Do you like apples, Miss Silverton?'

'I prefer a peach,' said Louisa, recalling the hothouses of her father's mansion. With some surprise, she realised it was the first time she had thought of home since reaching England.

'That's because you've never had an English pippin fresh from the tree.' Sarah fished a penknife from a pocket in her pantaloons and plucked an apple from the top of a basket. With quick, sure strokes she cut it into quarters and removed the core. She threw a piece each to Pip and Lucy and handed the third to Louisa before crunching down on the fourth herself with obvious relish. Louisa bit into the flesh. The crisp, clean fruit was full of flavour and so ripe that juice spurted out of her mouth and dribbled onto her chin.

'Oh, but that is delicious.' Louisa dabbed at her chin with her fingers. 'I have never tasted anything so sweet and tart at the same time.'

'The trick is not to peel it.' Sarah offered her handkerchief to Louisa for a second time. 'Most people won't eat the skin, but the sharpness of it brings out the flavour.'

Louisa wiped the juice from her chin.

'At least it's not blood this time,' Sarah remarked as she retrieved the handkerchief. 'Did I say I was sorry? I'm not always good at apologising.'

'I don't recall that you did.'

The words came out a little sharper than Louisa intended, mainly because the Honourable Miss Sarah Davenport didn't appear remotely contrite at nearly knocking her out cold. Sarah looked at her blandly.

'The incident might have been avoided had you been paying more attention.'

Louisa bridled.

'If that is your idea of an apology, it is a poor one. I only came out here because you refused to receive me like any decent person would. I suppose it was too much trouble for you to dress properly?'

'You do not approve of my attire?' Sarah's amused expression annoyed Louisa immensely. She did not enjoy being laughed at.

'I have never seen a woman dressed so… unsuitably.'

Sarah unloaded the first basket from the barrow and placed it by the door of the shed.

'What business brought you out here, Miss Silverton?'

'I have a message from Eleanor. She was not well enough to come and hopes to see you at Athelton, if you can spare the time.'

Sarah chewed her lip. 'Tell Eleanor I'll ride over tomorrow. But it must be early. I have an appointment regarding a quarry.'

'You plan to sink a quarry?'

The sinews in Sarah's neck stood in relief against her glistening skin as she heaved a second basket from the cart. Louisa felt a cool droplet of rain land upon her cheek and noticed the sky had grown quite dark.

'I do not. I know nothing of that business,' said Sarah. 'But we have gypsum here and limestone and I have been offered two hundred pounds for the rights to dig it up.'

'You would be foolish to accept such an offer,' Louisa began. Sarah dumped the second basket next to the first.

'You are rich enough, I suppose, not to care about two hundred pounds. But for me it is the difference between discharging an obligation or acting with dishonour. I cannot put a price on that.'

'Everything has a price,' Louisa insisted. It was one of her father's favourite maxims.

'That is a sentiment with which I cannot agree, Miss Silverton. It begins to rain and I must get these apples into the shed. Pray send Mrs Lowther my apologies. I am sure you are better at them than I. As you have so obligingly observed, I am not fit to be seen.'

Chapter Three

On returning to Athelton Hall, Louisa repaired to Eleanor's room to relay Sarah Davenport's message.

'How did you like her?' Eleanor asked, grimacing as she sat up.

'I do not imagine we shall be friends,' Louisa said dryly. 'I believe I offended her, although I was only attempting to offer advice.'

Eleanor's expression was part amusement, part alarm.

'What did you say?'

'I said she was being foolish. She could strike a much better bargain for the quarry, but she cut me off quite rudely before I could explain. She seems a most peculiar creature.'

'I hope you did not say so to her face?'

Louisa placed a lyre-backed chair next to her cousin's bed and sat down.

'I might have mentioned the unsuitability of her attire. Who would not remark upon a woman in riding boots and pantaloons?'

Eleanor shook her head and smiled.

'I don't deny that Sarah is different from other women. But the same has often been said of me. When we were children, she was the only one who treated me as if I were perfectly normal. Where others would be cruel, or avert their eyes out of pity, Sarah looked at me and talked as if I never had this hideous lump on my back. And… there are other things, for which she will always have my love and gratitude.'

Eleanor's eyes grew distant.

'As she is your friend, I shall do my best to be civil when she comes tomorrow,' offered Louisa, albeit with some reluctance.

'She is coming? Oh, but that's wonderful,' cried Eleanor, coming back to life. 'I shall retire early, so I might be well enough to receive her.'

Sarah Davenport rode over so early that the Lowthers and Louisa were still at breakfast when she strode into the room, the mud-stained hem of her greatcoat brushing against the black and white chequered tiles. She wore no hat and the scuffed toes of her boots thrust out from beneath the hem of navy-blue riding skirts with each long stride. In her left hand she grasped a hessian bag.

'You'll forgive me for arriving so early,' Sarah said, as soon as Louisa's uncle had made his 'how d'ye do'. 'I have business this afternoon that cannot wait.'

'We are quite used to your ways, Sarah,' said Aunt Lowther pleasantly. 'We are happy to see you at any time. You've met my niece, Louisa, I believe?'

Sarah gave Louisa a curt nod. 'How is Eleanor? Shall I go up?'

'Of course. Louisa has been most attentive, but I'm sure your visit will cheer Eleanor immensely.'

'I shall come with you,' said Louisa, rising.

'No need. I know the way,' said Sarah briskly, but Louisa followed anyway, refusing to be cowed by such flagrant discourtesy. As Sarah took the stairs two at a time, Louisa saw that her blue skirts were divided down the middle.

'You ride astride?' she exclaimed.

'What of it?'

'Isn't it improper?'

'Less so than falling off, which one is bound to do if obliged to perch side-saddle. To say nothing of the fact I might die from such a fall — but that is of minor importance when set against male ideas of decorum. I suppose you are happy to accept such a ludicrous proscription?'

'Me? I do not ride at all.'

Sarah looked at her with astonishment and said nothing further until they reached Eleanor's chamber. She greeted Eleanor with an affectionate embrace, kissed her cheek and proceeded to arrange and plump the pillows so that Eleanor could sit up and be supported.

'Still abed at this hour? People will think you an invalid,' she remonstrated.

'My back is a little sore,' Eleanor admitted. Sarah dropped the hessian bag onto her lap.

'I brought you apples. Nothing so wholesome as a Kenilborough pippin.'

'My favourite thing in the world!' Eleanor exclaimed eagerly, taking an apple from the bag. Sarah fished out her penknife, plucked the apple from Eleanor's hand and began to peel it.

'I thought it was better with the skin on,' said Louisa.

'Eleanor, for some unaccountable reason, prefers them peeled.' Sarah handed Eleanor a slice of white flesh. 'I have often informed her of her error, but she is such a headstrong, obstinate creature, she will never listen.'

'And you are such a dear, kind thing to indulge such reprehensible behaviour,' returned Eleanor with a smile.

'Let's have some light.' Sarah strode to the window and threw back the curtains. 'It is such a glorious day. Autumn is by far my favourite season.'

Louisa blinked as golden sunlight burst into the room and flooded across a brightly-coloured Scotch carpet.

'Whereas I much prefer the spring, when new life blooms,' said Eleanor. Sarah shook her head gravely.

'I cannot believe I am friends with such a strange, unaccountable creature as you. Ann is the same. She does not like the cold and barely ventures out of doors after September.'

'She would not like New York. Louisa tells me it gets so cold in the winter the river freezes over. And they have snow drifts taller than a carriage. Can you imagine?'

'I am not blessed with a strong imagination. That's why I detest poetry, although you will keep trying to convert me.'

Eleanor took a lacquered comb from her bedside table and used it to pin up her hair.

'Louisa has told me so many interesting things. It has been a great boon to hear such tales while I have been confined to my bed.'

'I am glad of it,' said Sarah, and Louisa was surprised to receive a glance of approbation. 'I wish I could come more often, but we have been so busy with the corn, and now we have the apples and pears to pick. And there'll be no rest before Christmas, for I must continue the improvements to the drainage before the ground hardens. But I am becoming tedious. I'm sure Miss Silverton does not wish to hear farming talk.'

'On the contrary,' said Louisa eagerly, for this was exactly the kind of topic she relished. 'I am most interested in how your estate works. I prefer talk of business above anything else. I too, have little time for poetry, although Eleanor has been trying to convince me of its merits.'

'Have a care, Miss Silverton. I might begin to like you.'

Sarah stayed with Eleanor for over an hour. As she observed the warmth and ease of their conversation, Louisa felt a pang of envy, yet the better part of her nature was glad to see how much her cousin was cheered by Sarah's visit. Sarah took her leave as abruptly as she had entered, standing up and pulling on her gloves as she said her goodbyes. She was halfway to the door before she turned back.

'Miss Silverton, yesterday you said I would be foolish to accept two hundred pounds for the quarrying rights to Kenilborough. May I ask why?'

Although not expecting to be addressed, Louisa was never short of an answer when the subject was trade.

'The value of limestone has been rising for the last year,' she said. 'Depending on how much stone is to be dug out, you might be underselling yourself greatly. I would strongly recommend you demand a profit share.'

Sarah's brow creased.

'But then I must wait for a return. I have instant need of funds to repay an obligation that weighs heavily upon me.'

'You should negotiate for both. Depending on the expected returns, an upfront payment may be warranted.'

'You have knowledge of the trade in stone?' Sarah raised both eyebrows.

'If a commodity is for sale, Louisa is intimately acquainted with it,' Eleanor assured her.

'Then, Miss Silverton, I wonder...' Sarah clenched and unclenched her gloved hands. 'I was inexcusably rude yesterday. I am used to depending on my own resources and failed to see that you were offering advice. I cannot afford to turn down any help that may improve our prospects. Might you be prevailed upon to accompany me to my meeting? To act as my advisor?'

'What, this very day?' Louisa asked in surprise.

'If Eleanor can spare you.'

'Oh, you must go, Louisa,' cried Eleanor. 'If you can help Sarah, you would be doing me the greatest service in the world.'

'I shall ask Mrs Lowther for the loan of her carriage,' said Sarah. 'As Miss Silverton does not ride, I must leave my horse with you.'

Chapter Four

All was swiftly arranged. Louisa suspected that Sarah Davenport never did anything slowly, and she had barely time to arrange her bonnet and find out her gloves before they were on the road to Kenilborough. During the journey, Sarah quizzed Louisa closely about stone and quarrying. She was an intelligent interlocutor, mining Louisa for information as if she were chiselling nuggets from a lode of gold. Louisa realised she had missed such talk since coming to England. She was surprised when the carriage stopped beside a stile in a drystone wall.

'We are here?'

'We must go the rest of the way on foot.'

The path was overgrown and Louisa's skirts were soon covered in thistle burrs and goose grass. Her calves began to ache and she struggled to keep up as Sarah strode on ahead, making no concession to Louisa being tired and out of breath, if indeed she noticed it at all. Louisa was beginning to resent such apparent ingratitude when they rounded a bluff and entered a steep gorge.

'Here we are,' said Sarah. Louisa took a moment to examine the cliffs of grey limestone that soared above them. The sound of picks clanging against rock echoed around the sunlit gorge. At the base of the cliffs a newly constructed timber shack sat next to a mud-clouded lake. As they skirted the lake towards the shack, Louisa plucked a specimen from a pile of rocks that had been hewn from the cliff and examined it closely. Her father had paid a small fortune for the finest limestone when extending their New York mansion the previous year. Louisa had questioned such extravagance, observing that cheaper stone would serve just as well. Mr Silverton informed her that the value of making a grand appearance could not be calculated, particularly when attracting investors.

A thickset man in a battered top hat and threadbare frock coat emerged from the shack.

'Ah, Mr Peters,' said Sarah. 'Permit me to introduce Miss Silverton, my assistant.'

Had Louisa breath left to protest at such a demeaning designation, she would have done so. Assistant? As if she were merely some hired functionary! Mr Peters invited them into the shack, which contained only a rude wooden table and two crates that served as stools. A bearded man in labourer's clothes rose hurriedly as they entered, brushing the palms of his hands anxiously against the sides of his trousers.

'My foreman, Mr Andrews,' said Mr Peters briskly. 'Now, your ladyship, I understand you wish to come quickly to a deal—'

'My stepmother owns that title,' said Sarah. 'Miss Davenport will do for me.'

'Absolutely, your ladyship,' said Mr Peters smoothly. 'I have here a banker's draft for two hundred pounds, as discussed.'

He was far too eager, Louisa thought. And, though she was used to having her wishes go unheeded, it seemed a dangerous step for someone hoping to do business with the Honourable Sarah Davenport. He removed a folded paper from inside his frock coat and presented it to Sarah with evident satisfaction. Sarah crushed the folded paper in her gloved hands and threw it to the ground without even looking at it.

'I have considered your offer and find it substantially under-values the property.'

'I think not,' said Mr Peters, carefully retrieving the banker's draft. 'I have been as generous as I can. I have listed the antici-pated yields here.' He took a ledger from the table and presented it to Sarah. She took it from him and handed it directly to Louisa.

'Miss Silverton, what say you?'

'What does the young lady think she knows about lime-stone?' asked Mr Peters in a condescending tone. Louisa placed her rock sample on the table so she might more easily peruse the first few pages, which were filled with columns of numbers and calculations.

'I think that you have quoted for low grade limestone when here is the very finest. And I estimate the tonnage per year will be triple what you suggest here.'

Mr Peters' confident smile slid from his face. He shook his head so hard his jowls wobbled.

'I dispute that. I dispute it most fervently.'

'Then we have nothing further to discuss,' said Sarah.

'Ah, let us not be hasty,' said Mr Peters, shifting his stance. He brushed his fingers against his mouth. 'I might consider another fifty pounds, on top of the two hundred. If it is indeed higher-grade stone, it would be worth the increase. Yet there are costs, all of which I must bear.'

Louisa could scarce believe he thought they would be fobbed off so easily. She was sure he would never have spoken in that way to a man.

'And Miss Davenport and her family must bear the noise and disruption,' she said. 'We will accept nothing less than a fifty per cent share of the profits and three hundred pounds, up front, for the quarrying rights.'

'Dear girl, what you ask is impossible. It would take ten years to recoup such an outlay.'

He addressed her in the soft cadence that grown-ups used when addressing children. But Louisa was confident in her calculations.

'I calculate, at a tonnage of a hundred per week, that you would break even within six-months. A year at the most.'

Mr Peter's eyes widened and a flush spread across his ample cheeks.

'But... well, even suppose those figures to be correct, which I dispute, your ladyship cannot think it fair to demand half the profits when all the labour and trouble will be on my side?'

Sarah's expression darkened.

'You forget that the land is ours, as is the stone,' she said. 'I can always find another contractor. Do not take us for fools, Mr Peters, just because we are women.'

He swallowed in the manner of a boy forcing down his least favourite vegetable and then closed his eyes.

'You will permit me to confer with my foreman?'

'Of course.' Sarah and Louisa stepped out of the shack and moved far enough away so they could not be overheard. The clanging of picks had redoubled. Louisa suspected Mr Peters had already begun working the quarry. If true, that would give Sarah even more leverage.

'What do you think?' Sarah ran her gloved hand over the top of her head.

'If he is a businessman, he should understand it is a fair deal.'

'Why ask for three hundred up front? Is it not too much?'

'Such men must have their small victories. We must let him feel he has bargained you down. He will insist on two hundred, which you will accept with great reluctance.'

Mr Peters emerged, hands thrust in his pockets.

'Would you be prepared to accept a quarter of the profits?' he asked.

'The profit share is not negotiable,' insisted Louisa.

'Not negotiable,' Sarah echoed with emphasis. Mr Peters attempted to outstare her. He failed. He extracted his hands from his pockets and folded his arms.

'Very well. Consider it agreed. However, I cannot move above the two hundred pounds that we initially discussed for the rights.'

Sarah wrinkled her nose and blew out her cheeks. She then made a show of looking about the gorge as though she were thinking, before squaring her shoulders and holding out her hand.

'You strike a hard bargain, Mr Peters. But if you can have the contract drawn up within a week, I will agree to it, subject to my lawyer's approval.'

After only a brief hesitation, Mr Peters shook her hand with a wry smile.

'Pleasure doing business with you, Miss Davenport.' He turned to Louisa and bowed. 'Miss Silverton.'

He and Mr Andrews took their leave, disappearing down the narrow path. Sarah sank onto a grassy mound and was silent for so long that Louisa asked if she was well.

'Quite well.' She shook her head. 'Miss Silverton, you are an absolute wonder.'

'High praise indeed, for a humble assistant.'

'You will forgive me for any offence, I'm sure. I had no idea what I should call you in such a case and seized on the first thing that entered my mind.'

'I accept your apology. Assuming it is one. With you, it is difficult to be certain.'

'Miss Silverton, you have no idea how much this means to me. Not only can I now meet the obligation I have already mentioned, but if the profits are as you envisage, I can see a way to clear Kenilborough of debt. It will not be easy, but today you gave me hope. That is such a precious thing, after striving so hard, and for such a long time, without knowing if one's efforts will ever be enough.'

Louisa was astounded to see Sarah's eyes brighten with tears.

'I'm glad to have helped,' she said quickly. 'And I really don't care that you called me your assistant.'

She realised that the rare experience of having her opinions valued and of being given an opportunity to prove herself was recompense enough. It was also pleasing to feel that she had performed with some distinction.

'What would you wish me to call you, should you have the choice?' Sarah asked.

'I will accept the title of friend, if you would be willing to bestow it,' Louisa suggested rather hesitantly, for she was unused to making or receiving such requests.

Sarah sprang to her feet and seized Louisa's hand in a firm grip.

'Nothing would please me more. Nothing at all.'

Chapter Five

Sarah Davenport sank onto a walnut shoe-rack just inside the kitchen door, peeled off her boots and set them aside. The leather was so old, the shafts flopped over like week-old flowers. She had been out all day in the rain and, because of her leaky footwear, her stockings were sodden and chafing.

She could not recall when she had last been truly at leisure. Five years ago, she had questioned the price they had paid for a new carriage horse. Her father had waved away her questions, informing her he left all such business to his steward, and if there had been a mistake, he was sure Mr Kingsley would put things right. Sarah had insisted on reviewing the accounts and had uncovered a terrible truth. Their steward, Mr Kingsley, had been systematically embezzling funds, and tradesmen and tenants had taken advantage of her father's leniency. Worse, their income was insufficient to meet their outgoings, thanks to the extravagance of the current Lady Kenilborough and numerous disbursements to her son. The family finances were like a wasps' nest, with debt built upon debt, the edifice so flimsy that any sudden blow would bring it crashing down.

Sarah had been dismayed, and not only for the sake of her family. So many depended on the estate: their tenants and labourers, the young men and women learning trades at the big house, eager to improve their lot, not to mention the loyal retainers whose pensions would be lost if Kenilborough went under.

Immediate action had been required. Since her father lacked the will and her stepmother refused to admit the seriousness of their situation, it fell to Sarah, then only sixteen years old, to take the reins. Their situation was so perilous, she was obliged to close the east wing and lay off a third of their staff. It was a painful duty. She had grown up amongst these servants, and Sarah's late mother had instilled in her daughters a firm understanding of the duty owed to all those who served Kenilborough. In dismissing them, Sarah felt deeply that she was betraying a sacred trust, but she could not afford to be sentimental. She served notice to each chambermaid and under-footman personally; anything else would have felt underhand and cowardly and Sarah was forced to harden her heart against appeals for mercy that she could not grant. To give in, even once, would set a precedent for others. She adopted a stern demeanour, as the only means to accomplish such difficult tasks. A similarly resolute approach was needed to manage other aspects of estate business, since many tenants and tradesmen were under the mistaken assumption that a young female aristocrat was an innocent lamb, waiting to be fleeced. Sarah's brisk, business-like manner soon set them straight. Mr Kingsley was dismissed, and what little remained of the embezzled money retrieved. Tradesmen's contracts were renegotiated and properties and possessions sold off. Still their debts remained heavy, and Sarah often felt as if she stood on the brink of a well with a slab of marble tied round her waist. It was a constant strain just to keep from being dragged under. Yet now, perhaps, there was hope, after the successful negotiations concerning the quarry.

The clock struck seven and Sarah realised she had only half an hour to dress. She berated herself for wallowing in self-pity, which served no purpose. After making a rapid toilette, she hurried into the dining room, adjusting her still-damp hair. Her stepmother glared at her balefully.

'Why must we always be waiting for you?'

'I am sure Sarah could not help it,' said Ann.

'I believe I am on time.' Sarah glanced at the carriage clock on the mantelpiece. It confirmed her statement, although she had barely a minute to spare.

'You are not wearing gloves,' Lady Kenilborough remarked.

'I prefer to save them for when we have guests.'

Her stepmother snorted through her nose in a manner that reminded Sarah of Jack, her hunter, when he scented a rat in the stables.

'Your disdain for your family is evident. Coming to dinner with your hair wet.'

'I cannot help it if it rained all day.' Sarah was in no mood to exchange incivilities with her stepmother. Only Lady Kenilborough retained a lady's maid and Sarah insisted that any time Mademoiselle Renarde could spare from their stepmother was given to Ann. Not that it was any sacrifice, as far as Sarah was concerned. It astonished her how many ladies were content to waste such a large portion of the day being poked, prodded and combed like some prize heifer, merely to take dinner with their own families.

Lady Kenilborough patted her own hair complacently. It had been styled upwards in ascending layers and plaits. To Sarah's mind, it looked like an overbaked cottage loaf but she happily admitted her own broad ignorance when it came to matters of fashion.

'The weather has been dreadful recently. I wish this rain would stop,' said Lady Kenilborough.

'I agree with you there,' said Sarah, seizing upon some rare common ground. She knew how much her father detested disagreements and her constant sniping with her stepmother was unfair to Ann, who was always obliged to play peacemaker. 'The low fields are causing me some concern.'

'Will they flood again?' asked Ann with a frown.

'Do not say such things,' pleaded Lord Kenilborough. 'To speak of misfortune is to encourage it — that is well known.'

'I am sure all will be well,' Sarah said reassuringly, although they had already lost half a field of winter turnips due to rot. If the poor weather continued, they might lose the whole crop and she would struggle to pay the next instalment on their second mortgage. Although perhaps she might appease the bank with projections of profits from the quarry. It had been a rare moment of good fortune that had placed Louisa Silverton in her path. There had been a refreshing frankness to Louisa's words and countenance, coupled with a diffidence rare in such an attractive young woman. Her advice, too, had been astute. Yet Sarah had marched her across miles of countryside with no thought to what the weeds might do to her skirts. In general, Sarah had no time for regrets, but she acknowledged that, in this instance, her urgent need for ready money had led her to be deplorably inconsiderate.

'We should invite the Lowthers to dine,' she said.

'You would permit us to entertain?' exclaimed her stepmother. 'After refusing to let me hold so much as a luncheon these past three months?'

'I propose only a small affair. Just the Lowthers and Miss Silverton. There would be very little additional expense.'

'If we are to give a dinner, it should be for the Mulcasters,' protested Lady Kenilborough. 'Who are the Lowthers, to be considered above an earl?'

'They are our friends,' Sarah insisted, unwilling to admit that she had another motive for the invitation. Dinner would be an excuse to know Louisa Silverton better and to acknowledge her assistance with the quarry. Sarah had debts enough. This one, at least, she might repay.

'I am sure Joseph would prefer we invite the Mulcasters,' said Lady Kenilborough sulkily. Sarah's grip on her fork tightened.

'What has my stepbrother to do with the matter?'

'He has a few days' leave and comes tomorrow. I am vastly pleased. We see him so seldom now he is in the army.'

Sarah would rather entertain a swarm of locusts than Joseph Pickering. They, at least, would move on once they had ravaged their surroundings.

'I am sure he will be delighted to meet Miss Silverton,' Ann interjected, before Sarah could give voice to her sentiments regarding her stepbrother.

'Her father is rich, is he not?' Lord Kenilborough remarked. 'Mrs Lowther informs me he owns a dozen factories and a vast fleet of trading ships.'

With that vital piece of information, all Lady Kenilborough's objections were swept away. Why, for such valued friends as the Lowthers, she would even condescend to write the invitation herself.

Chapter Six

On a chilly evening, ten days after she had visited the quarry, Louisa and the Lowthers were bundled together in the largest of the family carriages and heading to Kenilborough, where they were to dine.

'The invitation came from Lady Kenilborough,' said Mrs Lowther. 'It must be on your account, Louisa, for it certainly will not be on mine. I expect we have Sarah to thank, for she has the last word on such matters. When Lady Kenilborough first came to the country, she gave a great many dinners, but Sarah insists they can no longer afford such extravagance.'

'Then we are greatly honoured,' said Louisa.

'An honour I am sure you deserve,' said Eleanor with a smile that Louisa returned. Despite their short acquaintance, she had become extremely fond of her cousin. On the face of it, they had little in common. Eleanor had a poor grasp of mathematical principles and no knowledge at all of stocks and shares. Louisa had attempted to instruct her on the value of buying low and selling high, to which lectures Eleanor listened with great patience — certainly more patience than Louisa had when Eleanor expounded upon the joys of Cowper or Southey. But their differences of opinion did not seem important. It was a new and pleasant experience for Louisa to let conversations meander where they would instead of feeling she must always be useful. To know that there was someone who cared whether she was happy or sad and who delighted in her company was an experience that had been missing from her life. She had attempted to fill that space with numbers and calculations of profit, but she realised now it had been like filling a plant pot with pebbles. Nothing could bloom without some nurturing affection. This revelation did not change Louisa's opinion of romantic love. After what had happened with her mother, she distrusted it utterly, but for the first time in her life she regretted not having a sister.

'Lady Kenilborough does little to resolve the estate's difficulties, that's for certain,' Mrs Lowther continued. 'Sarah has instructed all the local milliners to give her nothing on credit.'

'Yet I believe she loves her son dearly,' said Eleanor.

'Oh, she would do anything for Joseph Pickering, although he is a most undeserving young man. I'm sure Kenilborough's situation was not so dreadful until Joseph came into the picture, bringing his gambling debts with him. The first Lady Kenilborough would never have brought such trouble to her family. Those poor girls. Such a tender age they were when their mother passed. Such a terrible blow — you, Louisa, will understand that.'

She spoke the last words with great sympathy, and it took Louisa some moments to realise what she meant. When she was twelve, her father had received a letter from the mistress of an almshouse. Mrs Silverton, abandoned by her lover, had sought her protection. She was gravely ill and hoped to be remembered to her husband. Mr Silverton had cast the letter upon the fire. A month later, another letter, exceedingly brief, informed him that his wife had passed away.

'Let your mother's fate be a lesson to you, Louisa,' he had said. 'Trust only what you can hold in your hand. Feelings or sentiment will not feed you, nor put a roof above your head.'

It was advice she had always followed, yet now, as their carriage slowed to take the shallow rise toward Kenilborough Hall, Louisa experienced the vaguely discomforting notion that perhaps she was not feeling what she ought. But, try as she might, she found it impossible even to recall her mother's face.

They were shown into a different room to that in which they had previously been received, although it shared the same air of faded elegance. Crewelwork chairs and tapestries retained only buff and indigo threads, any brighter colours having long since been bleached away by sunlight.

To Louisa's surprise, Lady Kenilborough greeted her warmly. Beside her, Sarah seemed ill at ease, tugging at the puffed sleeve of a grey linen gown which might have been fashionable once, but not for some years. Louisa reflected that she had looked far more at ease in her apron and pantaloons. Her sister Ann's dress was of a more recent style and newer material, with a pretty lace tucker protecting her modesty. Lady Kenilborough had not felt such a step was required, even though her neckline was so low that Louisa quite feared for her ladyship's safety. To the choker, she had added a thick gold chain with a large ruby pendant that nestled provocatively against her cleavage.

'Miss Silverton, I am delighted to introduce you to my son,' said Lady Kenilborough. 'Joseph, this is the young lady of whom I was speaking earlier.'

'The delight is entirely mine.' Joseph wore the bright red coat of an army lieutenant and pressed Louisa's hand to his lips with studied gallantry. 'I hope you are finding our little country to your liking.'

He had sandy hair and long side-whiskers, and was not ill-favoured in looks, although his broad-chested figure was of the kind likely to turn to fat in later life. Lady Kenilborough, enlivened by her role as hostess, introduced her husband. Lord Kenilborough was a slight man with thinning grey hair. He had Sarah's blue eyes, but Louisa detected nothing else of his eldest daughter in his limp handshake and vague expressions of welcome.

Louisa was eager to ask Sarah if she had completed the deal on the quarry, but found her attention appropriated by Lieutenant Pickering. He made every effort to engage her interest, attempting several topics in turn, but Louisa could only think that his gambling had led to Sarah and Ann living in such a poor way, and found it impossible to listen to him with more than tolerable politeness. After she had given him a few short answers, he offered a stiff bow and moved away. Seeing Louisa standing alone, Eleanor joined her, bringing Sarah with her.

'So, you have met my stepbrother,' said Sarah. 'His only interest will be in your money. But I see you have resisted his charms.'

'Since I do not intend to waste my time on men with no fortune, it was not difficult,' said Louisa. 'Although he seems very much the gentleman,' she added quickly, lest she be thought ill-mannered.

'The term gentleman is often abused, but never so much as when it is applied to Joseph,' Sarah remarked.

'Sarah tells me the papers for the quarry have been signed,' said Eleanor. 'I do not understand half of what she says about it, but I knew you would be pleased to hear it.'

'I am. Very much.'

'You deserve all the credit, Louisa,' said Sarah. 'If there is any way I can repay you, you need only ask.'

Louisa raised an eyebrow.

'That is a dangerous offer. It is like giving out a banker's draft with the value left blank.'

'I am not afraid,' said Sarah with a smile. 'Have you anything in mind?'

'I do. It is something that would require great patience and forbearance on your part.'

'Oh dear,' said Eleanor dryly.

'If Louisa has a favour to request of me, she need only name it.'

'I would learn to ride,' Louisa admitted. 'It was not required in New York, but in the English countryside it seems I am at quite a disadvantage. If I cannot ride, I must beg the carriage any time I wish to go out.'

'Have you never attempted it?'

'When I was a girl. I fell off on my first attempt and was too afraid to try again.'

'The only way to prevent fear taking hold is to get straight back on. Eleanor fell during her first lesson but did not let that stop her.'

Eleanor looked at Sarah with undisguised affection.

'I was crying so hard I could barely see, but you boosted me back on and led me round the paddock until I stopped weeping.'

'Alas, I had no such friend as a child,' said Louisa. Her father, being engaged elsewhere, had ordered one of the stable boys to teach her. When Louisa had fallen off, the shock of hitting the ground and the unfortunate circumstance of landing in a pile of steaming horse dung had caused her to bawl lustily. The stable boy had run off, fearful of punishment. Louisa had been left to wipe her own tears, pick herself up, and suffer the humiliation of presenting her excrement-covered skirts to the maid to be washed. She had not tried again.

'I would be happy to instruct you,' said Sarah. 'However, our stables are sadly depleted. I was obliged to sell most of the horses last year, but Ann will not mind lending us her pony. My hunter, Jack, is too headstrong for a novice. I am engaged tomorrow, but we could begin the day after?'

'So soon?' Louisa was concerned that two days would be insufficient to pluck up her courage.

'The less time you have to worry, the greater our chance of success.'

They were called in to dinner and Louisa found herself handed in by Lieutenant Pickering. Since she was to be his companion, she endeavoured to make amends for her earlier discourtesy, but he carried his resentment like a second uniform and parried her attempts at conversation with a brusqueness that far outstripped her own earlier behaviour. Her father had always taught her to strive for a doubling of one's investment. On this occasion, she felt she had received an even higher multiple.

Dinner was served at a polished walnut table, oval-shaped and large enough to seat fifty. Their small party was quite swamped by its grandeur, gathered as they were around one of the narrow ends. Louisa could see nothing lacking in the fare that was set before them. The service might have been quicker had there been another footman, but the food was of the best quality and excellently prepared. Yet Lady Kenilborough was not satisfied.

'I instructed Morris to prepare a sirloin of beef,' she complained, looking in vain for such a dish.

'I told her we would do well enough with lamb cutlets,' said Sarah. 'It being the end of the season, we have a surplus and cannot afford to let any go to waste.'

'I like nothing better than minted lamb,' said Ann diplomatically.

'Am I not to be mistress in my own home?' Lady Kenilborough asked her husband.

Lord Kenilborough coughed and held his wine glass up to the light. Having examined it closely, he set it down and proceeded to cut into his cutlets as if nothing had been said.

'It is exceedingly tender,' said Eleanor.

'The lamb should be tender, grazing on our best parkland,' said Lady Kenilborough. 'They make the place look so vulgar. And I am sure there is no need to have a pig farm so close to our drive. Lord Melgrove would not permit his parkland to be so abused.'

'Lord Melgrove has not our debts,' said Sarah.

Lady Kenilborough's fork clattered against her plate.

'Can you speak of nothing else, Sarah? I am sure we are all wearied to death by this incessant talk of retrenching and parsimony.'

'I will keep speaking of it until you take heed, madam. We are only in September and your allowance is already spent.'

Lady Kenilborough turned again to her husband.

'William, will you not intervene?'

'Sarah, I beg you will be more polite to your mother,' said Lord Kenilborough mildly.

'She is not my mother.'

A footman in red and gold livery cleared away Lady Kenilborough's plate, his face impassive. Louisa wondered if he was used to such disagreements.

'I am always kept in the dark,' continued Lady Kenilborough. 'I am told the harvest was exceptionally good this year, yet we dine on scraps. I can only think that Sarah has been squirrelling money away for her own purposes.'

'That is unfair,' protested Ann. 'Sarah barely spends a penny on herself.'

'Ah, well, yes. Ann has a point there, you must admit, my dear,' said Lord Kenilborough. His wife, however, was prepared to admit nothing.

'What of this quarry that is to be dug on our land? I heard talk of hundreds of pounds exchanging hands.'

'That is correct,' Sarah admitted. 'We made an excellent deal, owing entirely to Miss Silverton.' She raised her glass to Louisa.

'How much did you get?' Joseph asked casually.

Sarah took a sip of wine before responding.

'Two hundred pounds, which I received only this morning. I am vastly relieved, as it means we can at last settle our debts to the local tradesmen.'

'Two hundred?' Joseph turned to Lord Kenilborough. 'That

is the exact amount of a debt of honour that I am obliged to pay by the end of the month.'

'A debt of two hundred pounds!' Mrs Lowther's shock and disapproval were apparent to all in the room, and doubtless carried all the way to the kitchens.

'Not again, Joseph,' said Lord Kenilborough with a sigh.

'It was deuced bad luck. I was up by a hundred guineas at one time. One more hand in my favour and I would have been able to square my debts and buy back my black hunter, that was sold without my consent.' He gave Sarah a dark look.

'Sold, like much else, to buy your commission,' returned Sarah, crushing her napkin between her hands. 'I told you then that Kenilborough would never pay another penny on your gaming debts and I will be as good as my word.'

Joseph massaged the handle of his dinner knife between his thumb and his forefinger but said nothing further.

'It does seem a little hard-hearted, Sarah,' remarked her father.

Sarah threw down her napkin. 'Would you rather Mr Logan be put out on the streets, along with his family? His rent is in arrears thanks to the sixty pounds we have not yet paid him. And Richard Gates cannot repair his wheel until he receives what we owe him for our flour. If none of you care about the morality, then consider the damage to our reputation.'

'Ah, yes. Mr Logan, indeed. It would be most unpleasant,' agreed Lord Kenilborough.

'Let us speak of something else,' said Ann. 'We must think of our guests.'

She spoke gently but it was enough to halt the argument in its tracks. Sarah placed her napkin once more on her lap and tugged at it in a futile attempt to smooth out the creases. 'Ann is quite right. We should keep our family arguments to ourselves.'

'Oh, do not mind us,' said Mrs Lowther. 'I find this most diverting.'

'I will speak as I wish in my own house,' insisted Lady Kenilborough. 'I am sure Joseph may do so too, for this is his home as much as it is Sarah and Ann's.'

'I, for one, will endeavour to speak henceforth only of uncontroversial topics,' said Sarah, her eyes landing for a moment on Louisa, 'although I am at a loss to think of any.'

'Perhaps we might begin with the new corn laws?' suggested Louisa with a smile.

'Or Napoleon,' Eleanor added quickly. 'Who can disagree that he is a much-maligned creature who has only the best interests of Europe at heart?'

Such jocularities did much to rescue what remained of dinner, although Louisa noted that Sarah contributed little to the conversation. When they were done, Lady Kenilborough rose and led the women to the drawing room. Instead of sitting with the others, Sarah took herself to a window and proceeded to stare out into the darkness. Louisa took a step towards her, but found her elbow taken up gently by her cousin.

'I beg you would leave her,' said Eleanor in a low voice. 'At times like this, she is like a kettle whose lid has got stuck.'

Ann went over to the harp that stood in the corner of the room and began to play, while Mrs Lowther attempted to draw Lady Kenilborough into conversation. The volubility of one compared with the short, disinterested responses of the other would have diverted Louisa, had not her eyes so often been drawn to Sarah, who continued to stand with her back to them, clutching her elbows so tightly that her shoulder blades formed sharp points against the worn grey fabric of her dress.

The door opened and Mr Lowther came in. He called across to Sarah.

'Miss Sarah, your father begs you will join him in his office.'

Sarah turned slowly and pressed her lips together. With a decisive lift of her chin, she walked towards the door.

Chapter Seven

*L*ord Kenilborough and his stepson joined the others in the drawing room, bringing the clinging odour of pipe-smoke with them.

'Where is Sarah?' asked Ann. 'Was not she with you?'

Her father's eyes flew to the ceiling and then to the window.

'Ah. Yes. She was indeed, for a short while. But now she has retired to bed.'

'She had a headache,' added Joseph with a slight curl of his lip. Louisa felt a jolt of intense dislike. It was wholly irrational, and quite unlike her, but there was something cruel in his expression at that moment that made her stomach turn.

'Should not someone attend her?' she asked.

'I will go,' Ann said, rising from her harp. Joseph waved his hand dismissively.

'I've sent one of the maids. You know what your sister is like when she's in one of her moods. Best leave her to calm down.'

Ann sat back down and resumed playing, the gentle, cascading melodies providing a pleasant backdrop without being intrusive enough to prevent conversation. Joseph took a seat beside Louisa and leaned towards her.

'I fear I was out of temper earlier. I hope you will not think too ill of me.'

'After my own lack of courtesy, it would be hypocritical of me to hold it against you,' Louisa admitted reluctantly.

He crossed his legs and casually brushed away a speck of fluff that had caught in the nap of his pantaloons.

'Yet I sense you still disapprove of me.'

'I have no admiration for gamblers. I despise anything that generates such high losses.'

Ann began to pluck out a livelier tune, but it did not distract Joseph from their conversation.

'I understand your father is a man of business. Is not that just a different form of gambling?'

Louisa frowned. 'I do not consider it the same thing at all.'

'Why not? In each case a man lays out money, hoping for a return which may or may not be realised, depending on circumstance.'

Louisa wondered if there might be some truth in Joseph's assertion. She had often urged her father be more cautious, although she had seldom been able to persuade him. But surely it was not the same as staking money on the turn of a card?

'My father works hard and uses his skill and knowledge to make a profit,' she argued.

Joseph flexed his fingers.

'It is quite the same with cards. Skill and knowledge play an important part.'

'At the risk of being discourteous again, does it not therefore follow that you must be deficient in both? As I understand it, you keep losing. Perhaps you should give up?'

'Quite the contrary. After such a run of bad luck the odds must favour me hugely. Now would be the worst time to stop. I only need a stake but Sarah will deny me my chance, out of nothing but spite.'

'I cannot believe Sarah is spiteful,' Louisa said.

He gave a thin smile.

'You do not know my stepsister. Let me give you fair warning. You may think she is your friend now, but she gathers up companions and casts them off in the blink of an eye. You cannot rely on her.'

'Joseph, dear, what is that on your hand? Why, I do believe it is blood. I hope you haven't hurt yourself?' cried Lady Kenilborough.

Joseph twisted his hand. The side of his palm was smeared with pink. He licked the thumb of his other hand and rubbed at the stain until it disappeared.

'It is nothing. I cut myself shaving.'

'It comes of not having a valet,' remarked Lord Kenilborough, plucking at his necktie. 'I would have sent Butterworth to help you, but the poor fellow has enough on his hands with me.'

Lady Kenilborough shuddered. 'I hate the sight of blood.'

'Then it is fortunate I am in the army and not you,' said Joseph blandly.

'I wish you were not, with that dreadful Bonaparte fellow causing so much trouble.'

'Well, I must stick at it, for I have no other income, aside from what my dear stepsister remits to me. It sticks in a man's craw to come begging every time he needs a little money.'

He leaned back in his chair and crossed his legs. Louisa could not help but notice that his hessian boots were so new that the leather creaked as he flexed his toes. She thought of Sarah's patched boots and, unable to remain any longer by his side, she rose and went to the window that had been vacated by Sarah. All she could see in the black panes was her own reflection. A kettle with a lid stuck. She began to understand how Sarah had been feeling.

Chapter Eight

The next day, Lady Melgrove paid her long-awaited visit to Athelton. Mrs Lowther, always on the lookout for visitors, was first to spy her ladyship's coach-and-four.

'Now, Louisa, you shall see the finest example of the English nobility. There is nobody more elegant and refined than Lady Melgrove.'

'I shall be delighted to meet her.' Louisa took a steadying breath. She hoped that her untutored American manners would not embarrass her in such exalted company.

'And it is not only in her person that she excels,' added Mrs Lowther. 'Her taste is widely acknowledged to be without parallel; her judgement would put many on the bench to shame.'

'I fear you do not put cousin Louisa at ease, Mama,' said Eleanor.

'Oh, you must not be afraid, Louisa. I'm sure her ladyship will be delighted with you. You are a pretty little thing, even if you do have the most peculiar way with vowels. I am only repeating what is widely acknowledged. Lord Melgrove could not have chosen better. They had not been married a year before they had Vere. And then Henry came along, soon afterwards. Two strong, healthy boys — no husband could be more delighted.'

'Even her womb is faultless,' remarked Eleanor dryly. Louisa choked back a laugh and felt her nerves ease.

'Although I pity any mother who doesn't have a daughter,' Mrs Lowther said, with a fond glance at Eleanor. 'I'm sure your father would agree, Louisa. Or did he hope for a son?'

'I do not know,' said Louisa, 'although he did once remark that daughters cost less to raise than sons, which he certainly meant as a compliment.'

'I cannot imagine why anyone would make such a calculation,' said Eleanor.

Louisa looked at her in astonishment.

'I assure you, I know exactly how much it cost to rear me. How else can one estimate one's value?'

Eleanor broke into a peal of laughter.

'You are so droll, Louisa.'

'I do not intend to be.' Louisa could not fathom why Eleanor had found her statement so amusing. It made her wonder if her upbringing, which she had never before questioned, had been outside the usual model. She recalled, quite unexpectedly, an incident from her childhood. She had been five years old; she knew this for certain because she had just learned to master the calendar, having discovered an old diary of her papa's. In it, the occasion of her own birth had been noted thus, in her father's neat and regular hand: *Offspring, 6lb 2oz, healthy, female. Surgeon's fee, 2$.* The notation had been sandwiched between a noontime meeting with the harbourmaster and a two o'clock delivery of twenty cords of timber to the warehouse. It occurred to five-year-old Louisa that she was in arrears to her father for the two dollars that it had cost him to bring her into the world. She knew the great importance her father placed on these pieces of paper. Perhaps this debt explained why he eschewed her company? Determined to make reparation, she found out some blank paper and began to construct a pair of facsimile bank notes. With deep concentration, she outlined the pictures in charcoal and scratched out the text using her sharpest quill. She completed these little masterpieces by inscribing daisies around the margins for, at that age, Louisa believed there was nothing that was not improved by the addition of a floral border. She presented her finished work to her father with some pride. After barely a glance, he returned them to her with instructions not to interrupt him unless she had a scheme for making real money.

Their visitor was announced. Lady Melgrove was attired in the very latest fashion but, in contrast to Lady Kenilborough, there was no excess. Everything was in taste and proportion, her manners as much as her attire. She made some polite observations concerning the weather and extended an invitation to the Lowthers and Louisa to attend an evening party at Melgrove Park the following day. Her duty done, she lost no time in taking her leave. Louisa was relieved to have survived an encounter with such a paragon without shaming herself.

'The Mulcaster boys might be just the thing for you, Louisa,' said Mrs Lowther. 'Vere takes a great interest in the management of the estate. Henry is quite the sportsman. Their estate is larger even than Kenilborough and makes a vast profit. And Lady Melgrove had thirty thousand pounds before she married the earl, some of which is certain to be settled on the boys.'

'Will the Davenports be at the party?' Louisa asked.

'I doubt it. I am sure Lady Kenilborough would be over as fast as a milk maid can pump a teat, but the families do not get along.'

'Sarah does not approve of the substantial enclosures Lord Melgrove has made, and continues to make,' said Eleanor.

'And I suppose she made her opinion clear,' Louisa guessed.

'I am not sure why Sarah objects,' said Uncle Lowther, looking up from his newspaper. 'It is Lord Melgrove's land after all. I am surprised Sarah does not do the same with Kenilborough's common. Enclosing even a portion of the land would give them another twenty acres. Planted with corn, it would bring significant additional income. Louisa, I am sure, will be able to tell us how much.'

'It would depend on the yield, Uncle,' said Louisa.

'Let us say five quarters per acre.'

For Louisa, it was a simple calculation.

'A quarter of corn at current prices would be eighty shillings. A return of twenty pounds per acre. Even allowing for wages and other costs, they could clear an additional two hundred pounds profit annually. I am surprised Sarah would turn down such an opportunity.'

'She insists it would be a betrayal of her tenants, who use the land to graze their own livestock,' said Eleanor. 'Mama, do you think we might visit Kenilborough tomorrow? I would like to inquire after Sarah. It is so unlike her to be ill.'

'I do not think you will have time,' said Mrs Lowther. 'If Louisa wishes to make a good impression, we cannot be late for dinner at Melgrove Park.'

'Would that be considered a terrible crime?' Louisa asked.

The Mulcaster boys seemed excellent prospects and she did not wish to start off on a bad footing.

'Her ladyship would be too polite to say anything,' said Mrs Lowther.

'Although we would not escape entirely,' Eleanor remarked with a smile. 'Such a transgression would undoubtedly be met with silent disapproval. It is the privilege of the aristocracy and Lady Melgrove is extraordinarily proficient in the art.'

Louisa felt that it was a risk worth taking to put her cousin's mind at rest, and she stipulated only that they set off early so they might be certain of returning in time for their engagement.

'You must go without me, for I cannot bear to be rushed in my toilette,' said Aunt Lowther. 'At my time of life, it takes considerable effort to make a tolerable appearance.'

After an early breakfast, Eleanor and Louisa set off for Kenilborough, where they were informed that Miss Davenport remained indisposed and would not see anyone. Eleanor enquired after Ann and was told she had taken a walk to the nearby village of Hollaston.

'Would you mind if we went into the village?' Eleanor asked Louisa. 'I might look in at the linen-draper's. Mama would be cheered by a new muslin, I am sure, and we could look over the silks and bombazines. And perhaps we may meet with Ann. But if you have any concerns regarding our appointment at Melgrove Park, we shall return home at once.'

Louisa hesitated, for it was already past noon and she wished to make the best of her toilette before their evening engagement.

Yet Eleanor rarely asked for anything and so she agreed they should go.

Hollaston was a bustling village a few miles beyond the edge of Kenilborough's parklands. Its main street was full of carts and carriages. Labourers in their smocks and leggings mingled with carters who strode briskly about with bundles on their shoulders, halting only to doff their caps at genteel young ladies who clutched at their bonnets against a rising wind. The press of traffic forced their coachman to stop short of the draper's.

'Any sign of Ann?' Eleanor asked. She leaned out of the carriage window, but with the street so busy and the wind forcing everyone to bow their heads, it was impossible to recognise anyone among the crowd. Their driver nudged the carriage forward before a butcher's cart further down the road sprung a wheel and everything ground to a halt.

'Let us walk,' said Louisa, helping Eleanor down from the carriage. With her stooped posture, Eleanor found even such a trivial task difficult, but with Louisa supporting her arm they were soon safely down and it was only a short walk to the draper's. The shop was so busy that none of the attendants were at liberty. Louisa looked over the crowd, but there was no sign of Ann Davenport among the patrons. Nearby, two young women were looking through some calico offcuts.

'D'you think this would do for a new smock?' one of them said to her companion, holding the dark brown material against her waist. 'I think it will stretch, if I pull my belly in.'

'You can't be always holding your breath, Aggy. And it's torn, see?'

'I can soon stitch that. They might give it me for half a shilling less.'

'I thought you were rich now his lordship has paid what he owes.'

'Rich? Hardly. Half the money Miss Sarah brung yesterday is going straight into Charlie Booth's pockets for fixing our water wheel. The rest'll have to feed us until we can grind all the corn that's been waiting.'

Louisa's ears pricked up. Sarah had been well enough to visit the miller, yet too ill to receive them. Had she and Eleanor been deceived?

'Them at the big house should think of that, when they keep folks waiting for what's owed. But they know we can't say nothing, or they'll take their business away.'

'Miss Sarah was very sorry about it. Swore she'd never let such — now what was it? Rears, or summat like that. Said she'd never let rears build up again.'

'Now you're talking nonsense. Miss Sarah ain't the sort to be 'pologising. Everybody knows that.'

'She did, an' all. I was right there. Heard her meself.'

'Well, 'tis only right she should. Tain't right, making folks wait so long to be paid. Mr Logan was two days shy of bein' thrown out of his cottage.'

'I heard Mr Logan got his dues, same as Pa, and everyone else in the village that was owed.'

'That's all well, 'til the next time, and the time after that. All the while, her ladyship flounces about in all them jewels. Someone should teach 'em a lesson.'

'Well, p'rhaps someone did, for Miss Sarah fell off her horse on the way down.'

'She never did!'

'She did, too. Her face was all bruised up, right here.' The young lady placed her palm high up on her companion's cheek. 'Pa asked if she were all right and she were quite short with him. Said she'd been thrown on the bridge coming into town.'

"'Tis strange, is that. Ain't no finer rider than Miss Sarah, even among the gents, so everyone says. I ain't never heard of her bein' thrown afore.'

'I tell you, God's justice is what it is.'

She put down the calico and looked askance at Louisa.

'Come on, there's fine ladies waitin'. We'll not get served 'til teatime, and I've to be back in time to give Bessie her afternoon milkin'.'

As the young women hurried from the store, Louisa turned to Eleanor, swelling with indignation.

'We have been slighted. Sarah is no more ill than you or I. I do not know what we have done to deserve such incivility.'

'I'm sure there will be some explanation,' said Eleanor loyally.

Louisa could only think that Sarah did not wish to see them but hadn't the decency to explain why.

'We should not heed common gossip,' Eleanor continued. 'It is such a strange tale. That Sarah should fall from her horse quite astounds me.'

'The only unbelievable thing about the tale was the notion of Sarah Davenport apologising for anything.'

'I cannot think she would refuse to see me, without some explanation. We are such old friends,' Eleanor said with a frown.

Then it must be Louisa that Sarah was avoiding. Louisa could not recall anything she had done to earn such discourtesy and could only think that Sarah had regretted her promise to teach her to ride and had decided that casual rudeness was the most effective way to relieve herself of the onerous obligation. It was a rejection that felt surprisingly painful.

'Lieutenant Pickering warned me she was fickle. That she picked people up only to set them down. I took a dislike to the fellow and so I didn't listen, but he was right.'

'You are upset,' said Eleanor, as an attendant arrived to serve them. 'I shall write to Sarah and find out the truth of the matter.'

Their business was soon done. On exiting the shop, it began to spot with rain. Luckily, their driver had found a berth only a few yards from the shop. Louisa and Eleanor were hurrying towards the carriage when Eleanor disengaged her arm.

'Ann?' she cried. A young lady in a green pelisse was just leaving the milliner's. It was indeed Ann Davenport, her cheeks made rosy by the strong wind.

'Eleanor! And Miss Silverton. This is an unexpected pleasure. What brings you to Hollaston?'

'We came to inquire after Sarah,' said Eleanor. 'We called at the house and were told she was indisposed and would see no one. Not even such an old friend as myself.'

Ann looked down and placed her forefinger under the strap of her straw bonnet and adjusted its position, although Louisa detected no misalignment. The spotting of rain showed every sign of turning into a downpour. Eleanor insisted on offering Ann a lift home. Louisa added her own pleas to Eleanor's, although she was growing concerned about the time. A detour to Kenilborough would leave them barely enough time to get home and make any kind of toilette. After only minimal demurring, Ann accepted, and they were soon being jolted over the cobbled bridge that crossed the river as they left the village.

'I understand your sister had a fall?' Louisa said stiffly.

'Ah — did she?'

'You do not know?' Louisa was so incredulous that Ann bowed her head.

'You must speak with Sarah.'

To Louisa's surprise, Ann burst into tears. Eleanor threw her arms around Ann's heaving shoulders. Louisa could only think that the warnings she'd received regarding the aristocracy were well founded. It was impossible to know what to make of such strange behaviour. When they reached Kenilborough, Ann insisted they come in.

'I will fetch Sarah,' she said.

They were left waiting for nearly a quarter of an hour. The skies had cleared and Louisa eyed the setting sun, her foot tapping the floor. Ann returned alone.

'I am obliged to say that my sister is unable to receive you,' she said, so morosely that Louisa's rising anger melted in sympathy at Ann's obvious distress.

'We must be going in any case,' said Eleanor. 'Tell Sarah that I hope to hear from her soon. Send her my best love.'

Louisa felt no desire to send a similar message. Because of Sarah's behaviour, they would be late for their engagement at Melgrove Park. A bad first impression from which she might never recover.

As they walked back to the carriage, Louisa had the oddest sensation she was being watched. She looked up just as a curtain at an upstairs window flicked back into place. She climbed into the carriage and did not look back as the coachman spurred the horses into a brisk jog.

Chapter Nine

Melgrove Park had something of the French chateau in its steeply pitched slate roofs and ornate chimneys. The pale stonework had been recently cleaned and any shrubs that might have threatened its walls had been ruthlessly pruned back. Either side of a raised central block, shaded colonnades looked out onto a vast forecourt. Beyond the house, prettily landscaped parkland stretched into the distance. The effect was soothing and contemplative, with long swathes of turf and planes of reflecting water broken up by lines of mature trees.

Louisa had been grateful for the efficiency of her maid, Leah, in effecting a rapid toilette. Eleanor, too, had lost no time in preparing and despite the young ladies returning to Athelton Hall just a few hours earlier, the party arrived at Melgrove Park only fifteen minutes past the appointed hour. They were received in an airy, high-ceilinged chamber by Lady Melgrove, magnificent in a puce gown and pearls.

Benjamin Mulcaster, Earl of Melgrove, was a man of florid complexion with a significant paunch. He was attired every bit as splendidly as the countess, but his offhand, disinterested greeting indicated all the manners within their partnership belonged entirely to his wife. Their eldest son, Vere, was tall and spare, saying little as he leaned nonchalantly against the back of Lady Melgrove's chinoiserie sofa with his arms folded. As Mrs Lowther and Lady Melgrove exchanged pleasantries, Louisa felt Vere studying her. She held up her chin, not at all afraid to be looked at. She was wearing one of her favourite gowns, a dark red sarsenet with a brocade panel running down the front, and Leah had made excellent work of her hair, artfully arranging it to reveal just the right amount of neck.

'You will forgive us for being a little behind our time,' said Mrs Lowther. 'I take full responsibility—'

'It was entirely my fault,' Eleanor interjected, relating how they had visited Kenilborough and been delayed by offering Ann a lift. 'I could not, in all conscience, let her walk home in such a downpour,' she finished.

'Your father is in trade, I am told?' Lady Melgrove addressed Louisa, as if Eleanor had not spoken. 'Of what sort?'

Shocked at such casual rudeness to her cousin, Louisa took a moment to respond.

'His interests are varied, ma'am. My father is a great believer in diverse holdings.'

'Would you favour us with some examples?' Vere asked, settling his grey eyes upon her. 'I believe there is good money to be made in timber.'

'We hold several logging licenses, alongside a dozen factories.'

'Does your father own the factories outright, or are they leveraged?'

His gaze sharpened and she felt like an insect under a magnifying glass. She wondered whether he knew something of her father's current liquidity problems.

'My father believes only a laggard waits for one venture to pay off entirely before embarking on another,' she acknowledged. 'All our businesses are leveraged to some extent. You have an interest in trade, Lord Vere?'

'I prefer that capital is laid out for a return, rather than sitting idle. And I am sure there are better returns to be had than in farming, if one knows where to look.'

'Louisa is extremely knowledgeable about commodities and such like,' said Eleanor. 'Your ladyship would be quite amazed by her ability to calculate profits and losses.'

Lady Melgrove gave only a thin smile. Poor Eleanor, it seemed, had been marked out for the dreaded silent disapproval. And all thanks to Sarah Davenport, supposedly her best friend. The door burst open and a muscular young man strode in, still adjusting his coat, which was stretched tight around his shoulders but loose at the waist.

'Good of you to join us at last, Henry,' said Lady Melgrove.

'Sorry, Mater. I was on the trail of a buck and forgot the time. I had to circle round the hazel thicket, for he was a clever fellow and got wind of me down by the lake.'

He strode up to Aunt Lowther and seized first her hand and then Eleanor's.

'Mrs Lowther, Miss Lowther, delighted to see you. How d'you do?'

Mrs Lowther informed him they were quite well. He turned to Louisa.

'And who is this fine filly?'

Mrs Lowther performed the necessary introductions.

'Henry Mulcaster.' The young man announced himself as if he were arriving at a ball. Louisa tried not to grimace as he squeezed her proffered hand so enthusiastically her knuckles ground together.

'From America, eh? Capital. What sort of sport do you have? I heard chaps speak of something called a buffalo. Does your father partake?'

Louisa informed him that her father had no time for leisure activities.

'Unaccountable. We must get him over here and show him some true sport, eh? The fellow cannot know what he is missing. Do you hunt, Miss Silverton?'

Louisa admitted she did not even ride.

'Not ride? This must be remedied at once. I am at your service if you require an instructor.'

'Sarah Davenport has already offered to teach me. Although I am not sure if she meant it.'

'You need not worry about offending Sarah Davenport. She will hardly begrudge a fellow the honour of being your instructor. And it would be no trouble to me. I ride every day, for I'm utterly impossible until I've had my first gallop.'

'Sarah Davenport rarely says things she does not mean,' said Vere. 'I am surprised she has the time to give anyone instruction. Although she does like to tell the rest of us how we should conduct business.'

'That young lady should learn her place,' said Lord Melgrove crossly. 'Throwing opinions about as if she were shying coconuts at the fair, when our estate makes twice as much as Kenilborough.'

'Her approach is haphazard to say the least,' said Vere. 'I applaud what she has done with the water meadows, and the improvements in drainage are long overdue. I also heard she sent several wagons of apples to London this week, instead of selling at the local market.'

'Did she?' Louisa could not help but smile.

'But she insists on selling almost half her corn to the locals, even though the rate is much lower. You will not fathom it. Miss Silverton, I am sure your father would never sell for less than the best rate.'

'Certainly not.'

'Louisa and I were discussing the profits to be had from corn just the other day,' said Mr Lowther. 'She was quite of your opinion, Lord Vere, about the enclosures.'

Vere waved his hand contemptuously.

'And Sarah is too lenient with her tenants. Take that fellow William Burrows, who has Howton Farm. Anyone foolish enough to break his leg should be left to the poorhouse. There are plenty of good men, hale and hearty, who would willingly take that land, yet she forgave him his rent for half a year rather than throw him out.'

Lord Melgrove, whose stomach had been growling audibly for some minutes, whispered in Lady Melgrove's ear.

'Of course. Now that we are all at last gathered, we may proceed,' said his wife, rising to ring the bell. They were led into another roomy chamber, where an extensive supper of cold meats, cheese and other delicacies had been laid out on a sideboard. Louisa and Eleanor hadn't had time to dine before coming out and both picked up their plates eagerly.

'Allow me to assist you, Miss Lowther.' Henry dashed to her

side. 'You cannot possibly reach the eggs. And you must have some ham. No, I insist you permit me to fill your plate. You cannot stretch so far.'

Louisa could see that Henry meant well, but she also saw that Eleanor was embarrassed to have attention drawn to her infirmity. Oblivious to Eleanor's distress, Henry piled her plate high and insisted she take a seat near the fire. Although the fire was generous, it was dwarfed by a gleaming marble surround which featured the family coat of arms in high relief.

'We must not risk you catching a chill.'

'I assure you, my lungs are in excellent condition,' Eleanor protested. 'There is really no need for concern.'

Louisa joined her cousin, hoping to rescue her, if she could, from such well-intentioned persecution.

'I admire a girl with a healthy appetite,' said Henry with an approving nod at Louisa's well-stocked plate. His own was piled high with slices of cold beef topped with a large dollop of horse-radish sauce. Louisa looked around, hoping that Vere would join them. Of the two brothers, he was by far the more interesting to her. Being the eldest, he would be in line to inherit the estate and it was clear he had a head for business. But he was at present engaged in a discussion with Mr Lowther. Lady Melgrove, however, did join them, along with Mrs Lowther, and began to engage Eleanor in polite conversation, with no appearance of any resentment. It seemed Eleanor's penance was over. Indeed, such was Lady Melgrove's present civility to her cousin, Louisa began to wonder whether she had imagined the whole thing.

'Shall we make arrangements for your first lesson?' Henry asked, after chomping down on a mouthful of beef. 'We shall have you jumping fences in no time.'

'I am not sure...' Louisa began. She felt no obligation to Sarah after the way she had been slighted but was uncertain of the merits of placing herself in Henry's hands. Such eagerness for jumping fences made her nervous.

'I see how it is.' Henry wiped his mouth with a napkin. 'You have heard Sarah is the better rider.'

'On the contrary, I heard she fell off her horse yesterday,' said Louisa. Henry slapped his well-muscled thigh with the flat of his hand, making such a loud noise that a robin, who had been resting on the outer ledge of a nearby window, was startled into flight.

'Sarah Davenport is the finest horsewoman in the county. I cannot believe she would ever be thrown. You've been taken for a fool.'

Louisa recalled the flickering curtain at Kenilborough.

'I rather think I have,' she said coolly. 'I believe I will accept your offer.'

'A bird in hand is worth two in the bush, eh? You could come tomorrow. I've nothing better to do.'

Louisa looked towards Vere. Catching her eye, he gave a small bow, but continued his conversation with her uncle. Despite his present lack of interest, Louisa was eager to become better acquainted with such a promising prospect. The proposed horse-riding lessons would provide an excellent excuse to visit Melgrove Park. However, they had engagements for the rest of the week, and Louisa must first procure a riding habit. An agreement was therefore made that the lessons would commence the Monday following.

Chapter Ten

*E*leanor sent a servant with a note to Kenilborough, inquiring after Sarah, but he returned only with a reply that Miss Davenport remained too unwell to receive visitors. Louisa could see that her cousin was upset.

'This is a poor return to such a dear friend as you,' she said, angered on Eleanor's behalf, 'to not even send a note.'

'I own, I am concerned,' said Eleanor. 'I hope all is well.'

Louisa said nothing. Joseph Pickering had been right. Sarah could be charming and her character was an interesting one, but her uncertain temper and lack of consideration for others were not trivial faults. Louisa had faced enough rejection in her life not to lay herself out for more. She was glad she had accepted Henry's offer — if she waited for Sarah to make good on her promise, she might never learn to ride at all.

After a quiet weekend, Monday arrived, but it seemed that Louisa's lesson must be deferred, for Eleanor confessed to having had a restless night and felt unable to chaperone Louisa to Melgrove Park. Mrs Lowther, being a woman of large acquaintance, was already engaged elsewhere. Louisa's uncle set down his newspaper.

'I shall accompany you. Vere Mulcaster has a foal he wishes to sell. I will look at her while you have your lesson.'

A few hours later Louisa found herself eyeing a large horse that seemed determined not to look at her. Henry was stroking the broad white stripe that ran down the horse's nose with an affection rarely seen on the face of an unattached young man.

'Mabel is of Irish stock and she's a fine girl indeed. She will buck a little if you pull her too hard by the mouth, and if she sees a squirrel she's apt to jump, but nothing to signify.'

'That is not altogether reassuring.'

'Riding is as easy as walking once you get the hang of it. Up you go.'

His strong arms lifted her up with ease but she landed rather awkwardly on the side-saddle and struggled to obtain a comfortable seat. She was much higher off the ground than she had expected.

'Sit up straight, shoulders back. Don't look at the ground. Off we go.'

'Wait!' Louisa cried. 'I am not ready. I have not—'

But Henry was already striding away. With a shake of her head, Mabel plunged after him. The unexpected lurch was enough to unseat Louisa and throw her at once to the ground. Her ankle turned beneath her as she landed awkwardly on the hard dirt of the paddock.

'Good heavens! Off already?' cried Henry, handing Mabel to a groom and hastening to Louisa's side. 'Are you hurt?'

Louisa grimaced. With his help she stood up, but when she tried to put any weight on her ankle, pain shot up her leg.

'I did warn you that I was not at all proficient.'

'Deuce it, I did not think we should come to this before we got to the jump.'

'You were planning to have me jump on my first lesson?'

'For certain. Why, I was over my first log within ten minutes of getting in the saddle.'

'You might consider that not everyone shares your natural abilities.'

Henry lifted Louisa up and transported her with admirable speed to a day parlour, whose dark oak furniture displayed the curved lines and floral motifs of the Restoration. Her uncle, who had observed the whole sorry incident, followed them. The commotion drew the lady of the house and her eldest son. Louisa declined Lady Melgrove's offer to send for a surgeon.

'I am sure I will be well, once I have rested awhile.'

Lady Melgrove rang for a footman and bid him bring a glass of sherry, to soothe Louisa's nerves, and some cushions so that she might be made more comfortable.

In truth, now the shock was over, the pain in Louisa's ankle had receded, and she felt rather embarrassed by all the fuss.

'I suppose Henry took his usual elephant among the porcelain approach,' said Lady Melgrove.

'And broke the porcelain,' Vere remarked dryly.

'I shall fetch a poultice,' said Henry, before hastening away.

'I do not think it is broken,' said Louisa, surreptitiously arranging her habit to appear at best advantage. 'Uncle, perhaps you might call for the carriage? I would not wish to inconvenience Lady Melgrove any longer than necessary.'

'Of course.' Mr Lowther disappeared to do as she bid.

'I am surprised you entrusted your safety to my brother,'

said Vere. 'One should always consider the potential risk of any undertaking. I do not believe you have profited from this particular transaction.'

'On the contrary, I have been well rewarded, for I find myself in your company,' Louisa said with a smile. Her behaviour was more than a little flirtatious, but her father always said one must seize opportunities promptly when they arose. Her approach paid an instant dividend, for Vere took up a chair and placed it beside her.

'I am pleased to see your mind has not been affected by your accident. You have displayed admirable composure.'

'We New Yorkers pride ourselves on our grit. That and raised sidewalks, which permit us to walk where we choose and leave little requirement for travelling horseback.'

'I take it you have set yourself against riding?' Lady Melgrove remarked.

'I have tried twice and failed on both occasions. I would be a fool to venture a third time in the face of such strong proof of incompetence.'

'Then what shall you do with your time?'

'I thought it was well known. I am here to find myself a husband.'

Had Louisa been more experienced in the intricacies of society, she might have gathered, from the slight lift of Lady Melgrove's chin, that she had said something rather shocking.

'And how does that business proceed?' asked Vere, lifting an aristocratic eyebrow.

'I have identified an interesting prospect, but it is too early to know if it will bear fruit. I require more information.'

'Such as?'

'Whether the other party has sufficient capital and, of course, whether he wishes to invest.'

'You see marriage as a business proposition?'

'Almost all of them are,' said Lady Melgrove smoothly.

'I agree, Mother,' said Vere, 'but it is unusual to hear that position stated so openly by the young lady in question.'

'My father always says it is better to take a calculated risk than do nothing.'

'You might not comprehend every side of the calculation, Miss Silverton,' Lady Melgrove warned her. 'There is more traded in marriage than money.'

'You mean land or titles?' Louisa queried. The countess offered only an enigmatic smile in response.

'Can you give details as to the investment required and the anticipated returns?' asked Vere, before Louisa could ascertain to which unusual commodities her ladyship was referring.

'Any sum would be invested in my father's business. The higher the investment, the greater the return,' she informed him.

'I am sure you have a minimum in mind.'

'Is it chivalrous to offer the minimum for a lady's hand?' Louisa asked with an arch smile. Vere stood up.

'If it is chivalry you're after, you had better try Henry.'

At that moment, his brother returned with a poultice and Vere politely took his leave. Louisa was disappointed to see Vere go, although well pleased with her morning's work. She admired Vere's shrewd intelligence and approved his straightforwardness. An interesting prospect indeed! Henry was pleasant enough but after a quarter of an hour of him fussing about her, making endless apologies and inquiries, Louisa was relieved when her uncle came to tell her the carriage was ready to take her home.

Chapter Eleven

S arah Davenport was descending the stairs at Athelton, having spent a pleasant hour visiting Eleanor, when Mr Lowther entered the hallway with his niece, who was limping heavily.

'Good heavens — you are hurt!' she exclaimed. In an instant she was by Louisa's side, and together she and Mr Lowther manoeuvred Louisa into the breakfast parlour. Sarah demanded to know what had occurred.

'It is nothing,' Louisa protested as they deposited her onto a chaise longue. Mr Lowther, after explaining what had happened, left to instruct a servant to make up a poultice.

Sarah perched on the edge of a nearby ottoman, dismayed by the danger in which Louisa had placed herself. Henry Mulcaster was an addle-brained fool and a fall from a horse could be dangerous. Or even fatal.

'What the devil were you thinking, accepting lessons from Henry Mulcaster, when I had promised I would teach you?' she asked.

Gingerly, Louisa lifted her leg up onto the chaise longue.

Sarah caught a brief glimpse of a well-shaped calf and delicate ankle encased in smooth white silk before Louisa covered her exposed legs with the train of her riding skirt.

'You also assured me we were to be friends, yet the events of last week proved otherwise.' Her tone was bitter.

Without thinking, Sarah's hand flew to the scab above her left eyebrow. The skin around her eye was still tender, although the bruise, at least, was gone. She would never have ventured out in public otherwise. The incident had been shameful enough without everyone staring at her. Eleanor, of course, had been too considerate to ask what had happened, but it seemed she could not expect the same from Louisa.

'I hope you are not put off by a little incivility,' she said. 'Friendship is not something I offer lightly.'

Louisa's nose wrinkled.

'It doesn't seem much of an honour when you treat Eleanor so abysmally.'

'Eleanor knows I love her dearly and accepts my faults.'

'Eleanor has a sweet temper and will accept many slights that others will not,' Louisa remarked.

'That is very true.' Sarah bit her lip. It was clear that she had upset Louisa by her sudden withdrawal. Such a strong reaction surprised her. Sarah was well aware she did not endear herself to society and was convinced her acquaintances were generally relieved when she absented herself, understandably preferring the gentler company of her sister. 'If I have offended you, then I am sorry.'

Louisa's expression remained frosty.

'Well, that is something. But there is no "if" in the matter.'

'You are not content with my apology?'

'It is a poor one. As we both know, you are not very good at them. You offer no explanation, no reason for your behaviour.'

Sarah stared at the chequered floor. In general, she guarded her privacy in the manner of a medieval fortress; gate barred, portcullis closed and drawbridge up. Yet something about Louisa tempted her towards confidence. It was a surprising impulse and one Sarah distrusted. Some things she could never bring herself to disclose, and certainly not to someone who was angling to share a marriage bed with one or other of the Mulcaster boys.

'I must warn you, I cannot be friends where there is a lack of candour,' Louisa added, her colour higher than usual. The pinkness in her cheeks only increased the vibrancy of her complexion. In general, Sarah didn't care a fig what people thought of her, but she found Louisa's censure bothered her, possibly because it might well be justified.

'That is a shame,' she said. 'I have come to value your advice. I sent some apples up to London on your recommendation, along with a wagonload of pears. The extra profit permitted me to purchase some new boots. See?'

She thrust her leg forward, revealing a foot and calf encased in shiny black leather. Louisa's expression softened a fraction.

'I am glad of it. Your other boots were a disgrace.'

'I see they are not the only thing that is in disgrace,' said Sarah ruefully. 'I hope the Mulcasters will suit you better. They are rich, at least.'

'That is unfair,' Louisa protested. 'Friendship and marriage are very different things.'

Sarah could not comprehend why someone of Louisa's sense and intelligence was so set on selling herself for money. By all accounts, she was already richer than most of the English aristocracy. Her need to become even richer was like those old men who collect old coins, or butterflies, and could never get enough. Utterly nonsensical.

'Money cannot be your sole object in life, surely?' she said bitterly. 'What of honour, or compassion? I assure you Vere Mulcaster has none of the latter.'

She had not intended to speak so sharply, but the idea of Vere Mulcaster casting his cold, assessing gaze over Louisa made her stomach turn.

'Vere Mulcaster is a sensible man with an excellent understanding of investments,' Louisa argued. 'I could do worse. And after your behaviour this week, I will accept no lectures on morality from you.'

Sarah understood that further conversation would be useless. Louisa, it seemed, was set on her purpose. She rose from the ottoman.

'Then we have nothing further to say to each other. I wish you every success in your endeavours. I recommend rest and elevation for that ankle. Good day, Miss Silverton.'

She strode from the room just as Louisa's uncle returned with a servant, a poultice and a pot of tea.

Sarah made it back from Athelton just in time for dinner.

'I suppose we should be grateful that you bothered to appear at all,' said her stepmother. 'Hiding yourself away for a se'ennight as if you do not care to dine with us.'

'You forget that Sarah has been ill,' said Ann. Sarah shot her a warning look. Only Ann knew the truth about what had happened and Sarah had sworn her to silence. She wished now she hadn't gone out at all. After a difficult morning in the fields with her labourers, searching for the few turnips that hadn't rotted away due to the near incessant rain, there had been that painful interview with Louisa, brightened only by a rather delicious glimpse of Louisa's ankle, doubtless now wrapped in a poultice thanks to that thundering oaf, Henry Mulcaster.

'Lady Melgrove paid us a visit earlier,' said Ann, rousing Sarah from a pleasing fantasy which involved Henry being pelted by rotten vegetables in the village stocks. 'She had a new Indian shawl which she permitted me to admire. I do not think I have seen anything more beautiful, even when we were last in London.'

'I am surprised you can remember anything from town,' said Lady Kenilborough bitterly. 'It is three years since Sarah permitted us to go.'

'What did she want?' Sarah asked.

'We are invited to dine at Melgrove Park,' her stepmother informed her. 'There, at least, we shall be assured of a good dinner.'

Lady Kenilborough eyed the modest joint of pork that Mr Hogg, the butler, had set before her husband. It was dwarfed by the vast platter, which was intended for much larger roasts. Although she craved a glass of wine after such a trying day, Sarah poured herself some water. She had urged her father to drink less, both for his health and to save money, and felt obliged to set an example.

'I hope you will enjoy yourselves,' she said.

Lady Kenilborough's hand flew to a breast adorned, as always, with her large ruby pendant.

'You would decline Lady Melgrove's invitation?'

'I cannot commit to any engagements at present.'

'But you will be coming to the Lowther's ball?' said Ann. 'You will not let me go alone, surely?'

'Of course,' said Sarah, smiling at Ann's alarm. 'Who else will comfort those poor fellows who cannot obtain a dance with you?'

'You cannot refuse the Mulcasters in favour of the Lowthers.' Lady Kenilborough looked to her husband. 'It will be seen as a positive slight. Lady Melgrove was most particular that Sarah was to be one of the party, although I cannot think why.'

'You surprise me, for Lord Melgrove detests me and I assure you the feeling is quite mutual.'

'The Lowthers are also invited,' said Ann encouragingly. 'And Louisa Silverton. That must be an incentive to attend, for I know that you think well of her.'

'That was before she encouraged the attentions of Vere and Henry Mulcaster,' Sarah remarked. 'I thought she had more sense.'

'I have already accepted the invitation,' said Lady Kenilborough, looking to her husband.

'Ah, yes. I think…' he began, with a pleading look at Sarah. Seeing his pained expression, she relented.

'Very well. I will engage for one evening. But it must be after the ball, for I certainly haven't time before. And in future, I beg my stepmother will consult me before accepting invitations on my behalf.'

Chapter Twelve

*L*ouisa's ankle soon healed. She was glad of it, as plans for the ball were well advanced. The Mulcasters had accepted and Lady Kenilborough had responded to Mrs Lowther's invitation with unusual effusiveness, asking whether the invitation might also be extended to her son. Although Joseph Pickering had returned to his barracks in London, according to his mother he had been so delighted with Miss Silverton that he would seize any chance to further their acquaintance. Mrs Lowther was happy to oblige for, apart from the size of her hall, which was smaller than she would wish, her only other concern was the scarcity of gentlemen. She told Lady Kenilborough that her son was most welcome, as were any of his fellow officers.

'You do not seem pleased by the prospect of a ball,' said Louisa as she and Eleanor looked over some silks and painted cottons.

'Not even the prettiest patterns will disguise the hump on my back,' said Eleanor. 'I cannot help but feel exposed at such gatherings. And I am unlikely to be asked to dance. Who would wish to be seen with such a strange, warped creature as myself?'

Louisa protested violently, insisting there must be many gentlemen in the world who would value her cousin's intelligence and sweet nature.

'If so, I am yet to meet them,' said Eleanor. 'Do not think I feel sorry for myself. I have long accepted my lot in life. How paradoxical that, with my fortune, I am free to marry for love, yet it is impossible to find anyone who could love me.'

'That is untrue!' Louisa cried. 'I have only known you a few weeks and already I love you. Why, even the Honourable Miss Sarah Davenport claims to love you, although she has an odd way of showing it.'

'I do not doubt the sincerity of Sarah's affection.'

'I do not understand how you can accept such ill-treatment.'

Eleanor sighed.

'I only hope nothing is wrong. Sarah only behaves in this manner when she is troubled.'

'This has happened before and yet you remain friends?'

Eleanor set aside a bolt of pearl damask.

'The first time was when Sarah's mother died. She hid herself away and would not permit anyone except Ann to come near her. The second was when she was sixteen and she discovered the extent of her family's debts. For months we barely saw her and received nothing but short notes in response to our enquiries. She finds it impossible to ask for help, even when it is most needed.'

'Do you not find such pride distasteful?'

'None of us are perfect, Louisa. And you do not know what friendship Sarah showed me when we were young.'

Eleanor turned away and her shoulders began to shake. Louisa, dismayed at having caused her cousin such distress, flew to her.

'Whatever is the matter?' she cried, taking out her kerchief to dab her cousin's cheeks and searching through her reticule in the hope of finding some hartshorn. Eleanor reached for her tremulously.

'When I was fifteen, Sarah saved me from… from a terrible fate.'

Louisa wrapped her fingers around her cousin's and indicated she should continue. It was some moments before her cousin could collect herself enough to speak.

'My father employed a secretary for a time called John Percival. He was kind to me. He told me he had a blind sister, and that he understood how people treated those who were not like others. Foolish, innocent girl that I was, I believed him. Trusted him. Fell in love with him. When he asked me to marry him, I was overcome with joy. But my father, who saw his attentions for what they were, sent him away. I, of course, did not understand and when John wrote to me, begging to see me, I agreed. He bid me meet him on the road, just beyond our gatehouse. That should have raised my suspicions, but I could only think how much I loved him. The appointed hour was early in the day, while my family were still at breakfast, so it was easy to slip out. He was there with a carriage and said he'd come to take me to Gretna Green. Despite my love for him, I told him I could never agree to marry without my father's blessing.'

'Dear God!' Louisa began to have an inkling of what Eleanor was going to tell her.

'He grew angry and forced me into the carriage. I pleaded with him to let me go, but he put his hand over my mouth. It was clear he meant to take me away, against my will. I have never been so terrified.'

'I can believe it.'

'And then Sarah appeared, on horseback. She ordered John to release me. Only fifteen, like me, but she gave her command like a sergeant major. John laughed and ordered his man to drive on. Sarah bid the driver not to move and she was so impressive, even then, that he obeyed. John pulled out a pistol, pointed it at Sarah and ordered her to stand aside.'

'He did not!' Louisa's heart leapt into her mouth. 'What did Sarah do?'

'Looked him straight in the eye and asked if he intended to murder the daughter of a viscount. If so, she felt she should warn him that the entire county would be up in arms and he wouldn't make it as far as the turnpike before he was arrested. Whilst he was hesitating, she pulled me from the carriage and set me upon her saddle. The thing was, she was shaking, just as much as I. I felt it through my clothes. But she carried me safely back to the house. My father and mother saw my distress, and I could not hide such a thing from them. They begged Sarah to keep it a secret. To have been lured out by such a man was so shameful that, if the world knew it, my reputation would be gone forever. And she has kept that secret, for never a whisper of rumour ever reached us. She may be abrupt and a little prideful, but a truer, braver friend could not be met with.'

Louisa was moved by the story and swore never to say another thing against Sarah in Eleanor's presence. 'I feel ashamed to have taken offence at a slight so trivial when set against such a history. Who am I to accuse anyone of pride when I have been so full of it myself?'

'I am glad you understand,' said Eleanor with a tearful smile. 'I see I was right to tell you.'

'I am grateful to be entrusted with such a confidence. Be assured of my discretion. And, in honour of your sacrifice, I will do all in my power to mend things with Sarah.'

Eleanor flung her arms around Louisa's neck.

'That is what I wish for most in the whole world.'

'Do you think Sarah will come to the ball?' Louisa asked, once Eleanor had released her from the embrace. 'I cannot picture her in a ball gown.'

'Ann loves to dance and Sarah would never send her alone with Lady Kenilborough. I can tell you exactly what she will be wearing, for it is always the same. A green twill gown with narrow skirts in the old style.'

'I imagine she would much prefer to come in her riding skirts. Or pantaloons, even.' Louisa could quite picture Sarah gliding around the ballroom in trousers and frock coat, moving with energetic grace. It certainly seemed more likely than permitting herself to be led around by a man.

'I'm sure you are right,' said Eleanor with a smile.

'But why always the same gown?'

'Since she has no thought of getting married, she insists that, as long as she is presentable, she need not waste money on new gowns.'

'Does poor Ann suffer under the same proscription?'

'Oh no. Sarah will always find money for Ann to have a new gown and new gloves, while Sarah makes do with a pair that has been darned so often there is barely any original material left.'

'This is yet another example of Sarah's virtue that makes me ashamed to have doubted her character,' said Louisa.

'I think now you begin to understand her.'

Chapter Thirteen

*T*he evening of the ball arrived. The candles were lit, the musicians had been instructed and every upright chair in the house collected and placed along the walls of the large hall for the benefit of matrons and those unfortunate young ladies who failed to secure a dance partner. A wagonload of lemons had been brought up from London for the lemonade and the scent of freshly baked bread had been wafting from the kitchens since dawn. Five girls from the nearest village had been outfitted for the evening in clean caps and aprons to assist the regular staff. Despite such excellent preparations, Mrs Lowther was not without some disquiet. Being of a friendly disposition, she had found it impossible not to invite even the least of her acquaintance. She had not anticipated quite so many would be able to accept and had spent the afternoon walking up and down the hall in the hopes that the walls might miraculously expand outwards and that a hundred paces might turn into a hundred and fifty. The hall remained steadfast in its dimensions and Mrs Lowther was left with no option but to order a pair of large mirrors be hung at one end to create the illusion of space, if not the actuality.

'We shall have to be good neighbours and not mind knocking about together,' she said with a sigh. Louisa, having no responsibilities to interfere with her enjoyment, looked forward to the evening with lively anticipation. Tonight she would have the opportunity to size up every eligible young man in the area, as well as further her acquaintance with the Mulcaster boys. She wore a new gown, a glorious cream satin with delicate gold embroidery, and her hair was curled artfully and threaded with pearls. The empty hall seemed to be awaiting the guests every bit as eagerly as Louisa. Warm candlelight reflected from the polished parquet floor and gleaming windows, whose wine-coloured drapes had been tied back so that the window seats might be made available. The wooden panelling that covered the walls had been softened by the addition of pedestals bearing vases bursting with alstroemeria and gladioli from her uncle's hothouse. The musicians were warming up in the gallery above, rising flute scales and the scraping of bows against strings adding to the sense of anticipation. The distant clinking of china echoed down the narrow hallways as servants made their final preparations.

'You have a partner for the opening dances, I hope?' asked Louisa's uncle, after complimenting her appearance. Louisa was delighted to inform him that she had. Henry Mulcaster had ridden across to Athelton Hall the day after Louisa's accident to enquire after her and had seized an early opportunity to beg her hand for the opening dances. Although Louisa had been hoping his older brother would make that particular request, she was happy to secure a respectable partner with whom to open the ball. Vere had enjoined Henry to request the second pair of dances with Miss Silverton on his behalf. It was hardly gallant, but Louisa had to admit Vere's efficiency, for it saved him the trouble of calling at Athelton Hall himself. She hoped that his request meant he wished to continue their negotiations.

The guests began to arrive. The local vicar, Mr Longbridge, and his family were the first to come through the door, along with his new curate, an eager-looking fellow with a high fringe. They were followed by the Chesters, an extended family of shopkeepers and traders in wool. The young men proved eager to seek out Louisa and, by the time the Kenilborough party had arrived, she had but one space left on her card.

Lady Kenilborough wore a short-sleeved gown of pure white muslin, low cut and dressed with bright red ribbons. It would have looked well on a young girl at her first ball but ill-suited a matron of her more advanced years. On her arm was Joseph Pickering, and a handsome stranger in a captain's uniform was escorting Ann Davenport. The red coats attracted the attention of several giggling young ladies. Ann wore a gown of cerulean silk, the skirts broken up by broad vertical stripes of white linen. Around her throat she wore a necklace of deep blue sapphires captured in a band of delicately wrought gold.

'Ann, you look exceedingly well. Is that a new gown?' asked Eleanor.

'Sarah had it sent up from town,' said Ann, putting her hand to her throat. 'And she insisted I wear Mama's necklace, even though it is hers, for she said it would look better on me, but I am sure it does not.'

'I cannot disagree with your sister,' said the captain gallantly. 'Indeed, I dare not.'

'May I introduce Captain Williams,' said Ann, with just the hint of a blush. 'He has recently transferred into Joseph's regiment.'

'I am most grateful to you, ma'am,' said Captain Williams, addressing Mrs Lowther, 'for permitting Lieutenant Pickering to bring a stranger to your ball. I am indebted to you both for the introduction to such delightful company.'

Ann's green eyes sparkled as she looked over the crowded ballroom. Louisa was happy to admit, at least to herself, that Ann Davenport was the prettiest girl in the room. Her own nearly full dance card was insulation enough against jealousy and Ann was a sweet girl who deserved to be admired.

'I see Sarah is wearing my old favourite,' Eleanor remarked with a smile as Sarah joined them, wearing a plain twill gown the colour of holly leaves. She wore no jewellery and her gloves had been washed so often they were more grey than white.

'I would not wish to disappoint the masses,' Sarah returned, after kissing Eleanor on the cheek. 'I am aware what is expected of me.'

Louisa attempted to catch her eye so that she might express, if not by words then by her manner, that she was prepared to renew their friendship. At last, by means of a delicate cough and strategic movement of her fan, she was able to gain Sarah's attention.

'Miss Silverton, I hope you are well?' Sarah's greeting was perfectly cordial and Louisa was encouraged by the absence of any resentment. Equally, it lacked the warmth with which she had greeted Eleanor.

'Thank you, I am. Although I am uneasy at being the centre of attention.'

'You need not fear. You look very well. I am glad to see your ankle is mended.'

'I was hoping…' Louisa began, only to find her hand taken by Joseph Pickering, who requested the honour of the first dance.

She was happy to tell him she was already engaged but could find no reason to refuse him the last dance on her card. He bowed and turned away.

'It is damnably crowded,' exclaimed Lady Kenilborough, fanning herself furiously. 'Where is William? I must have a seat or I will be quite swept away. Good heavens, is that the Chesters? No wonder we are herded together like sheep. I expect they fill half the room by themselves. Why must Mrs Lowther invite all and sundry? I do not see Lord Melgrove. I expect the countess had the good sense to stay away from such a badly handled affair. Where is Lord Kenilborough?'

Her husband was a few steps behind her. He looked about as if he might find a way through the crowd if he could, but nobody paid any attention to his polite cough and murmured requests that he might come through, assuming anyone heard him at all.

'I believe I shall faint if I do not sit down,' Lady Kenilborough protested, loudly enough to be heard over the musicians, who had just struck up an introductory air.

'Permit me to assist.' Sarah seized her stepmother's elbow and with a forceful 'pardon me,' and 'I beg you would let us by,' followed by an abrupt 'much obliged' and other expressions of gratitude, Lady Kenilborough was brought swiftly through the crowd and deposited on a chair next to an open window. Louisa contemplated following, for she hoped to speak further with Sarah, but the crowd closed quickly around her and she had not a Sarah Davenport of her own to clear her path.

Lord and Lady Melgrove were announced and there was a general hush as everybody turned to admire the leading personages of the county.

'They are late,' Louisa murmured to Eleanor. 'We must show our silent disapproval, must we not?'

'Good heavens, no,' Eleanor whispered back. 'Silent disapproval is the preserve of the nobility. Among the lower ranks, it would be considered churlish.'

'Are you not offended by their tardiness?'

'Not at all. What is sinful amongst mere mortals is considered a virtue in the aristocracy.'

Eleanor dipped her head and smiled in the direction of the Mulcasters.

'That hardly seems fair,' Louisa whispered, confused by such illogical and one-sided rules. 'Does nobody protest?'

'The English are taught never to complain. It is instilled upon us from the cradle. Besides, we take pride in our traditions, no matter how ridiculous. Indeed, the more absurd the tradition, the more it is cherished.'

'That makes no sense.'

'Rationality, being a recent invention, is not yet widely embraced,' Eleanor said with a smile.

Thus enlightened, Louisa joined her aunt and uncle to greet their most eminent guests. Lord Melgrove made the briefest of salutations before disappearing in search of a card table. Lady Melgrove was very civil, and Louisa guessed she must be well used to making amends for her husband's rudeness. Lord Vere wore an immaculately brushed coat and highly polished boots. His spare figure was not as fine as that of his more sporting brother, but Louisa felt that the wife of Vere Mulcaster would have no reason to be ashamed of his appearance or his manners.

The arrival of the Mulcasters meant that dancing could begin. The musicians struck up a reel and Henry promptly took Louisa to the top of the set, followed by Ann and Captain Williams. There was some jostling for position beneath them, the room being so full, but at last the fortunate ladies with partners were separated from those who must sit and watch, and they began. Louisa soon regretted her choice of opening partner as she found herself flung about by Henry so dreadfully that her ankles were in as much peril as they had been when horse riding. He seemed unaware of his own strength and, while she could not fault his enthusiasm, his execution left much to be desired.

'What capital good sport this is,' he said, spinning her around so heartily that she almost overbalanced. 'I shall be as blown as if I'd ridden the hunt all day by the time we are finished.'

'Indeed,' said Louisa. 'Perhaps we might take the next dance more sedately? We are not all sportsmen.'

'Nonsense,' Henry cried. 'You'll soon catch the hang of it. Do they not have dancing where you come from?'

'None that are executed in such a manner.'

He promenaded her to the edge of the room and back so rapidly that she had to skip to keep up with him. The second dance, thankfully, was an Allemande, and not even Henry could make that into a gallop, although he tried his very best.

'I am surprised nobody has asked Sarah Davenport to dance,' Louisa remarked, observing Sarah sitting with Lady Kenilborough. 'She is quite handsome, don't you think, in her own particular way? And a viscount's daughter — were she in New York, she would never be without a partner.'

'Oh yes,' said Henry. 'She has an excellent figure. Fine proportions and strong shoulders. Vere and I have often admired it. I suppose the gentlemen are afraid to ask her. They are fools, for nobody speaks better about horses than Sarah. I shall ask her, just as soon as we are done.'

Louisa wished then that she had said nothing. Inflicting Henry on Sarah was unlikely to assist in the restoration of their friendship. At last the music stopped and her torment was ended. Henry handed her over to his brother. Vere moved with sedate economy, a welcome antidote to Henry's enthusiastic capering.

'How did you find dancing with my brother?' he asked.

'Exhausting.'

'I am relieved to see you survived uninjured, on this occasion.'

'I own that I had not considered there would be any risk to my wellbeing at a ball.'

'Reels are fraught with danger. I prefer a quadrille. Much safer.'

'Is that why you did not choose to dance until now?'

'Perhaps I do not care to stand up with any other lady?'

Louisa was delighted. This was a promising beginning.

'Have a care, Lord Vere — that sounded dangerously like flattery.'

'You are mistaken. I expressly wished to speak with you and find this the most convenient way to achieve that aim. I have been considering your proposition. This investment that I would make, as part of the marriage settlement — why must there be any marriage at all? If I chose, could I not invest in your father's company myself, without the encumbrance of marriage?'

'It would not only be an investment, but an alliance. In joining our fortunes, we will both be richer. At five percent, ten thousand pounds will return five hundred a year, but twenty thousand returns a thousand, for no extra risk or effort. And my father is never satisfied with five percent.'

'But the returns would not be entirely mine and nothing is guaranteed, especially with this ridiculous war between our countries. If I may be candid, it seems you are demanding payment for entry into the family business.'

'Is that not what happened with your mother?' Louisa returned briskly. 'We are being candid, are we not? Didn't she bring thirty thousand pounds to your estate?'

'For which she received a title and a home that few can boast of. Whereas I would be degrading myself into a family with no name and a scandalous history. I have been making enquiries. To compare my mother's marriage with this case is like trading a diamond necklace for a sack of turnips.'

Louisa could not bring herself to respond to such a comment and they walked up and down the dance in silence.

'I see that I have offended you,' said Vere.

'I doubt any young lady would take kindly to being likened to a sack of turnips.'

'I thought you were a sensible woman who was happy to speak of such matters in financial terms.'

'I take it then, that you decline any alliance?'

'Most emphatically. I hope that does not cause you any distress?'

'No indeed,' returned Louisa, although she could not deny that she felt something in her breast that pained her. Could it be that she had feelings for Vere? She looked at his calm face, his smile untouched by warmth. His cold judgement disgusted her. No, her heart had not been touched. But her pride had certainly been wounded by such an abrupt dismissal. And his allusion to her mother's scandal — that was painful and unexpected. And, she thought, ungentlemanly.

Chapter Fourteen

*S*arah detested balls. There was nothing to do but sit around and drink lemonade. Dancing was scarcely less tedious, for then one was forced into talking polite nonsense. Her time would be much better spent doing something useful, such as calculating rents, or planning crop rotations. At least Ann appeared to be enjoying herself, unlike poor Louisa Silverton, flung about so recklessly by that oaf, Henry Mulcaster. If Sarah had been a man, she would have stepped in, but she had been forced to sit by quietly and wring her hands together in lieu of wringing Henry's neck. Louisa looked exceedingly pretty with her fine gown and dark hair entwined with pearls and deserved better treatment. Captain Williams, she observed, was a much more attentive partner. He seemed a cheerful, well-meaning fellow and Sarah had been gratified to see him take Eleanor to the floor, a gesture that she knew her friend would feel deeply.

'May I have this dance?'

She was surprised to be addressed by Vere Mulcaster. Moments ago, he had been dancing with Louisa Silverton, who was now standing alone among the dancing couples looking confused, her face ashen. Sarah accepted his offer reluctantly. She envisaged no pleasure in dancing, but supposed it was preferable to spending any more time seated next to her stepmother.

'You should make more effort to please Lady Kenilborough,' said Vere, as he led her towards the top of the set. 'If you were better friends, she might be less strenuous in her efforts to supplant you and Ann in favour of her son.'

'She cannot harm us. The inheritance of Kenilborough has always been secured to the bloodline by deeds of settlement.'

'I would advise you to seek assurances that your father signed such a settlement and, if so, confirm its duration.'

'My father would not leave something so important to chance. Are we to dance, or did you only ask me so that you could lecture me?'

'You know your father best of course.' He cast a look in the direction of Lady Kenilborough. 'Even with a deed covering the house and estate, your father may dispose of his remaining assets as he pleases, and you can be sure he is importuned frequently in favour of your stepbrother.'

The dance began, and for some moments the steps took them apart from each other.

'My father would not be so perverse as to pass down Kenilborough without those possessions belonging to it,' Sarah insisted, when she was back in his company. 'A house without its furniture? Without the paintings and tapestries that delineate our family's history? Most gentlemen aim to please their dance partner. This is a poor beginning.'

'I regret my advice is unwelcome. I think only of your interests. You must know that I admire you greatly.'

'I know no such thing. We rarely speak except to argue.'

'I never waste time debating with people I do not respect. I assure you, I shall not speak of enclosures tonight. I promised my mother we should not disagree, and I plan to avoid those topics where we are in dispute.'

'Then what on earth are we say to one another?'

'I have a subject in mind, one I flatter myself you will be gratified to hear.'

'You set yourself quite the challenge.'

Once more the movements of the dance parted them, and then brought them back together.

'I will bring myself at once to the point,' said Vere. 'I propose you and I join the estates of Kenilborough and Melgrove Park by marriage.'

Sarah was so astonished by his utterly unexpected declaration that, for a moment, she was unable to speak, and was grateful that the dance was simple enough that she could follow the steps without conscious thought.

'You are surprised,' Vere remarked.

'I am. I had thought you interested in Louisa Silverton.'

His lip curled in a manner that made Sarah want to strike him.

'The colonial upstart? So eager to throw herself at me. I put her in her place. I suppose you know that her mother ran off with her surgeon? It was quite the scandal.'

He reached for her hand, but she snatched it away.

'I did not. What business is it of mine? Besides, Louisa Silverton is not to blame for the faults of her parents.'

Once more the dance separated them, which, Sarah thought, was fortunate for Vere. Poor Louisa, to have been on the receiving end of Vere's barbs. No wonder she had looked so pale when they had parted. She scanned the room for Louisa's pearl-bejewelled hair but was unable to find it among the crowd.

'Let us return to the topic at hand,' said Vere, as the dance brought them back together. 'I had thought my offer would be welcome, especially after the recent loss of your turnip crop. It is true we have never been the best of friends, but you have qualities I admire. With my guidance and capital, you could restore the fortunes of Kenilborough. Together, our two estates would command considerable respect. Your lineage cannot be faulted. I flatter myself the same is true of mine. And,' he added in a lower voice, 'I assure you that, beyond the getting of an heir, I would not trouble you with those duties that generally fall to man and wife. My tastes lie elsewhere as, I suspect, do yours.'

Sarah pressed her lips together. Even if, at that moment, she was picturing a certain attractive American in a satin gown, a shapely bosom swelling above a gilded neckline, she refused to blush like a schoolgirl in front of Vere Mulcaster.

'As part of the marriage settlement, I would ensure the inheritance of Kenilborough was secured for our heirs,' he continued. 'You need no longer be concerned about Lady Kenilborough's stratagems. Ann would always be welcome at Melgrove, or Kenilborough, should we choose to live there once your father is no longer with us. I must, however, stipulate that Joseph Pickering never set foot in the house once it is ours. He is a detestable man.'

'You would find no disagreement from me there,' Sarah said, roused into speaking at last. 'But I have resolved never to marry.' The idea of vowing to love and obey Vere Mulcaster repulsed her. And yet, could she afford to refuse an offer that would save her family from possible ruin? Could she really be so selfish?

'Do not answer me now,' Vere said, as if reading her thoughts. 'I am sure that, with time, the merits of my proposal will become apparent. You are too intelligent to dismiss them out of hand.'

The dance ended, and Sarah was glad to walk away. Her emotions had seldom been in such turmoil. So many conflicting ideas strove for dominance: detestation of Vere, pity for Louisa, dread that she might, at some point, be forced to accept Vere's offer. Most disturbing of all was the way her body had reacted so strongly to the image of Louisa in her mind. It had taken everything in her power to control herself and remain impassive under Vere's penetrating gaze.

Chapter Fifteen

*L*ouisa's next dance was with the young curate from the village, who was eager to lecture her on the merits of spirituality and charity amongst the rich, and generously offered hints as to which ambitious young churchman might be the worthiest recipient of such charity. He was followed by George Chester, the eldest of the Chester boys, who paid his attentions in the style of a fellow who had ventured a few shillings on a bet at extraordinarily long odds, knowing that his horse was lame. As she was gently but firmly dashing the hopes of the intrepid young Chester, Louisa noticed that Sarah was dancing. In her dark green dress, she stood out from the other young ladies, most of whom were wearing white or pale colours like Louisa. The tight lines of her dress revealed her slender hips as she danced and, although her bosom was not as full as Louisa's, it was sufficient to soften her otherwise lean frame. To Louisa's surprise, Sarah was accompanied by Vere Mulcaster. They moved up and down the dance, deep in conversation. Seeing them together, Louisa felt a jolt of something unpleasant in her stomach and wondered if she was quite as indifferent to Vere as she thought. Then she recalled his allusion to turnips and any regrets were instantly stifled. She wondered what Vere and Sarah could have to discuss. Whatever it was did not please Sarah, for she frowned and the instant the music stopped she left her partner and went to sit with Eleanor and Mrs Lowther.

Supper was followed by more dancing. Louisa saw that Henry had persuaded Sarah to dance, and her eye was often drawn to them, for she was intrigued as to how Sarah would deal with Henry's exuberance. She was quite astonished to see Henry moving with the careful, precise steps of a young boy who had been permitted to dance for the first time, his head down as he frowned in concentration. It was as if his mother had told him he was to stop playing about and be serious. Louisa wondered how Sarah had managed to bring about such a transformation. She could only think that Henry was growing tired. She certainly was. By the time it was Joseph Pickering's turn, Louisa was so weary that she asked if he might forego the pleasure of dancing in favour of resting her aching feet.

'You are hard-hearted to ask a fellow to give up the pleasure after I've been waiting all evening,' he protested.

'I fear there would be little pleasure in dancing with me in my current state.'

'You gave me a promise. I intend to hold you to your word. Besides, there is a particular matter I wish to discuss with you.'

With a sigh, Louisa permitted herself to be led, once more, to the dance, trying not to feel how much her slippers were chafing her heels. After dashing the hopes of the curate and George Chester, here was another impecunious champion that she must disappoint. At least the hall was no longer quite so crowded. The

Mulcasters had departed not long after the refreshments and several other families had followed them.

'May I say, you are looking extremely well this evening?'

'You may.' Louisa granted him a tired smile. It was certainly better than being compared to a sack of turnips.

'I flatter myself that we make an enviable couple. You would not find me an unattractive husband, I think.'

He pulled her closer to him. His coat reeked of liquor and tobacco smoke. Louisa, with great firmness, pushed him away.

'You move with too much haste, sir. We barely know each other.'

'I am a man of bold actions.'

'I am sure that is admirable in a soldier. But less so in courtship.'

'You are a young lady set on marrying for practical reasons. I would find it very practical to be relieved of my debts, which are most pressing.'

'I see the advantage to you. It is less clear what I would gain.'

'Besides the charm of my company?'

'I'm afraid that is an asset you greatly overvalue.'

'Then let us speak no more of charm. In a few years, I expect to be installed as the master of Kenilborough.'

Louisa looked at him in disbelief, but he seemed utterly serious.

'Surely Lord Kenilborough's daughters are to inherit the estate? Or at least have stewardship until one of them produces an heir?'

'Between you and me, there is no deed of settlement in the case, which means my stepfather may dispose of Kenilborough as he wishes. Who knows if either of my stepsisters will ever marry? I can't imagine anyone would take Sarah on, and Ann has barely been in society. Lord Kenilborough will soon see that a guaranteed male heir is the sensible choice. Be assured, once Kenilborough is in my hands, Sarah and Ann will be sent away. My wife would not be burdened with the responsibility for their upkeep.'

A movement took them away from each other, for which Louisa was glad, for his presence made her positively ill. However, the inevitable flow of the dance soon brought them together again.

'You frown at me,' he said. 'Perhaps you are concerned that it may be many years before you would become the mistress of Kenilborough. I assure you, the viscount is not in good health, and I take every opportunity to leave his windows ajar and ply him with strong drink. I cannot see him lasting more than a year or two.'

'I pray you will stop,' cried Louisa, pulling away. 'Every word you speak disgusts me.'

He started back.

'I do not understand your contempt. Any sensible girl should be delighted at such an offer.'

'Then I will enlighten you. To speak so casually of depriving two women of their inheritance — to delight in the idea of casting them from their home! To express an active wish for the death of the man who has taken you in as a son. Any one of these would be reason enough to despise you, even if you did not casually gamble away money earned by the hard work of others. You are a contemptible man. I would not marry you if you were a duke with ten thousand a year.'

She made to step away from the dance, but he clamped his hand around her wrist.

'I will not forget this.'

'I hope not,' she said. 'I want no repeat of these grotesque offerings.'

She wrenched herself free of him and he walked away, taking the stink of tobacco with him.

Chapter Sixteen

$\mathcal{T}$he last dances were done and the musicians began to pack away their instruments. Louisa joined her aunt and uncle in the entrance hall to see off the remaining guests. Eleanor had already retired, fatigued by the heat and the crowds. Louisa wished she could do likewise, but since the ball had been in her honour, she felt duty-bound to remain with her aunt and uncle until all the guests were gone. By some misfortune, a delay to Lord Kenilborough's carriage meant that his party were left waiting when everyone else had gone. Joseph Pickering stood by his mother's side. Louisa could not bring herself to look at him. There was no sign of Sarah amongst those waiting in the chilly hallway, although Louisa could have sworn she had been there just a few moments ago. Louisa regretted that there had been no chance for them to speak, no opportunity to renew their friendship. Ann declared she was too weary to stand any longer. Almost before she had uttered the words, Captain Williams brought her a cushioned chair, which Ann accepted gratefully. Louisa eyed it with undisguised longing. At that moment, Sarah appeared with another chair, and this one was for her. Oh, blessed joy!

'Sarah Davenport, you are an angel,' she said as Sarah handed her into the cushioned seat.

'It is only a chair,' Sarah remarked. Perhaps Louisa imagined it, but she thought Sarah's hand, strong and warm, lingered on her own for a fraction longer than required.

'Had you danced as much as Louisa and I, you would appreciate the depth of our gratitude,' said Ann.

'I am also tired, but nobody thinks of me,' said Lady Kenilborough. 'I must suffer in silence.'

'If only that were the case,' Sarah murmured.

The sound of approaching hooves was greeted with relief by everyone.

'At last,' exclaimed Lady Kenilborough. 'Insupportable that a viscount should wait so long for his carriage.'

'I am sure I would have done something,' said her husband. 'But I was uncertain who I should speak to on the matter. Still, all is well now.'

'Something is amiss.' Sarah cocked her head as the carriage pulled up. She hurried out into the night and pulled up the foreleg of the horse nearest to her and examined its hoof, and then did the same with the rear leg.

'What can she be doing?' Lady Kenilborough exclaimed. 'She will ruin her gown.'

'Helios has thrown two of his shoes,' said Sarah, returning. 'He cannot pull the carriage in such a state.'

'Surely it does not signify. We must get home,' said Lady Kenilborough. 'Cannot he be shoed tomorrow?'

'I will not risk laming one of our best horses.'

'Mr Lowther, I'm sure, can provide a substitute,' her stepmother insisted.

'Alas, all our horses are down at the farm,' said Mr Lowther. 'We cleared the stables ahead of the ball so that we might accommodate the carriages of our guests. I'll have my groom take Helios to the smithy in the morning, but it seems you must stay with us tonight.'

'I will find some accommodation in the village,' said Captain Williams. 'I would not impose, being so little known to you.'

'I won't hear of it. You are quite as welcome as anybody here, after your kindness to Ellie,' said Mrs Lowther, ringing the bell. 'I will show Lady Kenilborough to her room myself. Louisa, will you take Ann and Sarah to the guest chambers? The room with the Queen Anne bed and the one opposite are aired. I will have the maids fetch water and linens.'

'Of course,' said Louisa, delighted by the opportunity to at last speak with Sarah.

'I can find my own way,' said Sarah abruptly, pulling her cape around her shoulders. 'I shall take Helios back to the stables. I will not entrust him to the fool who put him in harness in such a pitiable state.'

She vanished into the darkness. Louisa took Ann to her appointed chamber at the far end of the north wing and returned to her own, which was close to the main stairs. She lost no time in undressing, snuffing out her candle and retiring to bed. Yet, despite her weariness, she could not sleep. At first, she blamed the noises about the house. Footsteps clicked and clacked down the corridors and doors opened and closed as the servants dealt with the needs of their unexpected visitors. But soon enough, all was quiet, and still Louisa could not sleep. The events of the ball spun round in her head. After such excited anticipation, it had proved a vast disappointment. She had failed to secure anything approaching a proposal, at least from anyone suitable. Her father would be disappointed, which caused her some distress. But something else nagged at her. She did not question her father's plan to marry for money. It was practical and necessary and she valued herself too highly to engage herself to anyone who lacked a healthy fortune. But money could not be all, she realised. She could never consider marrying such a man as Joseph Pickering, not for all the money in England. And Vere Mulcaster met every standard she and her father had agreed upon, with a title in addition, yet she was relieved not to be spending the rest of her life facing his aristocratic condescension over the breakfast table.

A door creaked, so close that Louisa's heart leapt into her mouth. A flickering light revealed the door to her chamber had been opened.

'Who is there?' she asked nervously. 'Sarah, is that you?'

There was an overpowering odour of tobacco. The candle seemed to float towards her and behind it loomed a broad, powerful shadow.

'I told you I would not forget.'

She could do no more than gasp in horror as Joseph Pickering set down his candle and climbed onto her bed. She tried to move away but his weight was on the coverlet and the taut sheets pinned her down.

'Get out,' she cried, reaching desperately for the bell pull. A strong hand grabbed her arm, another pressed against her neck, pinning her down.

'If I get you with child, you'll have to marry me,' he said. His hot breath scoured her cheek, the sweet odour of port mingling sickeningly with the reek of tobacco. She tried to push him away but he was too strong.

Something moved behind them and another circle of light broke up the darkness. Joseph started back, and Louisa felt blessed relief as his weight lifted from her chest.

'Get away from her, Joseph.' Sarah's eyes gleamed like blue opals in the candlelight. Her dark gown appeared black in the gloom.

'This is no concern of yours.'

'Step away, I say.'

He alighted from the bed and moved away. Louisa sat up, tears of relief stinging her eyelids, until she realised he was not heading for the door, but to the fireplace, where he seized a heavy iron poker from among the fireside tools.

'It seems I must teach you another lesson, Sarah,' he said.

He swung for Sarah's head. Although her throat still felt tender from Joseph's weight, Louisa cried out a horrified warning, but Sarah had already stepped aside. Lifting her arm, she brought her heavy candlestick crashing down on Joseph's brow. The impact dislodged the candle, whose flame died as it hit the ground, plunging the room into near darkness. There was a heavy thud.

'What was that?' Louisa gasped. 'Sarah?'

A shadow moved towards her and Louisa let out a stifled scream, her heart racing.

'All is well.' Sarah lifted the candlestick that Joseph had left on Louisa's nightstand and carried it towards the fireplace. Joseph lay flat on his back, unmoving. Louisa forced herself to leave the bed, clinging to Sarah's arm as they gazed down at him. Blood oozed from a gash in his temple, forming a dark, glistening pool on the wooden floor.

'Is he dead?' Louisa whispered.

The horror of that possibility caused her legs to buckle. Sarah, taken away and charged with murder. Perhaps even sent to the gallows. The Lowthers would be disgraced and their house scorned as the scene of such infamy. And all because of Louisa.

'Let us see,' said Sarah. She leaned down and pressed her fingers against the inside of Joseph's wrist. Louisa did not know how she could bear to touch him.

'Alive.'

'What shall we do?'

There was only the merest hesitation.

'I suppose we must fetch a surgeon.'

'I will ring the bell,' Louisa offered.

'No,' said Sarah. 'He must not be found here. You are blameless, but a soldier in the chamber of an unmarried lady — it will be talked of. We must move him.'

'Where?'

'My chamber. I will say we had a disagreement. Nobody would doubt that.'

'But what of your own reputation?'

'I am his stepsister. People will be less likely to leap to conclusions. Also, unlike you, I am fully dressed.'

Louisa looked down and saw that her nightgown had been torn, exposing her shoulder. She reached for a shawl and pulled it around herself, shivering. She felt Sarah's hand upon her elbow.

'Louisa, you must be brave. I am not strong enough to carry him myself. Can you bear to help, do you think?'

Louisa eyed the lumpen shape by the hearth and tried not to be sick.

'I believe I might take his feet,' she said with a shudder,

looking at Joseph's boots, so new and shiny. 'I could not bear to touch his flesh.'

Sarah seized her stepbrother beneath his armpits and Louisa grabbed his ankles. He was so heavy his body sagged between them, the seat of his pantaloons scraping along the floor. Step by agonising step they moved him, Sarah going backwards as she led the way. So encumbered, they could not carry a candle and were forced to go blindly down the inky black corridor until Sarah whispered for them to halt.

'Wait here while I fetch a candle.'

Louisa's heart clenched.

'Don't leave me alone with him,' she pleaded. A warm hand seized hers and she was led back down the corridor to where a faint cast of yellow light signalled the entrance to her bedroom. The candle retrieved, they returned to the body.

'I do not think I can do more,' said Louisa, her legs suddenly weak. She felt an arm around her waist.

'Come. It is better he is found in the corridor in any case. I should have thought of that earlier, had I been fully myself.'

Sarah led Louisa into her own chamber, placed her onto the bed and draped a blanket around her trembling shoulders, before lighting another candle from the one she was carrying.

'Wait here. I must fetch your uncle.'

She closed the door behind her, leaving Louisa alone. Some few minutes later, Louisa heard footsteps approach, and then muted voices right outside the door. She hugged the blanket round herself but couldn't stop shivering. The footsteps receded and Sarah returned.

'My stepbrother has been taken to his room. Your uncle sits with him and Captain Williams has gone for the surgeon.'

Louisa looked up at her in confusion.

'How came you to rescue me?' She dared not imagine what would have happened had Sarah not appeared. Sarah sat down on the edge of the bed. In the near darkness, it was impossible to read her expression.

'I wanted to know how Helios came to lose two shoes. One of the grooms reported seeing Joseph in his stall. I looked closer at Helios' hooves and saw his shoes had been pried off. Joseph must have done it as a means of keeping us here. I was on my way to confront him when I saw the light in your room. It seems he planned everything so that he might… Well, let us not speak of that.'

To even think of what might have happened was too dreadful to contemplate and speaking of it was quite impossible. Yet Louisa was surprised that Sarah was capable of such delicacy. Even more surprising was to feel an arm slip around her waist, although it was most welcome. She permitted herself to fall against Sarah's warm, lean body.

'You are shivering. We must get you into bed.'

Louisa's fists closed around the blanket, pulling it even tighter around her.

'I could not bear to return to that room. Not while he is still in the house.'

'Then you must stay with me.'

Even once she was between the sheets with the coverlet placed over her, Louisa could not stop shaking.

'When we were children and the winter was at its coldest, I would lie with Ann and keep her warm,' said Sarah softly. 'Would you allow me to do the same for you?'

Louisa felt a burst of gratitude and nodded, wishing very

much to be held. Sarah quickly removed her dress and slid in next to Louisa, heat radiating from her body as if from glowing coals. Louisa rested her head against Sarah's chest and felt an arm circle round her. The up and down motion of Sarah's breathing, together with the steady thud of her heart, which Louisa could hear beneath her ribs, calmed Louisa's fevered spirits and lulled her into sleep.

Chapter Seventeen

*L*ouisa woke from a sleep so deep it took her some moments to know where she was. She could tell by the grey hue of the light filtering around the drapes that dawn was just beginning to break. She was alone, although the sheets beside her were still warm where Sarah had lain. She rose and went to the window, pulling the curtain aside. The guest chamber overlooked the stable yard, in which Mr Lowther's carriage was standing ready, four black horses shaking their heads in their harnesses as a plainly dressed coachman held the reins. A bulky figure in a red coat stepped from the lee of the house, his head swathed in a white bandage. He was accompanied by Louisa's uncle and Captain Williams. When he reached the gig he turned, and Louisa's throat closed over. Joseph Pickering, his face mottled with hatred, was not looking at Louisa but at someone on the ground floor. Even so, Louisa let the curtain fall with a sharp inhalation. She heard the carriage move off and risked another peek. Sarah now stood in the yard with Mr Lowther, watching the coach depart. As Louisa let out a heavy breath, relieved to know that her tormentor had gone, the two figures turned back to the house. Sarah applied the heel of her hand to her forehead, and Louisa felt a pang of compassion. Always, it seemed, Sarah took it upon herself to perform the most onerous tasks. But who, in turn, cared for her? Even someone as strong as Sarah must, at times, yearn for comfort. To be herself held, as she had comforted Louisa through the night.

It was too early for the fires to have been lit and Louisa felt the chill from the floorboards against her bare feet as an icy draught crept around her ankles. How different from the still-remembered warmth of Sarah's embrace. At that moment, Sarah glanced up at the window and Louisa gave her a small wave, a gesture that by no means expressed the strength of her feelings. A few minutes later, Sarah entered the chamber.

'You saw?' she said. 'He is to be returned to his barracks. Captain Williams has assured me we will not see him again for some time.'

'I owe you more than I can express.'

Sarah plucked at the bodice of her dark green dress, which was exceedingly crumpled and secured by a hurried and haphazard arrangement of ties. She seemed unwilling, or unable, to meet Louisa's gaze.

'I do not deserve your gratitude. I have long known what sort of man Joseph is but said nothing.'

Sarah drew back the curtain and stared at the overcast sky, pressing two fingers of her left hand against her eyebrow, the same one that had been cut after her supposed fall. Louisa felt a jolt of horrified realisation.

'You didn't fall from your horse, did you? It was him.' Bile burned her throat as she recalled the blood on Joseph's hand the night Sarah had retired with an apparent headache, and the casual way he had cleaned it with his thumb. Sarah said nothing but the lack of a denial told Louisa she was right.

'My business on the estate requires that I command respect,' Sarah said at last, still gazing out of the window. 'I cannot abide to be pitied. If people knew I had been beaten down in such a manner '

Louisa longed to reach out to her, but the stiffness of Sarah's posture did not invite interaction.

'Why would he behave so monstrously?'

'Because he takes pleasure in it. And because he wanted the two hundred pounds from the quarry, which I refused to give him.'

'Lord Kenilborough cannot approve of such violence?'

'My father prefers to think that such things do not happen. But I should have spoken. If not for my pride, you might have been forewarned. Although I never imagined Joseph Pickering would be overtaken by his passions.'

'It was not passion that brought him to my chamber,' said Louisa quietly. 'He made me an offer of marriage, which I refused. He... he thought getting me with child, or even just the shame, would leave me with no choice but to accept him.'

Sarah turned to Louisa, her blue eyes flashing.

'This comes of selling yourself like cattle at a market. You, who are so capable. If money is your object, why not gain it through your own efforts, instead of sacrificing yourself on the altar?'

Her sudden change of demeanour startled Louisa.

'You think so ill of marriage?'

'I do. To surrender oneself to another, to cast off free will and rights to property — these are offerings fit for a god, and I have found men to be only too mortal.'

Louisa felt obliged to defend herself.

'I have the right to decide how I should be happy. Accumulating money has always given me pleasure. Why should I deny myself?'

'And what...' Sarah broke off, unusually hesitant, '...of love?'

'A poison that destroys reason and leaves its victims nothing but pain and misery,' Louisa asserted.

'What dreadful experiences have led you to such a view?' Sarah asked. And then, more tenderly, 'I hope you have not let your heart be broken by Vere Mulcaster?'

'Vere? Indeed I have not.' Louisa was surprised by the question. Sarah examined her closely.

'At the dance, you seemed distressed as you parted.'

'He declined my offer to ally our fortunes. I regretted it as an opportunity lost, but nothing more. I did not venture my heart in the business.'

'Then why this mistrust of love?'

'I have good reason. My mother was seduced into ruin. And Eleanor — you know what happened to her, when she was younger. How she was fooled by that man.'

'That only shows the error of loving in the wrong place. Eleanor's heart was blameless — only the object was at fault.'

'You believe in love, then, but not in marriage? That is a strange position. Especially from you.'

'Me?' Had Louisa believed Sarah capable of blushing, she might have thought the redness spreading across her cheeks to be something of that kind. As it was, she supposed Sarah's heightened colour must be due to the exertion of having recently climbed the stairs.

'I cannot believe you will ever surrender your heart, Sarah. You think only of Kenilborough.'

'I will never apologise for doing my duty.'

'Duty, money. In your case they are the same thing. Why, then, do you censure me?'

'It is not censure, exactly. But I pity anyone who disavows love.'

'I love Eleanor, very much,' Louisa protested.

Sarah's head flicked upwards mockingly.

'We both know there is no merit in loving Eleanor.'

Louisa clutched the back of her neck, too fragile to bear Sarah's condemnation.

'Why must you always be so quarrelsome and contrary?' she protested. 'Last night you treated me with such kindness, but now you speak as if you despise me. I cannot decide what opinion you have of me.'

Sarah's expression softened.

'You might do better to know your own mind before concerning yourself with what others think. Rest assured, I do not despise you. Although I find you every bit as perplexing as you appear to find me.'

Chapter Eighteen

'You asked me to wake you early, Miss Sarah.'

'Thank you, Meadows.'

It was still dark, but Meadows had brought a pair of candles, leaving one on Sarah's bedside table and placing the other next to a bowl of warm water on the dresser. Sarah cast aside her coverlet and, after running a damp cloth over her face and neck, she dressed swiftly and headed to her office, a small chamber on the first floor of the Tudor tower, with blackened planks for flooring and wattle-and-oak walls. Its only furniture was a sturdy writing desk, permanently open, and a studded leather chair whose green covering was faded and cracked. A leaded window faced onto the south driveway with a varnished oak seat beneath. The room was chilly for she had not ordered a fire, and sleet spotted the outside of the glass.

Sarah searched her desk for the letter she had received the previous afternoon from Mr Peters. She had yet to see any return beyond the initial two hundred pounds, or even a projection of future profits. Yet wagons full of top-quality limestone had been travelling from the quarry to Hollaston for more than a month.

Mr Peters' letter warned her to expect no returns until next autumn. She was certain he was swindling her but, despite what she had learned from Louisa, she felt insufficiently prepared to confront him. She spent the morning poring over newspapers and pamphlets on quarrying and prices that could be expected for different grades of limestone but found it impossible to comprehend.

Sarah rubbed her eyes. Of course, she knew someone with the knowledge and intelligence to help, but she was reluctant to trouble Louisa after what had happened at the ball. Sarah had made a point of staying away from Athelton, concerned that her presence would only remind Louisa of that horrifying incident. And it was not only concern for Louisa that made Sarah hesitate. She did not trust herself around someone who had such a disconcerting effect on her body and her mind. It was not the first time Sarah had felt a physical affinity to a woman. She knew she was different from most women and had never felt an ounce of attraction for a man. Vere Mulcaster, it seemed, had divined this. Yet her feelings for Louisa were more potent by far than any she had previously experienced. Even thinking of her sent Sarah's blood stirring in a way that threatened reason. She could not afford to indulge such a powerful infatuation. It was hard enough to gain the respect she needed to run the estate without embroiling herself in anything that might lead to scandal. Her responsibilities came first. But did the estate not now need Louisa's help?

Frustrated at her own indecision, Sarah ordered the gig and drove herself to Athelton. Sleet coated the ground in a thready white blanket. The weak sun failed to break through a hazy sky and the chill in the air was made worse by swirling gusts of wind.

Sarah was glad of her greatcoat and sturdy riding boots, regretting only that she must wear skirts rather than more practical pantaloons. Although prepared to defy convention within the grounds of her beloved Kenilborough, Sarah knew better than to do so outside the estate. Being a woman was handicap enough when it came to doing business without giving the men she dealt with even more reason to despise her, or worse, ignore her as some mad eccentric.

Mrs Lowther was out visiting, but the servant showed Sarah into a panelled drawing room where Eleanor and Louisa were sitting next to a crackling fire.

'Sarah,' cried Eleanor. 'What a lovely surprise.'

Louisa sat slumped in a chair, a blanket over her knees. Shadows bloomed beneath her eyes like bruises. Sarah felt an intruder in the face of such obvious distress.

'You are unwell.' Sarah half turned to leave. 'I should not have come. I shall leave you to rest.'

'No, please,' said Louisa, sitting up. 'The distraction is welcome.'

'Louisa has not been herself since the ball,' said Eleanor, stepping across to pick up the blanket that had slipped from Louisa's knees. 'She must have over-exerted herself.'

'It is nothing,' said Louisa, her dark eyes locking onto Sarah's as Eleanor tucked the blanket once more around her. There was a fragility about Louisa's appearance that concerned Sarah greatly.

'I came seeking your help,' she admitted. 'But if you are unwell, it is of no consequence.'

'For you to ask for help, I know it must be important,' said Louisa, light kindling in her eyes. 'I beg you will tell me.'

Sarah explained the situation with Mr Peters.

'We must see him at once,' said Louisa, rising, the blanket slipping once more to the ground. 'You must exert your rights.'

Alarmed by the paleness of her cheeks, Sarah sought to dissuade her.

'I cannot think of asking you to come. It is bitterly cold out, and you are so cheerful and cosy here by the fire.'

'It is my spirits that afflict me, not my flesh. And I cannot be cheerful when my friends are being swindled.' Louisa looked around. 'Let me fetch my bonnet and cloak.'

She appeared instantly brighter and Sarah no longer felt guilty about coming. If only there was something besides money and profit that could raise a similar warmth in Louisa's countenance, or induce such a spring in her step. What, mused Sarah, might be the effect of a lover's kiss?

Eleanor offered to join them, although expressing doubt that she would be of much use.

'I came in the gig,' said Sarah, reining in her wayward thoughts. 'There is only room for two.'

Chapter Nineteen

*S*arah turned the gig onto the newly laid track that linked the quarry to the nearest lane. An ox-hauled wagon headed towards them from the direction of the quarry and she manoeuvred the gig aside to let them pass.

'Here is a chance for you to find out the truth,' said Louisa. 'There is no better source of information than workmen.'

She had said little during the journey, bundled up in blankets against the cold at Sarah's insistence. Sarah had felt it prudent to concentrate her full attention upon driving. Helios, who was stationed between the shafts, had never received so much correction or guidance from his mistress in all his years of service. Sarah recognised one of the men leading the oxen as Mark Greenfield, whose family were among her tenants.

'Good day to you, Mark,' she said pleasantly.

'And to ye, Miss Sarah,' he returned.

'Have you a moment to speak?'

Mark squinted his eyes against the wintry sun.

'We can't stop, Miss Sarah. We've to get to Hollaston and back, ready fer next load.'

'This won't take but a minute. How many cartloads will you take today?' she asked, blowing on her cupped hands in an attempt to warm her frozen fingers.

'Two.'

'And how many carts are there?'

'Four in all.'

His companion, a muscular man with a thick beard, glared at them over the heads of the oxen.

'Foreman don't like us talkin', Mark,' he muttered. 'Not to the sort o' young women that hang about in the lanes.'

Beside her, Sarah felt Louisa's shoulders jerk and she heard a suppressed snort of amusement.

'I have been called many things, but never in my life have I been mistaken for that kind of woman,' Sarah snapped. 'My father owns this land and our family retains a half-share in the quarry. I'll forgive your insolence on this occasion, but do not repeat it, if you wish to keep your position.'

The man rubbed his calloused palm against the back of his neck.

'I meant no offence, milady,' he muttered.

'Your name?'

'Gibbs, milady. Samuel Gibbs.'

'And were you involved in making the track, Gibbs?'

'Aye. Took a month of hard labour, haulin' and rakin' over all them chippings.'

'How many men?' asked Louisa.

'Two dozen, I reckon, weren't it, Mark?'

'Aye. I'm sorry, Miss Sarah, but we must get on.'

'Of course,' said Sarah. 'Your father, I hope, is well? And your mother and sisters?'

'Aye, Miss Sarah. 'Tis good of you to ask.'

The ox cart moved on, and Sarah continued to the quarry, where she was greeted by a surprised Mr Andrews. The foreman carried a thick ledger in his hand which, rather foolishly, he attempted to hide behind his back.

'Mr Andrews,' said Sarah with a cold smile. 'I would see that ledger.'

'Mr Peters won't like it,' he stuttered.

'You do not wish to break the law, Mr Andrews,' said Louisa. 'Miss Davenport's father is a partner in the business and she is entitled to view all papers and accounts pertaining to it.'

'Do not make me fetch my lawyer,' Sarah added. The threat was enough for Mr Andrews to hand over the book. Louisa scanned it quickly.

'Well?' Sarah asked impatiently.

'We must speak with Mr Peters,' said Louisa. 'At once.'

At first, Mr Peters attempted to obfuscate things with talk of wages and cost overruns.

'The track. I had fifty men on it, for two months,' he protested. 'There'll be no profits until next year.'

Sarah informed him that she had it on good authority it took one month and only two dozen men.

'Even so, we have yet to break even.' Mr Peters shook his head with a benevolent look, as if to suggest she had been very foolish. Sarah nodded at Louisa, who produced the ledger.

'Where did you get that?' asked Mr Peters, his voice rising.

'The simple fact, Mr Peters, is that you have attempted to

swindle Miss Davenport,' said Louisa. 'It is quite clear. You see, here, in this column? Mr Andrews has obligingly noted the price obtained for the sale of every batch of limestone. With your advance sales, the business is already in profit to the tune of a hundred guineas.'

'I have spoken with my lawyer and we are taking steps to revoke your rights of access,' said Sarah. 'Even now, he is reviewing offers from other contractors.'

She reflected that her lawyer was extremely busy for someone who moved with all the haste of a calving heifer and took to napping most afternoons. But she did not think Mr Gregory would object to being falsely accused of doing work where he had not. Just as long as he didn't expect to be paid for it.

Mr Peters' face turned grey.

'Please — I have invested every penny. If you revoke the rights, I'll be ruined.'

'That might be the first true word you've spoken to me today,' said Sarah bluntly. Mr Peters took out a handkerchief and began to mop his brow.

'All right. I admit, I tried to take more than was my due. Any fellow would try the same. It's part of doing business.'

'Not any business you do with me.'

'I'll make it up. I'll pay you everything you are owed,' he said, wringing his hands in desperation. 'I misjudged you, Miss Davenport. Miss Silverton, too, I see. I am not a man who repeats mistakes. I beg you. Give me another chance. If not for me, then for the workers. If I am ruined, I cannot pay their wages.'

His duplicity made Sarah's blood rise and she was about to inform him that he deserved no such consideration when she felt Louisa's hand on her arm.

'Do not be hasty,' Louisa advised in a low voice. She looked at Mr Peters and his foreman. 'Gentlemen, a moment please?'

'You think I should give him a second chance?' Sarah protested as the two men stepped away. 'After what he has done?'

'The business itself is well run. And those other contractors you spoke of are likely to be as bad as Mr Peters, or even worse.'

'True. And it's not as if I've actually contacted any other contractors.'

Louisa's lip curled upwards.

'You were bluffing? I did not think you could be so devious.'

'It seemed a necessary deception.'

Louisa broke into laughter, a sound that gladdened Sarah's heart.

'We shall make a trader of you yet.'

'Once again, I am in your debt,' Sarah told her.

Louisa reached out a gloved hand and laid it on Sarah's. 'I could give you a thousand pounds and never repay what I owe.'

She spoke low and hoarse and there was a tenderness in her dark eyes that Sarah longed to return by some word or deed. But they were not alone, and there was business to be done. She cleared her throat and beckoned Mr Peters.

'I shall give you one last chance,' she informed him sharply. 'But only if I receive the money owed me.'

Mr Peters agreed with alacrity. His air of condescension had been supplanted by profound respect. He invited her into the quarry office, a substantial timber building that had replaced the rickety shack where they had first shaken hands. He counted out fifty guineas, Sarah's half share of the profits, into a leather pouch.

'It seems we are at last on a true footing, Mr Peters. Let us continue in this vein, shall we?'

'Yes, Miss Davenport,' said Mr Peters. 'May I say, once again, how grateful I am to be given this second chance, of which I am so undeserving.'

'Quite—' Sarah began, stopping short as one of her stable boys burst through the door, gasping for breath, his face red and splotchy.

'Noah?' she exclaimed. 'Whatever is the matter?'

'Miss Sarah. The big 'ouse — yer wanted.'

Sarah's heart quickened.

'Is it my father? Or Ann?' But Noah had used every last breath in his lungs to reach her and could speak no more.

'I must go!' Sarah cried. 'It will be quickest by foot. Noah, once you are recovered, drive Miss Silverton back to Athelton.'

The boy nodded breathlessly.

'Wait,' Louisa began. 'You have not taken your money.' But Sarah was already hurrying towards home. Spurning the track for a shorter route across field and meadow, she broke impatiently through long grass, crushing their ice-coated blades, paying no heed to the brambles that tugged at the hem of her coat. When she reached Kenilborough, a large wagon was parked by the entrance to the east wing which, for the first time in years, was open.

'What the devil…?' She ran under the carriage porch, up the stone steps and into the cavernous entrance hall. In the corner, Sarah's groom, Thomas, was being restrained by a giant man with a patch over his left eye, from which a jagged pink scar emerged and cut through his poorly trimmed stubble like the crack atop a loaf of bread. Two other men were lugging a framed painting of her mother across the veined marble floor. Mr Hogg was attempting to block their path, but the men were much larger than he and the butler was being driven backwards, the bottom corner of the portrait pressed into the pit of his stomach.

'Stop!' Sarah cried. 'How dare you?' The men hesitated and Hogg used the opportunity to wrestle the portrait from their grip. A scrawny figure emerged from the shadows, smoothing parallel strands of dark hair over a bulging cranium.

'Who are you?' Sarah demanded.

'Name's Cossington. I've a writ for his lordship. I'm sure you don't want these gennlemen to cart him off to gaol, so I took it upon meself to take yer valuables instead.'

'My father?'

'He signed a bill of mine three years ago and neglected to pay the interest. Bein' a kind-hearted gennleman, I bin rollin' it over, but when I heard about the loss of yer winter harvest, I thought I'd better come and help meself, while there's still summink left. I hired these gennlemen, whose fees'll be added to the principal.'

Despite Cossington's assertions, Sarah was reasonably sure the men with him were not gentlemen.

'How much?' she asked wearily.

'The bill was for a hundred pearnd, but it's double that now, what with interest and penalties.'

'Wait here,' she said, pressing her lips together. 'Thomas, if you wish to take up the sport of wrestling, please do so in your own time.'

A red-faced Thomas at last threw off the large fellow who was holding him, the shoulders of his coat crumpled and torn at one of the seams.

'Nothing is to leave this house until I return. See to it, Hogg.'

'Yes, Miss Sarah,' said Hogg with perfect equanimity, although he and Thomas were vastly outnumbered.

En route to her father's study, she passed a footman carrying a loaded tea tray.

'Tanner, fetch Forrester immediately. Tell him to get to the east entrance and look as dangerous as possible. You and Brock are to go too.' Brock was their second footman.

'But her ladyship…' Tanner looked down at his tray.

'Will have to wait.'

Sarah hurried to the Tudor tower and rapped on the door to her father's study.

'Go away,' he said peevishly. She tried the door and found it locked. 'I have no money, I beg you will leave me be.'

'Father, it is only me.' A moment later she heard a key turn and her father opened the door just enough so that he might peer into the dim landing.

'Are they gone? That dreadful ratty fellow and his crew of reprobates?'

'Not yet. What's this about a bill? We agreed you would sign no more.'

Her father let out a sigh and released the door so that she might enter. He waggled his fingers towards some papers that dangled over the edge of his desk, as far away from his chair as they could be without falling to the floor. Sarah perused them quickly. A bill, signed by her father, and a writ, permitting the bearer to take objects to the value of two hundred pounds, or, if such items were not forthcoming, to escort his lordship to the nearest sponging house.

'It was three years ago. I had quite forgot. Joseph arranged it all. He told me he must fight a duel otherwise. I could not permit that, of course. Margaret was exceedingly distressed, you understand. But I was firm. I told Joseph it was the last time, just as you instructed me, and I have been as good as my word.'

'Oh, father! Three years — why did you not tell me?'

'Please, Sarah, do not be angry with me. This business is most upsetting. The fellow spoke of gaol. I am not in good health, as you know, and those are such cold, damp places.'

He collapsed into a chair, his collar awry and his face pale. Sarah strove to suppress her exasperation.

'I will deal with this matter,' she said, crumpling the bill in her fist. 'But please, father, assure me there are no more.'

'I swear it,' he said fretfully. 'Do not berate me. You know how much I hate being browbeaten.'

'Lock the door behind me,' she instructed. 'Permit no one but myself to enter.' She cut across the courtyard to return to the entrance hall via the cloister door. Her mother's portrait was propped against the wall by the open door, guarded by Hogg and a perspiring Thomas.

'Yer've spoke to yer father, have yer?' said Mr Cossington. 'Yer'll instruct yer servants to get out of my way.'

'I ain't movin,' said Thomas stoutly.

'Nor I,' said Hogg.

'You should thank them,' Sarah informed Mr Cossington. 'They have prevented you breaking the law.'

'I think you'll find my papers are in order,' said Cossington with a smile that would have done credit to a weasel.

'I accept the debt is owing. However, you cannot take the paintings. Nor any plate, china or furnishings. We have a loan, stamped and assured, upon which they form the collateral.

Removal of any of these items would be considered theft, and Hoare's Bank would pursue you to the full extent of the law.'

Mr Cossington tilted his head.

'Yet you accept the debt, Miss Davenport?'

'It seems I must.'

'Then what are we to do? We could take yer father, but I do not think the King's Bench would suit his lordship. Perhaps there are movables that might fit the bill, eh? I hear your sister has some fine dresses.'

Sarah felt her bravado dissipate. She had no means to pay the writ. But for her father to be dragged away, like a criminal? It could not be borne.

'I have an alternative proposal.' These words, spoken with a distinctive colonial drawl, came from the porch.

'Louisa?' Sarah exclaimed, disbelief mingling with another emotion she couldn't quite place. Louisa jangled a leather pouch.

'How about a hundred and fifty guineas, paid now, in final settlement of your writ?'

Chapter Twenty

*L*ouisa's imagination had supplied all manner of reasons for Sarah's urgent summons and she could not countenance returning to Athelton without ascertaining what was wrong. She had ordered Noah to take her to Kenilborough, where they found Sarah surrounded by thief-takers.

'Louisa?' Sarah repeated. 'Did not Noah take you home?'

'You forgot the money Mr Peters had for you.'

'So I did.' Sarah's expression brightened momentarily before growing dark again. 'But fifty guineas, it seems, will not be enough.'

'The young lady said a hunnerd and fifty?' Mr Cossington observed. Louisa eyed him with distaste.

'I shall write you a cheque for a hundred pounds, to be drawn at Silverton's Bank in London. You may collect it at your leisure.'

'Silverton's? Yes, I know it.'

'I couldn't possibly permit it,' Sarah insisted stiffly. Goodness, but the woman could be infuriating. Could she not see Louisa wished to help?

'You would prefer to be in debt to this moneylender than to me?'

'Ah, then you are offering me a loan?' Sarah's expression was unreadable. 'At what level of interest?'

'I… had not thought,' Louisa stammered in confusion, for her intention had been to gift Sarah the money. Her previous self would be appalled at such disregard for profit, and her father would hardly believe it. Had Louisa's sojourn in England changed her so much?

'Ahem,' interjected Cossington. 'I feel obliged to observe that even a hunnerd and fifty pearnd don't cover the interest and penalties.'

'Let me see the writ,' said Louisa. Sarah, after only the briefest hesitation, handed it to her.

'Fifty pounds profit is a more than fair return on a bill for a hundred pounds. Your rate of interest is flagrantly illegal,' she told Mr Cossington, after looking over the bill.

'Yet his lordship agreed to it.'

'You can take what I offer or leave with nothing,' Louisa insisted. 'Given the estate's difficulties, you would be advised to take what you can.'

'Miss Silverton makes a good point,' Sarah acceded.

'Would you really give up fifty pounds certain profit?' Louisa brought a cheque from her reticule and asked Hogg for a pen and ink. Two footmen appeared at the main door, along with a gamekeeper who carried a cocked shotgun in his hands. One of the thief-takers stepped forward and whispered something in Cossington's ear. The moneylender pulled his lips back from his teeth, flicked his eyes from side to side and then adjusted his coat. He held out his hand to receive the clinking leather pouch and Louisa's hastily written cheque.

'Very well. A pleasure doing business with yer, Miss Davenport.'

'I cannot say the same,' Sarah said. 'You might use some of the money to buy a hat. The top of your head is extraordinarily displeasing. If you enter our lands again, you will be charged with trespass.'

Cossington and his men departed.

'I did not mean… it just came out. It needn't be a loan,' Louisa said, concerned that Sarah had misunderstood her intentions.

'Nevertheless, I will repay you,' said Sarah. 'Only it may take some time. Oh, Hogg, you may leave that,' she added, as Hogg was about to remove the picture that had been in the middle of the dispute. 'I would look at it awhile.'

'A striking woman,' said Louisa, after Hogg had bowed and departed, taking the footmen and the gamekeeper with him.

'My mother. Painted not long after she married my father.'

The first Lady Kenilborough looked only a few years older than her daughter was now. She shared Sarah's strong jaw, although her colouring was lighter and her eyes were hazel instead of blue, returning Louisa's gaze with calm clarity. Around her neck was the necklace of blue sapphires that Ann had worn at the ball.

'When she was alive, although we had debts, they were never out of control. How I wish…' Sarah stopped and pressed her clenched fist to her lips. 'But you also lost your mother, Louisa. You must know how it feels.'

'I wish I did,' Louisa admitted. 'But the truth is, I never really knew my mother. And… she never showed any desire to know me.'

What a dreadful thing to admit: that she was such a faulty specimen of humanity not even her own mother could cherish her. A lump settled in her throat. Sarah's hand landed gently upon her shoulder and Louisa felt the heat of her whispered breath on her earlobe.

'You are loved, Louisa. You are known, and you are loved.'

Sarah's words sent a warm thrill prickling through every bone and sinew in Louisa's body. Never before had words of that nature been addressed to her, and never with such sincerity. For a moment, she was quite overcome. A door opened from the south wing and Ann put her head around it, a quizzical look upon her face. Louisa pulled away from Sarah, dabbing her damp eyes with her fingertips.

'What is happening? Where's Tanner? Where is our tea?' Ann saw Louisa and her hand went to her throat. 'Is something wrong?'

'Nothing of consequence,' said Sarah, calmly taking her sister round the waist. 'We shall take tea now.' She looked to Louisa. 'Miss Silverton, I hope you will join us before you return to Athelton?'

Chapter Twenty-one

*I*t was the day the Davenports were to dine at Melgrove Park. Sarah dreaded the visit, even though Eleanor and Louisa would be there. Vere Mulcaster would be expecting a response to his proposal, and she did not feel she could reject him outright. After the loss of the winter turnips and paying off Mr Cossington, she was finding it almost impossible to keep the estate afloat. The money from the latest quarterly rents would provide some relief, but if the summer corn harvest should fail, or even fall short of an excellent crop, they would be ruined. Could she, in all conscience turn down a perfectly respectable offer of marriage — one that might save her family?

She dressed with more than usual care. The old favourite would have another airing and she found out a pair of evening gloves that, although not exactly new, were at least more white than grey. On impulse, she asked a rather surprised Mademoiselle Renarde if she might arrange her hair. Whether she was to face down the Mulcasters, or submit to their advances, she might as well look her best. Or perhaps, whispered a voice within her breast, you hope to please another?

'Miss Davenport,' said Lady Melgrove, distinguishing her immediately upon their party's arrival. 'I am glad you have come. Vere was concerned you might not be able to prise yourself away from the estate.'

Vere, who was standing at his mother's side, gave a straight-backed bow. He wore a navy waistcoat with polished silver buttons, and a matching frock coat, adorned with the subtle embroidery that was the current fashion. Everything was perfectly fitted, and there was not a speck of dust or dandruff in sight. In appearance, he was all that a country gentleman should be, but Sarah knew the ruthless streak that lay behind the façade. The idea of being married to him left her nauseated. And yet, did she have a choice?

'I am very well,' said Lady Kenilborough, after waiting in vain to be asked. Lady Melgrove turned instantly towards her.

'Lady Kenilborough, a thousand apologies. I thought my husband was attending you.' The earl was engaged in a heated discussion with his butler. Being unable to catch her husband's eye, Lady Melgrove proceeded to make amends to Lady Kenilborough for his incivility, leaving Ann and Sarah to be entertained by Henry and Vere. Sarah plucked at the sleeve of her gown, feeling constrained by the thick twill.

'Are not the Lowthers coming?' she asked, after looking around the room in vain.

'I am surprised to hear that you have not yet dredged the stream beneath your low fields,' said Vere. 'Have you not learnt from the loss of your turnips?'

'At present, we have not funds to undertake the work,' Sarah admitted stiffly.

'Sarah, I'm sure, don't want to talk business,' said Henry. 'Will you be hunting this year?'

'I cannot risk Jack getting injured by such tomfoolery.'

'You may borrow any of my hunters, you know.'

'I doubt I shall have time for trivialities.'

'How about shooting? We've still a few weeks left for pheasants. I imagine you'd be a fine shot if you cared to try it.'

'I think it unwise,' said Sarah impatiently. 'I am a disagreeable creature and might be tempted to injure someone if I had weapons to hand.'

'I should never call you disagreeable,' said Henry gallantly.

'Even though I have just referred to your favourite pastimes as trivialities and tomfoolery? You are remarkably hard to displease, Henry. I am afraid that is not universally the case.'

A servant announced the Lowthers. Sarah's attention was drawn immediately to the door. There was Eleanor, eyes down and pensive, as she always was in company. Behind Eleanor came Louisa, hands clasped in front of her waist, her step almost as reticent as her cousin's. She wore a red dress with a brocade panel down the front. The colour suited her dark colouring and the cut emphasised her full, yet well-shaped figure. Sarah felt a soft hiss of regret escape her lips, which she covered with a cough. Why did Louisa have to look so beguiling on the very evening she must stiffen her resolve and commit her future to Vere?

'Miss Silverton, I see you are wearing the same dress as on your last visit,' said Vere as Louisa and Eleanor joined them. 'I hope this does not signal any downturn in the family finances?'

If Louisa could not afford a new dress at present, it could only be due to the hundred pounds paid over to Mr Cossington. Never had Sarah greater cause to lament the ruined finances of her family estate.

'Take no notice of my brother,' said Henry. 'Miss Silverton could wear that dress every day and delight any man with a pair of eyes in his head.'

'I am quite used to your brother's brutal honesty,' said Louisa smoothly. 'I do not mind it. Indeed, I find it preferable to insincere flattery.'

'But my flattery is extremely sincere,' insisted Henry, bemused when everybody laughed.

'We had such a long ride of it,' Lady Kenilborough said in a voice that carried across the chamber. 'Why must there be cattle in the lanes instead of in the fields, where they belong? If they must be moved, it should be done in the morning, when nobody is about.'

'You would never think of shooting Lady Kenilborough?' Henry said in a staged whisper.

'You would be unwise to provide me with a gun in her presence,' said Sarah, plucking once more at her bodice. She felt uncomfortably hot. With spring approaching, the evening was mild, but for some unaccountable reason Lady Melgrove had a vast fire roaring in the grate. 'Who could miss such a prime target?'

Lady Kenilborough's glittering orange sarsenet gown had certainly caught the light of the candles.

'Surely you are not serious?' Louisa exclaimed.

'I am sure she is not,' said Eleanor.

'Sarah does not mean anything,' said Ann. 'I have rarely heard her speak such nonsense. I cannot think her quite in her right mind.'

'Dear Ann. I am mortified that you mistake my attempts at wit as insanity. I shall henceforth speak only with great seriousness.'

'That was wit, was it?' said Ann mildly. 'I mistook it for speaking your mind, as you so often do, irrespective of the feelings of others.'

Sarah looked at her sister and Louisa thoughtfully. On reflection, she saw that speaking openly of shooting her stepmother, even in jest, was in poor taste. She could only blame the heat and her frustration with her current situation for such an ill-judged outburst.

'Wit is over-valued,' said Vere. 'Like fool's gold, it may please the undiscerning but is ultimately worthless.'

Sarah squeezed Ann's hand. 'I shall attempt it no more,' she said contritely. 'I am quite ashamed.'

Ann's smile told her she was forgiven. Sarah blessed the fortune that had given her such a sister.

Vere took Sarah into dinner, fighting off Henry, who was obliged to offer an arm each to Louisa and Eleanor. Sarah was amazed that there could be any discussion, for she was certain Henry had by far the best of the bargain.

'Might I expect an answer to my proposal?' Vere's low tone was covered by the clatter of the servants bringing in the white soup. 'Am I to become the happiest of men?'

'Were you in earnest, I would remark that you have a peculiar notion of happiness. If we were to be married, we would be forever in dispute.'

'Does that mean that you refuse?'

The moment she had dreaded had come, where she must sacrifice her future to a man she despised. She happened to glance across the table. Louisa was looking at her intently. Had she overheard? Louisa pressed her lips together and appeared to give a small, but insistent shake of her head.

'May I have some more time to consider?' Sarah asked.

'Indecision is not usually part of your character,' said Vere disapprovingly.

'Marriage is a significant undertaking, particularly for a woman.'

'What are you speaking of, Vere?' exclaimed Henry from across the table. 'You and Sarah had better not be talking of quarters and yields.'

'You have found us out,' said Vere with a tight smile.

'His father is just the same,' said Lady Melgrove. 'I can never get my husband's attention once his steward is in the room.'

'It is a wife's place to know when to speak and when to keep silent, my dear. You are an excellent exponent of the art. A model for any young woman,' said the earl, with a pointed look in Sarah's direction. His spouse chose not to make a reply, excepting the slight raising of a perfectly sculpted eyebrow. Across the table Sarah caught sight of Eleanor attempting to hide her amusement behind a well-placed napkin. Vere signalled to the footman to remove his half-finished bowl of soup.

'I cannot wait forever,' he said. 'I must have your response by Easter, or I will withdraw my offer. I understand you have a mortgage repayment due around that time. Perhaps that will tip the scales in my favour.'

Although every dish had been cooked to perfection, Louisa had little appetite, and was relieved when Lady Melgrove rose to lead the ladies to the drawing room, leaving the men to discuss topics deemed unsuitable to ladies' ears. Lady Kenilborough congratulated their hostess on her dinner.

'We always eat well. Lord Melgrove is most particular in that regard,' her ladyship replied complacently.

'I blush at what Kenilborough can offer these days, although Morris would make great efforts if you could be persuaded to return the visit.'

'I do not expect a reciprocal invitation, given your unfortunate situation,' said Lady Melgrove graciously, leading them to an arrangement of chairs and sofas near the fire. 'Miss Lowther, won't you take this chair? It is closest to the fire.'

Eleanor sank into the proffered armchair. Louisa knew that the journey from Althelton had wearied her cousin and was grateful for her ladyship's consideration. Eleanor, although a little pale, returned Louisa's expressions of concern with a half-smile and waft of her hand to indicate she did not wish a fuss to be made.

Sarah did not sit, but instead took a turn around the room, her posture stiff and shoulders tense. Once she had been assured Eleanor was comfortably settled, Louisa joined her.

'Will you tell me the cause of your restlessness?' she asked, distressed to see Sarah so ill at ease. Sarah stopped to glare at one of the tall windows, or perhaps at something beyond. The sinews in her neck stood so proud they formed a throbbing hollow at their base.

'What makes you think I am restless?'

Louisa resisted the urge to smile.

'Eleanor once explained the signs. Won't you confide in me? I would help if I could.'

'It is not a problem that can be solved by money. At least, not by a hundred pounds.'

The harshness of her tone pained Louisa.

'Is that your opinion of me? As just another banker from whom you must beg money?' Louisa protested. Sarah pressed her fingers to her temples and Louisa wondered, fleetingly, if an apology might be forthcoming. Sarah's jaw worked and then she half turned her head towards Louisa.

'The truth is, I find myself in a position where my heart is absolutely opposed to my duty.'

'Your heart?' Louisa asked falteringly. The air in the room seemed to thicken.

'Vere Mulcaster has asked me to marry him. I thought perhaps you overheard our conversation?'

Louisa flushed.

'I couldn't be certain what I was hearing. It seemed so unlikely.'

Sarah's lip quirked.

'Unlikely that anyone would want to marry me? I cannot dispute that. Many would agree with your assessment.'

'That you would consider accepting,' Louisa clarified.

'You are not distressed on your own account?'

'Me?' Louisa queried weakly. What was Sarah trying to say?

'You were once hoping for the honour yourself, were you not?'

Louisa flushed.

'And you chided me for it. I hope you refused him. Indeed you must!' she cried.

'And plunge my family into penury?' Sarah asked bitterly, turning her attention once more to the window.

'There must be another way to save the estate.'

'God has a strange sense of humour, Louisa. I have been praying for a miracle, and he has sent me one. Should I turn it down, just because it is not to my taste?'

'Yes. You must. Promise me you will.'

'I can make no such promise,' Sarah said tightly.

Before Louisa could plead her case further, the door opened to admit the gentlemen.

'Well, my dear,' cried Lord Kenilborough. 'Look who is arrived. A pleasant surprise for you, I collect?'

When she saw who accompanied Sarah's father into the room, Louisa felt every ounce of blood drain from her chest.

'Joseph?' Lady Kenilborough rose from her chair. 'Why is he not in his regimentals?'

Louisa's ears filled with the sound of waves, pounding against a rocky shore. She felt Sarah's hand wrap around her own, and she clutched it so tightly she must surely be cutting off any flow of blood to Sarah's fingers. Sarah did not flinch, moving only to step forward to place herself between Louisa and the new arrival. Louisa swayed forward and rested her forehead between Sarah's shoulder blades. Sarah's body was so steady and strong that Louisa had a sincere belief that not even a hurricane could dislodge her, though it might sweep through the sumptuous drawing room and take everything else in its path.

After a while, the rushing sound in Louisa's ears subsided sufficiently for her to hear the conversation.

'You sold out?' Sarah exclaimed. 'After we sacrificed so much to secure your commission? Even your mother gave up half her allowance.'

'I had debts of honour to be discharged. If you had paid them when I asked, I would soon be boarding a transport ready to lay down my life for king and country.'

Just the sound of his voice was enough to make Louisa quake.

'In any case, I refused to serve under that Welshman, who

thought himself better than I. The fellow is a pauper. His family could barely scrape together the money for his lieutenant's commission. They had not the money for a captain's step.'

'Then he must have earned it,' Sarah observed.

'He led a bayonet charge at the Battle of Salamanca,' said Ann softly.

'What will you do with yourself now, Pickering?' someone asked. Louisa dared not raise her head to see who had spoken. She thought it might be Lord Melgrove.

'I shall help with the estate.'

'We need no help from you,' Sarah snapped

'But you have been struggling for so long, Sarah. It really is past time I took up the reins.' Joseph's voice was soft and mocking.

It was Louisa's turn to have her hand crushed between Sarah's clenching fingers.

'What business have you to make such declarations?'

Footsteps padded across the carpet towards them.

'You have not heard?' Joseph was now so close, Louisa could smell the stale tobacco on his clothes. She put her hand across her mouth for fear she would be sick. 'My dear Sarah, I am, by your father's permission, to change my name to Davenport. We are to be brother and sister after all.'

Chapter Twenty-two

fter the party at Melgrove Park, Louisa fell into low spirits. Joseph Pickering's sudden reappearance had shaken her, as had Sarah's revelation that she was seriously considering marrying Vere Mulcaster. She knew Sarah would do anything to save the family estate, but the idea of them together was deeply painful. Louisa supposed it was because Sarah had become a dear friend, one she was reluctant to lose. 'You are known, and you are loved.' Louisa could still remember the thrilling sensation that had surged through her blood in response to Sarah's words. On reflection, it was more likely that Sarah had been thinking of Eleanor and Aunt Lowther than expressing any feelings of her own. Louisa had seen the depth of Sarah's affection for those she loved — for Eleanor and for Ann. Such devotion was not given lightly, and certainly not to a recent acquaintance like Louisa. For all her life, Louisa had longed to be loved and cherished and she was deeply grateful to her cousin and her aunt, who treated her with delicate kindness during her current period of despondency. Why then, did she feel as if something even more precious had slipped from her grasp?

Mrs Lowther ascribed her low spirits to homesickness and was delighted when a letter arrived from Louisa's father. It was only the second she had received since leaving New York. Louisa opened it with trepidation, for in the previous letter her father had informed her of increasing setbacks to the business, not least the British blockades keeping his fleet trapped in the Chesapeake.

My own girl,

I write in the hope that you have made progress in your endeavours. Our trade continues to be plagued by these blockades and some of my creditors have issued warrants, forcing me north to Boston, to avoid the thief-takers. I am sure these lily-livered fools would never have taken such a step if not for the recent collapse of the Lehigh scheme, which has rendered our canal shares worthless.

Even though I must hide, I will not be frightened into submission. Once the Jupiter gets through the blockades with its cargo of coffee and cocoa, all will be well. I refuse to sell our house or my timber licenses below their value, just to pay off warrants that may soon be cancelled.

Have you news for me? If you have succeeded in your endeavours, a written undertaking, evidencing your engagement, should be enough to have these warrants set aside. If, however, you have had no luck in the country, I urge you to go at once to London, which is filled with the class of men that I particularly admire. Indeed, I wonder if you might better have tried there first, for when fishing it is best to try the largest pond.

I have written to Mr Levitt who, you may recall, is my partner in Silverton's Bank and runs it on my behalf. He has many acquaintances in trade and finance. I am sure among them will be just the sort of fellow we are after. You must proceed swiftly. It is imperative that you secure an engagement before news of my troubles reaches England.

Yours, as ever,

Papa.

'What is it?' asked Aunt Lowther. 'You are as white as a duck's egg.'

Louisa was full of self-recrimination. Her father had given her one, clear task, and she had failed. Now he was in danger. A danger she might have prevented, if she had tried harder to charm Vere Mulcaster, or even taken a chance on Henry. Instead, she had let herself be distracted by the lure of friendship, with all the unexpected emotions that had raised, instead of concentrating on the matter in hand.

A few days later, a note arrived from Mr Levitt inviting her to stay with him and his wife in Portland Square. In anticipation of her accepting this proposal, he had arranged for a post-chaise to be waiting for her at the Cross Keys Inn at Spenwick a fortnight hence, under the assumption that Mr Lowther's carriage could be spared to carry her thus far. Such efficiency pleased Louisa. If London contained men such as Mr Levitt, she might yet perform her duty to her Papa.

Her aunt and uncle were happy to promote anything that might secure their niece's happiness and agreed that she had more chance of finding a rich husband with an appetite for investment in London. The allotted fortnight passed swiftly, and Louisa was hard pressed to take leave of all her new acquaintances. She called at Kenilborough, relieved to be told that Joseph

Davenport was out, but disappointed to discover that Sarah, too, was not at home. She received kind expressions of friendship and good wishes from Ann Davenport, along with murmured regrets from Lord Kenilborough and his wife. Louisa waited several hours in the hope that Sarah might return, but to no avail. In the end, she asked Ann for pen and paper, that she might leave Sarah a note.

However, when it came to putting words down on paper, she didn't know quite what to say. She very much wished to repeat her warnings against marrying Vere Mulcaster, but recognised the hypocrisy of such advice, given her own plans. There were no logical objections to be offered against the match. Indeed, there were so many sound and sensible reasons why Sarah should accept Vere's proposal that Louisa grew ever more certain it was inevitable. She contented herself with wishing Sarah well, regretting how imperfectly such formal, polite expressions conveyed her true feelings. She also outlined her concerns about Joseph and his plans to usurp both Sarah and Ann, warning Sarah to keep a close eye on her stepbrother's interactions with Lord Kenilborough. Sealing the note seemed distressingly final and Louisa lamented that she must depart the country without taking leave of the person to whom she owed so much, even if that person stirred such conflicting emotions in her breast.

Once her visits were complete, it only remained to take leave of her hosts. Although thoroughly convinced her path was the correct one, it dawned on Louisa that, should she prove successful, she must return to New York and be separated from the Lowthers forever. She had never imagined she would find such dear friends and extracted a firm promise from Eleanor that they would correspond. They parted with a tearful embrace.

Chapter Twenty-three

Portland Square, London, March 1813

Mr Levitt and his wife had recently leased a splendid house in Portland Square and furnished it in the most fashionable style. Sumptuous Indian rugs stretched between the freshly papered walls of every parlour and no expense had been spared in the acquisition of fittings. The wardrobes and cabinets smelled of beeswax, the silk upholstery gleamed like new minted pennies and the nap of the plush velvet drapes was so pure it revealed every passing touch. Such sparkling exuberance formed a notable contrast to the comfortable, mismatched furnishings of Athelton. Even the faded grandeur of Kenilborough bore no comparison.

'The bank must be prospering,' said Louisa. 'I hope this means you will be able to relieve my father of his present difficulties.'

'Alas, it is not possible,' returned Mr Levitt, regretfully. 'The business is fundamentally strong, but I have recently given out several large loans at an attractive rate — with the war in Spain, there is great demand, and the reserve is already lower than Mr Silverton stipulated as a minimum. I am confident things will ease in the next few months, but for now I can do nothing.'

'Nothing at all?' Louisa did not think she could bear to live surrounded by such opulence while her father was threatened with a debtor's prison.

'Would that I could spare something from my own purse,' said Mr Levitt, 'but after fitting up this house, my own situation is much like that of the bank, and my credit is exhausted. I see you frown — I acknowledge that our surroundings appear extravagant, but it is vital to make a good showing. Which is why you must stop demurring and accept the hundred guineas I drew against your father's account. You must have the finest gowns and hats, and whatever.'

'I would rather send the money to my father.'

'He would not wish it. He would agree that this particular hundred guineas is better invested in our business at hand. We are all relying on your success, for Mr Silverton promised that I might put a portion of your wedding settlement into the bank to bolster the reserve.'

Mary Levitt was a pretty young woman with rosy cheeks and dimples and was as eager as her husband to further Louisa's aims. On Louisa's very first evening, a dinner party was got up for the purpose of showing her off to Mr Levitt's friends, all of them bankers, goldsmiths or merchants. The invitations favoured those who had yet to achieve the blessed state of matrimony and thus, except for Louisa and the lady of the house, the table was made up entirely of gentlemen. The conversation was of bonds and commodities, leases and percentages. The rumours of a coming peace with France were dismissed as pernicious nonsense, spread by those who were jealous of the profits made by men who knew how to conduct business in times of war. Louisa listened eagerly and her questions regarding current commodity prices, or whether certain stocks might be recommended or avoided, were complimented for their perspicacity.

'I don't know how you can care for such dreary talk, Louisa. It takes me back to the time I was ten and poring over my lessons,' remarked Mary at breakfast the next morning. 'I always found them most disagreeable. I am sure I was never any good at my sums and my governess would smack me over my knuckles for not knowing the answer.'

'You forget that such dull business pays for all your fine dresses,' said her husband.

'How could I forget when you and your friends talk of nothing else?'

'What would you prefer to speak of, my dear?'

'We might ask Louisa if any of the gentlemen met with her approval,' said Mary. 'Tell me, Louisa, did you prefer Mr Fulton with his two factories, Mr Lampeter with his West Indian estates, or Mr Packham with his twenty thousand pounds?'

'You are very knowledgeable for someone who is not interested in matters of business,' said Louisa with a laugh.

'Mary is always well-informed when it comes to money,' said Mr Levitt dryly. 'It is only the making of it that wearies her.'

'One can enjoy a fine cake without knowing the ingredients,' said Mary. 'The only thing I need to know about money is how much I might have.'

'And how you might spend it,' added her husband.

'Louisa, please explain to my husband that a young lady must have pretty clothes and somewhere pleasant to sit.'

Louisa held up her hands.

'Please, do not draw me into your dispute. I am a guest here and would not endanger that position by taking sides.'

'Very politic.' Mary's full mouth puckered into a pout. 'I notice you have not yet responded to my question. What think you of Mr. Packham? He did not speak much, but his eyes were often upon you.'

Louisa remembered Mr Packham very well. A soberly dressed fellow with narrow, sloping shoulders, she had first noticed his eyes. Being blue, they had reminded her a little of Sarah Davenport's. His conversation had been rational and his attentions perfectly polite and appropriate. By the end of the evening, she had decided his eyes were paler than Sarah's and not so arresting. Neither was his company as enlivening, but she reminded herself she was looking for a husband, not a friend. Did she really wish to marry someone as challenging and unpredictable as Sarah? Someone who could make her feel so vexed one moment, yet so grateful the next? The very idea set her heart fluttering violently in her chest. With Mr Packham, she suspected she would never have to guess what was on his mind or wonder what his opinion of her might be.

'I have great hopes for Mr Packham,' said Mr Levitt. 'His capital will be just the thing for us, instead of languishing in The Funds as it is now. But he is a damnably cautious fellow and unwilling to commit.'

'I am sure Louisa could convince him if she wished,' said Mary. 'I shall invite him to dine on Friday.'

'Excellent,' said Mr Levitt. 'Mary is a great one for catching husbands, Louisa. Your business could not be in more expert hands.'

Chapter Twenty-four

*E*ver since the dinner at Melgrove Park, Lord Kenilborough had locked himself away in his chamber, pleading indisposition. Sarah suspected he was avoiding her and so she intercepted Brock as he was carrying up her father's breakfast tray.

'There you are at last, Brock,' said her father, sitting up the instant she opened the door. 'I am quite famished.'

'I am glad to hear you have an appetite,' said Sarah, setting the tray down next to his bed. 'It means you cannot be very ill.'

'Oh, Sarah, it is you, is it?' her father said with no small alarm.

'You cannot hide from me forever.'

'I thought I might attempt it,' he responded with a sigh. 'If you are going to remonstrate with me, may I at least eat my breakfast first?'

'Certainly.'

She perched on the bottom of his bed until he had eaten his poached eggs and taken a fortifying gulp of coffee.

'I am surprised you are not already gone out,' he remarked at last. 'Are not you busy with the spring planting?'

'I wished to speak with you first.'

Her father dabbed a napkin against his mouth. 'Very well. Say what you must. But be gentle, I implore you.'

'What is this business about Joseph changing his name? I have consulted Mr Gregory and he tells me that it confers no legal status. But how must it appear to those outside the family? It will look as if you intend to make him your heir, which cannot be the case, not with the deed of settlement.'

Her father licked his lips and plucked a plug of stray wool from his blanket.

'Father, there is a deed, is there not?'

'There was,' he said carelessly. 'It lapsed two years ago.'

Sarah looked at him in horror. Louisa had been right to warn her. 'How can that be?' She attempted to fix him with her gaze, but he refused to raise his head.

'It was signed by my father on his majority. A new one was drawn up for me to sign at my own coming of age, but your grandfather died just before my birthday and so there was no immediate need to bother with a new settlement.'

'No need? Do not you see how vulnerable this makes us? If the banks were to call in their loans, we would be forced to sell.'

He continued to worry at his blanket. 'That is why Margaret and I thought you would welcome a brother. Joseph might help you, if only you would permit him.'

'Never. You know how careless he is with money. We would be ruined within a year. You must see that?'

'If he were given responsibility, I'm sure he would do better.'

Sarah rose.

'Father, I insist Joseph does not interfere in estate matters. I will not be undermined.'

'Very well,' he said with a heavy sigh. 'Since you ask it, I will speak to Margaret and she will square everything away with Joseph.'

'And the settlement?'

'I shall look into it.'

Sarah leaned forward and kissed his forehead. 'Thank you,' she said. 'Now that is settled, I hope you will find yourself sufficiently recovered to join us for dinner.'

'Ann, you seem in good spirits,' Sarah remarked that night at dinner, observing an unusual glimmer in her sister's eye.

'Eleanor and Mrs Lowther visited us today.'

'I'm sorry that I missed them.'

'They go to town next month and have extended an invitation for us to join them.'

Sarah hated London. Such a crowded, malodorous place. Nothing but pressing business could ever drag her there.

'I shall be far too busy with the planting,' she insisted.

'I thought you would say that,' Ann replied. 'I would very much like to go, but if we cannot afford it, I shall, of course, decline.'

Sarah detected a blush on Ann's cheeks and a suppressed eagerness, far greater than a trip to town would usually excite.

'You hope, perhaps, to meet with Captain Williams?'

Ann's colour deepened. 'He goes to Spain. I'd like to wish him luck before he departs. And I look forward to seeing Louisa again. What is it — a month since she left?'

'Four weeks to the day,' Sarah responded absently. Louisa

had been often on her mind. Sometimes, it was merely a passing interest, to wonder what she might be doing. On other occasions, usually at night, her thoughts strayed to more intimate pastures. But what of that? Louisa had left with almost no warning, in open pursuit of a prosperous marriage. Sarah hoped she had more pride than to chase after someone who had not the courtesy to say goodbye in person. She realised Ann was still looking at her with eager hope.

'You must accept, of course,' she said with a smile. 'The Lowthers will carry most of the expense, but you will need some pin money.' Where they would find it, Sarah did not yet know, but she could not bring herself to deny Ann her request. Her sister deserved a chance to enjoy herself for once.

'I might have been invited,' protested Lady Kenilborough. 'Mrs Lowther knows how much I enjoy town. I have many friends there.'

'We cannot afford the expense of two visitors,' said Sarah. 'My sister must go alone. I hope, Ann, that you will pass my compliments on to the gallant Captain Williams.'

'And to Louisa, of course.'

Sarah coughed.

'Certainly. Assuming she remembers us.'

Chapter Twenty-five

M r Packham was invited often to dine and Mary
Levitt did all she could, by feigning the need to
speak with servants, or excusing herself on other
business, to provide that cautious gentleman with an opportunity
of making declarations. Yet, when manoeuvred into a position to
speak with Louisa alone, love was not first among Mr Packham's
concerns.

'I hope you do not take me for a fool, Miss Silverton,' he said,
smoothing down an errant lock of hair at the back of his head
with a pale hand. 'I am honoured to be the object of such an
intelligent young lady. And could I be certain these attentions are
not intended to trap me in an unwise scheme, I would be eager
to seek their furtherance. But I have no presumptions about my
own attractiveness. I am a dull fellow and am certain you could
find a more charming man to amuse you.'

'Perhaps I might,' said Louisa with an encouraging smile.
'But equally, there are more handsome women in the world than
I. With your fortune, you might catch a much prettier creature.
One with a more elegant figure, certainly.'

'Your appearance is quite unobjectionable.'

'For sure, nothing pleases a woman more than to be considered unobjectionable.'

He failed to catch her playfulness, continuing as if she had not spoken. 'But I must wonder why your friends are doing so much to encourage me into a declaration.' He glanced towards Mr and Mrs Levitt, who had helpfully manoeuvred themselves beyond earshot. 'I hope you do not mind me speaking plain.'

Louisa twined her fingers together. 'Mr Packham, I, too, shall speak plain. Recent events have forced my father into over-leveraging himself. I assure you, our portfolio is worth a great fortune, but at present we need capital and are looking for someone who can see the long-term benefits of investing.'

As a child of numbers, Louisa abhorred misrepresentation of any kind and was determined to state their position honestly. Mr Packham attempted once more to tame his errant lock with the flat of his hand.

'And you do not concern yourself with the passions of the heart? I am not a fellow with a strong bent for the romantic.'

'I would rather marry a man of sense and propriety than an amorous fool who would fritter away my fortune. As for men of passion, I would be concerned that anyone prone to such strong feelings might find their attentions straying to another object once we were married.'

'This is just the sort of talk I admire,' he said approvingly. 'I hope, however, that you will take no offence if I take a little time to consider.'

'One should not take such an important decision without careful consideration,' agreed Louisa, although frustrated at his cautious approach. Soon afterwards, he took his leave. When

Louisa reported what had transpired to Mr and Mrs Levitt, both were sanguine that Mr Packham might soon be brought to a proposal.

It was not the only reason for optimism. Eleanor had written to inform her that the Lowthers were coming to London and would call upon Louisa as soon as they were settled into lodgings. Eleanor hinted that she hoped to bring a surprise that was sure to please Louisa. Louisa was intrigued, although the promise of seeing her cousin again was delightful enough.

After a few days of rain, Louisa awoke to a clear blue sky, and decided to take a walk in the nearby park. The air was bright and crisp. White and purple crocuses were blooming and tulips were in bud, hinting at a future display of bright reds and sunny yellows. After a refreshing walk, she returned to discover she had been called upon in her absence.

'Miss Lowther and her friend, Miss Davenport, were here, but could not wait. They have taken a house in Fenchurch Street,' Mary informed her. 'We are invited to dine there tomorrow night. I must have a new dress. How delightful, to sup with the daughter of a viscount.'

'Eleanor!' Louisa exclaimed, her heart bursting with joy. 'She is already in town? And with Sarah? How wonderful.'

'I suppose you shall quite neglect me now your friends have come, though I have done so much to secure Mr Packham,' Mary said with a sharp laugh.

Louisa coloured, for she could not pretend that she preferred Mary's company to Eleanor's, whose warmth and kindness she had missed. As for Sarah, she felt a quiver of anticipation at the thought of their reunion that she was at a loss to comprehend.

'I am surprised Sarah would leave Kenilborough and come to town for pleasure,' she said. A fleeting notion that it might be on her account sent a warm sensation quivering along her ribcage. However, when they arrived at Fenchurch Street, all was explained, for it was not Sarah but Ann Davenport who had accompanied Eleanor to town. Louisa did her best to hide her disappointment, which was surprisingly sharp. Fortunately, Mrs Lowther's effusiveness gave her time to compose herself.

'And we are delighted that dear Ann has joined us,' finished Mrs Lowther, after telling them all the news from the country. 'Since Lord Kenilborough no longer keeps a house in London, we asked the girls to come with us. We do not mind a little extra expense. It was Eleanor's idea. She has been quite pining since you went away, Louisa. Sarah would not come, however. Too busy, as always.'

'Poor Sarah — always working. She never thinks of herself,' Eleanor remarked.

'But we hope we may see her soon, for she mentioned she must come up to see her banker.'

'I am afraid I am a poor substitute,' said Ann with a sigh. Eleanor protested she was no such thing and Louisa, guilty of having had exactly such thoughts, added her own protests with particular enthusiasm. They spoke eagerly of the plays they might see and the concerts they hoped to hear.

'I cannot do as much as the girls would wish,' said Mrs Lowther. 'My legs are swollen from the journey and I fear it will be some days before I may go out.'

'I would be delighted to act as chaperone,' offered Mary.

'That is kind of you, Mrs Levitt. We plan on staying only for six weeks and I am eager for them to be seen. Ann, in particular, has been shut away in the country, just when she should be in society.'

'You could not do better,' remarked Mr Levitt. 'There is nobody better at exposing young girls to society than my wife.'

'If I cannot secure a marriage proposal for the daughter of a viscount, I shall hang my head in shame,' said Mary, with a complacent look at Ann.

Ann protested against such a favour, although her countenance suggested she was eager to see what London society had to offer.

'I fear you will not find it so easy for me,' said Eleanor with a smile.

'I relish a challenge,' Mary returned blandly.

Chapter Twenty-six

$\mathcal{A}$nn, Eleanor and Louisa were soon at every recital, play or public assembly that tickets could be got for and attending any party for which invitations might be secured. The highlight was Mary securing vouchers for a masquerade at the famous Almack's, which they attended in the garb of highwaymen, or rather highway-women, for a lady wearing breeches in public was unlikely to meet with the approval of Almack's patronesses. Tricorne hats had been borrowed from Mr Lowther's footmen and the braiding carefully removed with nail scissors. Mr Levitt and Mr Lowther had agreed to the loan of their greatcoats, leaving only the masks to be purchased. Mary had proposed a more elaborate costume involving swan feathers, but Louisa had insisted upon something cheaper, concerned for her purse, and that of Ann, who she knew had little to spend. They were accompanied by Mr Levitt. Mrs Lowther was still troubled by her swollen legs and Mr Lowther preferred to remain at Fenchurch Street with his wife.

'I wonder if we will see Packham tonight?' Mr Levitt said to

Louisa as the ladies took their tickets from the Master of Ceremonies and ascended the grand staircase.

'Mary was at pains to inform him we would be here,' Louisa returned.

'How does your scheme progress?'

'Mr Packham is not a man who moves swiftly.'

'You must encourage him,' said Mr Levitt. 'Only yesterday, a corn trader came to me, begging for five hundred pounds on any terms. He has secured a contract to supply Wellington's army and needs only capital to transport his goods. I had to turn him down. Any terms, mark you, and I had to turn him down. If we had Packham's money, I could lay it out immediately, to great advantage.'

'I thought you were first to bolster the reserve,' Louisa said, frowning.

'Your father would not wish me to turn down such an opportunity. We must make haste. If we do not catch Packham swiftly, he will fix upon a rival's hook.'

Louisa offered her opinion that, to continue his analogy, Mr Levitt might do better to ensure his ship was seaworthy before filling it with fish. He patted her hand.

'Louisa, you would do better to leave matters of business to men and direct your efforts to the catching of a husband.'

It struck her then how similar Mr Levitt was to her father. Both would listen to her views only as long as they coincided with their own. Although they professed to admire her talents, she was nothing more than a novelty to them, useful to have to hand if some difficult calculations were required. However, they would never entertain the idea she might make a greater contribution. With regret, she knew there was no point in speaking further.

They reached the top of the sweeping staircase and entered the vast ballroom. Along the outer wall were too many fireplaces to count. Layered crystal chandeliers and huge mirrors sent fragments of light dancing across the walls and the floor, whose chalked pattern was already half gone, worn away by the feet of young men and women as they searched for friends or made new acquaintances. Elaborate costumes of swan and peacock feathers rippled in the warm air, mingling with ancient gods of Greece and Egypt. The voices of the multitude merged into an indistinct rumble, resembling a weir at high flood.

'Oh, there is my particular friend, Mrs Davis,' cried Mary, hastening towards a young woman who sported a pair of swan's wings on her back. The crowd was so thick that she was soon lost to their sight. A pair of highwaymen approached. One of them removed his mask to reveal the handsome countenance of Captain Williams.

'I see we have been visited by the same muse, Miss Davenport.'

'It was Louisa's idea,' said Ann, removing her own mask with a broad smile. 'So ingenious — it saved us vast expense.'

'Indeed. Although with such opulence on display, I feared at first that we might be mistaken for actual vagabonds and be arrested on the spot.'

'How did you know it was us?'

Captain Williams was too polite to look at Eleanor, whose distinctive shape was in no way hidden by her disguise.

'I was drawn by such an extraordinary example of sense and good taste in terms of costume. I might have guessed it was you. Might I introduce my friend, Kirk? He is Scottish, but I'm sure you will not hold that against him. There's not a finer fellow in the country, for all that he chose the navy over the army.'

His companion raised his mask and bowed. He was not so handsome as his friend, his nose being rather fleshy and his forehead jutting over thick, sandy eyebrows, but his greeting was polite and well expressed.

'Kirk is soon to return to his ship. I am trying to get him out as much as I can while he is in town.'

'Do you like to dance, Mr Kirk?' asked Eleanor.

'I much prefer dinner and good conversation,' said Mr Kirk. 'But I'm grateful to Williams for taking pity on me. Once I am aboard ship, the food will be vile and I will be among fellows who will speak only of the weather and gunnery practice.'

'I, too, prefer conversation to dancing,' said Eleanor. 'But I could not turn down an opportunity to see the famed Almack's ballroom.'

The crowd at the top of the stairs thickened and they were pushed deeper into the ballroom. A lady encumbered by great plumes of peacock feathers passed by them, so deep in conversation with her companion that she did not notice when her costume brushed across Eleanor's face, causing some disruption to her hair.

'Madam, I beg you would take more care,' said Mr Kirk. His rebuke was mildly given, but the lady in question seemed displeased to be spoken to in such a way. She stopped and turned. The top half of her face was covered in an elaborate mask of gold leaf.

'I was not at fault,' she drawled. 'Perhaps if your companion stood up properly, she would not be so much in the way. But I see now she is a cripple and cannot help it. I am surprised you have come, madam. Your costume does not hide your deformity and no gentleman will dance with you.'

Eleanor's flush would have been visible even if she had still been wearing her mask.

'Madam, that is remarkably impolite,' said Mr Kirk. 'I insist you apologise.'

'Who are you to demand an apology from Lady Anisborough?' protested the befeathered lady's companion, who wore the robes and mask of Anubis.

'Such incivility would be unacceptable even from a queen,' said Mr Kirk. 'But all will be well, if her ladyship would only acknowledge her words were ill-judged.'

'She said nothing but the truth. You will permit us to move on, sir.'

'If her ladyship is unwilling to apologise, then perhaps I should demand satisfaction from you?' said Mr Kirk, his colour rising.

'I beg you would not,' said Eleanor, gently placing her hand on his arm. 'A little disorder to my costume is nothing to the distress I would feel if anyone came to harm. It is such a trifling matter.'

'Miss Lowther is quite right, Kirk,' said Captain Williams.

'Typical Scotch belligerence,' muttered Anubis as Mr Kirk drew aside to let them pass. Ann and Louisa flocked around Eleanor.

'Are you well? Would you prefer to go home?' Ann asked in concern. 'I will attend you with great pleasure. You need only ask it.'

Louisa reached out to rescue a dislodged hairpin before it fell to the floor, and placed a steadying hand on Eleanor's shoulder as she did so.

'But you were so looking forward to dancing, Ann,' said Eleanor, as Louisa fixed her hair back into place with the pin. 'And we cannot leave Louisa alone.'

'Do not fear for me,' said Louisa, reluctant to give up the chance of meeting with Mr Packham. 'Mary is somewhere about.'

'It would be most unfortunate if you were to leave,' said Mr Kirk, 'for I was about to ask you to dance, Miss Lowther.'

'You need not take pity on me, sir.'

'It is you that would be taking pity on me. I am unworthy of the lady who can give such a sweet-natured response to such a slight. But, as I have oft said to my gunner, a long shot is better than none. Have you the courage to stand up with such a ruffian?'

Eleanor dipped her head and smiled. 'I would welcome an opportunity to show Lady Anisborough she has not frightened me.'

'And when you tire of Kirk, I hope you will stand up with me,' said Captain Williams. 'We shall show Lady Anisborough how greatly she has erred. Miss Davenport, I expect you are already engaged?'

Ann was delighted to inform him that she was not, and the four of them went together to the dance. Louisa watched with satisfaction as Mr Kirk treated Eleanor with great respect and delicacy, doing all that he could to protect her from any repeat of the unfortunate incident with Lady Anisborough. Ann and Captain Williams made an elegant couple and drew many admiring eyes. Louisa looked about the room and thought she made out the slanted shoulders of Mr Packham among the cos-tumed figures. She lifted her mask, so that he might recognise her. After a few moments, he raised his hand and headed sedately towards her. Unaccountably, Louisa's mind conjured up a vivid image of Sarah Davenport striding into the breakfast room at Athelton. She shook her head and smiled. As if Sarah would ever set foot in such a place as this.

Chapter Twenty-seven

Mr and Mrs Lowther could not hear of the service Lieutenant Kirk had paid their daughter at Almack's without wishing to thank him. Mr Lowther also desired to become better acquainted with Captain Williams, for whom Ann Davenport had clearly developed a preference. He felt it only prudent, being *in loco parentis*, to discover what he could concerning the prospects and character of the dashing young soldier who had captured Ann's interest. After consulting with his wife, it was agreed they would invite the young men to dine at Fenchurch Street.

Since Mr Kirk would not be long in London, an early date was agreed upon and invitations sent out. Louisa and the Levitts, of course, must also be invited, and Mr Levitt was so keen to advance Louisa's future happiness that he secured an additional invitation for Mr Packham. Mrs Lowther was delighted to oblige, for the party would now comprise an equal number of ladies and gentlemen.

Captain Williams and Lieutenant Kirk were already present by the time Louisa arrived with the Levitts and Mr Packham.

Their red and blue coats provided a vivid contrast to the muted pastels favoured by the young ladies. Louisa had purposely donned a plain white gown that she had worn several times before, knowing that Ann and Eleanor could not afford a new dress for every engagement, and not wanting to make them feel inferior. Ann looked well in a patterned muslin Louisa recalled her wearing at Kenilborough but not, as yet, in London. Eleanor wore a primrose dress with Vandyke edging on the neck and sleeves that Louisa knew to be one of her favourites, together with a pearl necklace. Her pink cheeks showed she was not unmoved by the presence of Lieutenant Kirk at her side. Captain Williams was seated by Ann.

'The Lowthers are comfortably off, I see,' said Mr Packham, taking a seat beside Louisa. 'Does this house belong to them, or do they rent?'

'Do you inquire into the finances of everyone you meet?'

'It is only prudent to find out what one can. One never likes to be taken by surprise.'

Ann laughed at something Captain Williams had said.

'And what of your investigations into me?' asked Louisa. 'Do they continue?'

'I have not yet found anything to cause alarm,' Mr Packham returned. 'Although I hear that Silverton's recently sold a substantial amount of gold. I hope that augurs nothing ill?'

'I am sure it does not. Mr Levitt tells me he has taken on some new creditors of late, at a high rate of interest. That would necessitate some loosening of reserves.'

She was distracted by another peal of laughter from across the room. Even Louisa's uncle had joined the conversation, and anything that induced Mr Lowther to set aside his newspaper must be interesting indeed. She felt a pang of envy at missing out on such enjoyment. Eleanor was smiling and shaking her head and Mr Kirk was pleading with her about something. Mr Packham continued to restate the many reassurances Mr Levitt had given him concerning the Silverton company and Louisa was thus prevented from joining what appeared to be a lively conversation on the other side of the room. She was glad when dinner was announced. Although Mr Packham, with grave propriety, attached himself to her, they were a small enough party that if anything amusing was said, she was bound to hear it, even if she were seated between Mr Levitt and Mr Packham, who were sure to speak only of profit and business. A few months ago, nothing would have pleased Louisa more, but her time in England had given her a taste for other styles of conversation.

'I did not realise you had friends in the nobility,' said Mr Packham, with a nod towards Ann.

'Does that count in my favour?' Louisa asked with an arch smile. Not for the first time, he failed to realise she was being playful.

'Any connection with people of influence is of value. Is the viscount active in the Lords? Does he vote on matters of trade? Do you think Miss Ann might be prevailed upon for an introduction? I'm sure a fee could be arranged.'

Uncomfortable at discussing Ann and her father as if they were commodities for sale, Louisa turned the subject. As wine was being poured in preparation for the first course, there was a distant jangling of a bell.

'Surely that cannot be for us?' exclaimed Mrs Lowther.

'I am not expecting anyone,' returned her husband. 'Who would call at such a late hour?'

His question was answered when a footman announced Miss Sarah Davenport. Her name was barely out of his mouth when Sarah marched past him wearing a travel-stained coat, her gloved hands aloft.

'Mr and Mrs Lowther, I know the hour is unconscionable, but the instant I realised I was in Fenchurch Street, I could not pass your door without looking in. But I see you have guests. I would never have burst in like this if I had known you had company. I am on my way to the Bridge Inn to take a room. No, Mr Lowther, you must not get up on my account, I deserve no such consideration.'

However, the gentlemen had already risen and Ann flew to her sister.

'I disturb your dinner,' said Sarah, catching the onrushing Ann in her arms. 'I shall only beg your indulgence for an instant, that I might give my dear Ann a kiss.' She planted her lips against her sister's cheek. 'And dear Eleanor too.' Releasing Ann, she bent over Eleanor's shoulder and gave her a kiss of equal warmth. Louisa looked up eagerly, hoping to catch Sarah's eye, and perhaps receive a similar greeting. But Sarah seemed determined not to acknowledge her.

'Will you join us, Sarah?' said Mr Lowther. 'We are not yet begun.'

'You are monstrously kind as always, but I would not wish to disturb such a charmingly equal arrangement of ladies and gentlemen.'

'Oh, but you must stay,' cried Eleanor, 'Mama, you must insist upon it.'

'I cannot,' said Sarah. 'I have come straight from the road and my white gloves are at the bottom of my bag.'

'Never mind that,' said Mrs Lowther. 'And I will hear no more talk of you going to the Bridge. You will stay with us. Ann, you won't object to sharing with your sister, I'm sure.'

'Nothing would give me greater pleasure,' said Ann, her eyes shining.

'We have other friends here,' added Mr Lowther, injecting a little formality into the proceedings. 'Louisa, of course, you know.'

The tremors in Louisa's stomach that had started up at Sarah's unexpected entrance grew wild enough to make her breath catch in her throat. Sarah nodded vaguely in her direction, but her eyes moved quickly on as Mr Lowther introduced the rest of the party, leaving Louisa feeling bereft. She regretted now that she had worn such a plain dress. She was sure it did not flatter her.

'Have no compunction against accepting Mr Lowther's invitation on our account,' said Lieutenant Kirk. 'Not when there is such friendship in the matter.'

Sarah fixed her blue eyes upon him.

'What do you know of my friendship with these people, sir?'

'I have heard much spoken about Miss Sarah Davenport.'

Sarah raised an eyebrow.

'Yet you still wish me to join you? It is heartening to know our navy contains men of such courage.'

'The army will not be shamed by the navy,' said Captain Williams. 'I venture to second my friend Kirk.'

'And I would take it as a favour if the Honourable Miss Sarah Davenport would take a seat by me,' said Mr Packham sedately. 'I flatter myself that as an acquaintance of Miss Louisa Silverton, who I understand is a friend of the family, you would not think it inappropriate for me to make such an offer.'

Sarah stared at him. Had it been possible, Louisa would have sunk into the ground with shame.

'Although,' he added, perhaps realising that he had said something amiss, 'I would not wish to offend. As a man of means with a reputation for probity, I apologise if I have committed an error.'

'I am much obliged, Mr Packham, but I would not deprive Miss Silverton of such a worthy companion.'

'Sarah, you must sit by me.' Ann indicated with the palm of her hand that Sarah should sit to her left.

'Capital idea.' Sarah shrugged off her coat, beneath which she wore the grey linen dress with puffed sleeves she had worn for the dinner party at Kenilborough. She took up a chair and inserted it to Ann's right, between her sister and Captain Williams. 'Our gallant captain will not object to a temporary retreat, I hope.'

'Certainly not,' he said, with a slight tilt of his glass to show her he understood what she was about and a smile that said he did not resent her for it. 'What brings you to town, Miss Davenport?'

'I come to visit my bank. Or rather banks, for we have accounts with several.'

'You spread your risk. That is very wise,' said Mr Packham.

'I'm afraid in our case, the risk is all with our lenders.'

'Is Silverton's among them?'

Sarah's eyes flicked towards to Louisa, but only for a moment.

'It is not, but you must read nothing into that. My family are set in their ways and if a bank isn't at least a hundred years old, we will not touch it.'

'May I ask what rate of interest you are being charged?'

asked Mr Levitt. 'I am sure I could make a good case for Silverton's.'

'You can hardly expect me to divulge such information.' Sarah gave him a cold look. 'I expect my bankers to have the utmost discretion in my affairs and I pay them the same courtesy.'

Mr Levitt held up his hands with a smile.

'You cannot blame a fellow for trying.'

'I require some advice in investments,' said Mr Kirk. 'I am due five hundred pounds in prize money. A modest sum by your standards, I am sure, but I have no other fortune and would like to put it to work.'

'You must deposit it with us, mustn't he Louisa?' said Mr Levitt. 'We offer two points above the Funds.'

'You will not receive a better offer, Mr Kirk,' said Louisa, gratified that Mr Levitt had heeded her advice. Securing deposits was the quickest way to increase their reserve.

'What news have you from home, Sarah?' asked Mrs Lowther. 'Your father and Lady Kenilborough are well, I hope?'

'I shall report all in due course.' Sarah looked pointedly around the table. 'But do not ask me to speak of home when there are clearly affairs of much greater interest occurring here in London.'

Chapter Twenty-eight

After dinner, Sarah begged to be excused to find out a pair of white gloves. Ann offered to go with her. The rest of the ladies retired to the drawing room to await the gentlemen.

Ann and Sarah took an age to reappear, arriving only moments before the gentlemen came in. Louisa wondered what had kept them away so long. Sarah Davenport was surely not the sort of woman to dally over choosing a pair of gloves. Coffee was brought in and Sarah insisted on serving, declaring it was the least she could do for interrupting their party.

'I would be grateful, Louisa, if you would assist me,' she added.

Louisa was surprised, rising just in time to avoid the attentions of Mr Packham, who was making a direct line for her chair.

'I hope I do not take you away from a more attractive companion,' said Sarah, adjusting her long gloves.

'I wondered if you were avoiding me.' Louisa took up a cup and saucer.

'I did not wish to interfere with your continuing efforts to secure a husband.'

'Endeavours of which you still disapprove, I gather.'

Sarah swirled the coffee pot forcefully enough to rattle the lid.

'You left us rather suddenly. Was your business so urgent you hadn't time to take leave of your friends?'

'It is hardly my fault you were not at home when I called,' Louisa protested.

'Very well, I shall make no more of it. I was recently informed that I am contrary and quarrelsome and I am striving to mend my ways.'

'Whoever would dare accuse you of such things?' Louisa asked innocently, holding out a cup to be filled. Sarah dispensed the coffee and added a dash of cream.

'Unaccountable, I agree. And that is not all that baffles me.'

'Oh?'

'I hear you have been very kind to Ann.'

A few days before, Louisa had found Ann in floods of tears. With all the entertainments arranged by Mrs Levitt, she had spent all her pin money and was convinced she must spend the rest of her stay locked away in Fenchurch Street. Moved by her distress, Louisa had insisted on giving her twenty pounds from her own purse.

'That shocks you?' Louisa gave the filled cup to Lieutenant Kirk and picked up an empty one.

'I did not think you would continue to give out money without demanding a return. I have not forgot I already owe you a hundred pounds. I will repay you as soon as I can, but must beg your indulgence for a few weeks, or perhaps a little longer.'

'You must not think of paying me back. I certainly do not expect it.'

Not if it would mean you accepting Vere Mulcaster, she added silently.

Sarah raised her eyebrows in exaggerated surprise.

'You see why I am puzzled. Such generosity is hardly compatible with the ruthless pursuit of profit.'

Sarah spoke lightly, but her words echoed her previous accusations.

'That is unfair!' Louisa exclaimed. 'I admit to loving profit in the way you love apples, or as others might take pleasure in poetry. But I would never use my friends as a means to make money.'

'Do your new acquaintances share those sentiments?' Sarah eyed Mr Levitt as he retreated with his coffee.

'I am sure Mr Levitt is an honourable man. My father would not trust him if he were not.'

'I hope all is well?' Sarah lowered her voice. 'I heard that Silverton's Bank is selling bullion.'

Louisa felt as though a tiny worm was burrowing inside her stomach. The last thing she and her father needed was some pernicious scandalmonger, attempting to do the bank harm.

'I beg you will not repeat what you have heard. You are the second person to speak of it this evening and nothing is more dangerous to a bank than rumour.'

'Then you can be assured of my saying no more on the matter. And Mr Packham — is he also of unimpeachable integrity?'

'Have you cause to doubt it?'

'No indeed. Someone so insufferably dull is unlikely to have the imagination for immorality.'

'He speaks a great deal of sense,' Louisa protested rather feebly, for she could not deny that Mr Packham's conversation lacked liveliness.

'Who wants always to be speaking sense?' Sarah began, her voice rising. But then she checked herself. 'But I am heading into dangerously quarrelsome waters and I was supposed to be mending my ways. I should not criticise your choice of acquaintances, especially when you have been such a good friend to my sister.'

'I will not take marriage advice from anyone who is seriously considering a proposal from Vere Mulcaster,' Louisa could not help but remark.

Sarah took a moment to lay out some saucers.

'I have resolved to refuse him.'

Her declaration delighted Louisa so much that, without thinking, she threw her arms around Sarah's neck and kissed her on the cheek.

'I am relieved to hear it.'

Sarah stiffened.

'What?' asked Louisa, disengaging. 'Is it forbidden in England to display affection in public?'

'It is not widely encouraged.'

'How then should one communicate such feelings?'

'A handshake might do,' Sarah offered cautiously.

'A handshake?' Louisa's lip twitched in amusement.

'Quite so. A warm handshake.' Sarah followed her comment by a brisk nod, as if convinced by her own conclusion.

'I would accept your premise, if I did not know you were dissembling,' said Louisa, still amused. Sarah lost grip of a cup, which clattered against a saucer. With much deliberation, she centred the cup with her gloved fingertips.

'In what manner am I dissembling?' she asked.

'Did you not embrace Ann and Eleanor when you arrived? And kiss them, too?'

'That is different. Ann is family. Eleanor no less so.'

'Oh, to belong to such a family,' Louisa said with a wistful sigh. Sarah looked as if she might respond but she was importuned by Mr Levitt, who desired a refill.

'How long do you stay in London, Sarah?' Mrs Lowther called from her seat. 'Will you have time to take in the assembly rooms?'

'For a few days only.' Sarah's voice was scratchy and she cleared her throat before proceeding. 'There is much to be done at home. But I have packed the old favourite, in case it was needed.'

'You deserve some pleasure. The young ladies have been having a fine time, excepting that unfortunate business with Lady Anisborough.'

On hearing what had occurred, Sarah favoured Mr Kirk with a look of earnest gratitude. Mrs Lowther sighed.

'Although I will be unable to accompany you. The physician fears my legs favour gout and must be elevated whenever possible.'

'I would be delighted to chaperone you, Miss Davenport,' offered Mary.

'The idea is quite preposterous,' Sarah remarked. 'It is a strange custom, is it not, that I am permitted to manage my father's estate and do business on his behalf, yet I cannot go to a dance with my friends and my sister without a chaperone. But that venerable role may fall to Mrs Levitt, who is younger than I, simply because she is married and I am not. I mean no offence, Mrs Levitt.'

'I am sure I take none,' said Mary, in a tone that said the opposite.

'I hope Lord Kenilborough is well?' asked Eleanor.

'He has been much fatigued in recent days and stays often in his rooms. We were concerned enough to call Mr Matthews.'

'Dear Papa,' said Ann in alarm. 'Should I come home?'

'I do not believe he is in any immediate danger. You must not think of forfeiting your time here.'

'It would be no sacrifice, if I could be of assistance to Papa.'

'I am sure it would be no sacrifice at all, now that Captain Williams' regiment is to be called away,' said Mrs Levitt with a bright laugh. Ann blushed furiously.

'You go to war?' Sarah turned to Captain Williams.

'I do,' he replied. 'But I would not speak of such unpleasantness when we are having such a delightful evening.'

'I'm sure we always love to speak of war,' Mary remarked airily. 'Mr Levitt's friends hope it will last many years yet.'

'It is only that there are opportunities to be had, in the supply of goods,' Mr Levitt explained quickly. 'Packham's uncle made his fortune supplying rum to the navy.'

'I wonder, is it moral to make profit out of strife and death?' ventured Eleanor.

'I have no objection to fellows that supply necessary goods,' said Captain Williams. 'The bravest soldier is no use on an empty stomach, or if he lacks a pair of stout boots. But I cannot abide profiteers that bleed the army dry for poor quality goods or take money for food they never intend to supply. They care not for the suffering of others. Such scoundrels deserve to hang.'

'Hear, hear,' said Lieutenant Kirk. 'I can't begin to say how much trouble we've had with rotten pork and watered-down grog.'

'My father believes it is bad business to sell faulty goods,' said Louisa. 'There might be short term profit, but the loss of reputation is too costly.'

'Your corrupt fellow cares not for reputation, for he knows to change his name at the first sign of trouble,' said Captain Williams. 'He will create a new business, leaving his investors high and dry. And there are other ills that occur from the unalloyed pursuit of profit, slavery being chief among them.'

'You will find few men of trade who would support that view,' said Mr Levitt. 'None that are successful. Nor landowners either, I'd wager,' he added with a bow in Sarah's direction. Sarah's expression grew dark.

'Kenilborough holds no lands in the West Indies, not since my grandfather sold his plantations. He could not countenance the measures required to ensure a profit.'

'You must regret that decision. I know of several country estates whose incomes depend entirely on their West Indian holdings.'

'My only regret is that my family ever had such holdings at all. I am convinced that the African trade will be remembered as the most shameful chapter in our history.'

'Until we stop the disgrace of a person considering another man as his property, we will forever be building our fortunes on immorality,' said Captain Williams.

'I suppose that means you think me a villain for inheriting money made from rum,' said Mr Packham stiffly. Louisa flushed at this point, for her father had also traded in rum. From an early age, she had known the price of sugar and molasses to the cent, but until now she had never considered the human cost. How could she have been so blind, so thoughtless?

'We are all guilty,' said Captain Williams. 'It is impossible, the way things are, to be completely dissociated from the products of such iniquity. The cotton of my shirt, the wine in this glass may all, at some point, owe their origin to the work of slaves. But that should not prevent us seeking to abolish such an injustice. And I would never invest directly in such a cruel business.'

'Is not soldiering an equally cruel business?' Mr Levitt remarked.

'Perhaps,' said Captain Williams. 'But sometimes necessary. This Bonaparte fellow must be stopped. Kirk will agree with me.'

'My reasons are not so noble as yours, Williams,' said Lieutenant Kirk. 'I have loved the sea ever since a fisherman took pity on a lonely orphan boy and took me out in his boat. I am never as happy as when I am aboard my ship. There is an equality among sailors that one does not find ashore.'

'I thought that rank was everything in the navy,' said Mary, dimpling her forehead. 'Is not the captain like a god, handing down judgement from on high?'

'That is true,' said Mr Kirk. 'I did not explain it well. What I mean is that, except for a few regrettable examples, everyone on a ship earns their place by merit. If you do your work well, nobody cares who your parents are, or if you have dark skin or a hare-lip. Africans, Spaniards, Lascars — all are valued, if they do their duty.'

'How different to London society, where appearances are everything,' said Mary, complacently fingering her diamond bandeau. 'Heaven help the poor woman who goes out in last month's fashion.' She glanced at Sarah. 'Or that of a previous age.'

'Perhaps I should consider joining the navy,' said Sarah dryly. 'Although I doubt the equality Mr Kirk speaks of extends to women.'

'You might solve your problem by purchasing a new gown,' said Mary. 'I would be happy to provide the name of a good modiste. But society can only be a trial for unfortunate creatures like poor Miss Lowther. What happened at Almack's is proof of it.'

'Not all society,' said Eleanor composedly. 'When I am at home, or with Sarah, I feel quite as content as Mr Kirk aboard his ship. And,' she added, with a fetching blush, 'I have felt the same blessing this evening.'

'As have I,' said Mr Kirk.

'God bless the good ship Lowther,' said Sarah, raising her coffee cup. 'And all who sail in her.'

Chapter Twenty-nine

'Louisa looked pretty tonight,' Ann remarked, as she and Sarah prepared for bed. 'Did not you think so?' she added when Sarah did not make an immediate answer.

'I have always considered her handsome.'

'You never said so, at least not to me. Tonight her complexion was remarkably fine. I must ask if she uses Gowland's, or anything of that kind.'

'It could not have been stimulated by the insipid Mr Packham,' Sarah remarked. 'I cannot compliment Louisa on her taste in suitors.'

'You speak as if you were jealous of Mr Packham.'

Sarah tugged off her gloves and flexed her fingers.

'I am. Exceedingly so. How I wish we had a rich uncle to leave us twenty thousand pounds.'

Ann said no more, but as they lay down on the bed together, her words lodged themselves in Sarah's mind. Jealousy was a detestable emotion, but could she acquit herself? She had certainly found it difficult to observe Louisa with that slope-shouldered fool. The sight had affected her so strongly that she had almost failed to acknowledge Louisa's presence, a discourtesy she had instantly regretted, perceiving that Louisa had been justifiably surprised and hurt by the coolness of her greeting. And hurting Louisa was the last thing in the world she wished to do. No, what she wished to do to Louisa was quite different. An image of full, pale breasts swelling enticingly above cream satin lurched into her mind, accompanied by a sudden heating of her blood. How she had fooled herself, believing she had come to town to visit her banker, when Louisa had been ever foremost in her mind. After seeing her tonight, undeniably attractive even in the plainest of dresses, Sarah knew it was no longer possible to suppress her feelings. Since becoming acquainted with Louisa, she had lived in a heightened state of being. Every moment seemed charged with meaning, every scent enhanced, every opening door bearing the possibility of Louisa.

She longed to present herself as a rival to Mr Packham. She was aware of certain women who lived together as companions but were rumoured to share a closer connection. Sarah now acknowledged that, if she were to share her life with anyone, she wished it might be with Louisa, whose prowess in trade and finance would be the perfect partner to Sarah's knowledge of estate business. In addition, since knowing Louisa, Sarah had become more aware of the feelings of others and more willing to listen to advice. She was aware of how frequently she caused offence but wasn't always certain why. She sensed that Louisa could help her understand her own deficiencies and soften her sharp edges. Where many were too afraid to point out Sarah's faults, Louisa had never hesitated to inform her when she erred. It showed her to be a woman of spirit as well as intelligence, although that should surprise nobody. It took strength of mind and courage for a young lady to travel to a foreign land with only a maid for company. Yet Sarah felt much more than mere admiration for Louisa's character. She longed to hold Louisa in her arms, to claim her as her own. But it was a quite absurd fantasy. She could hardly expect Louisa to give up her own hopes and shackle herself to Kenilborough's troubles.

And yet, there had been that kiss. Sarah pressed her fingertips to the cheek that had felt the press of Louisa's lips. Was that not encouragement that Louisa might have some affection for her, beyond friendship? To not know, suddenly, was torture. On the morrow, she must go to Louisa and lay out her feelings. It was better to know at once whether Louisa welcomed the passions that raged in Sarah's breast than to live in this constant state of agitation. She could not continue as she was. She had already abandoned her duty to come to London, drawn by a desperate need to see Louisa. It was time to grasp the nettle and let the consequences be as they may.

Chapter Thirty

$\mathcal{L}$ ouisa took breakfast with Mary, who seemed inordinately pleased with herself.

'Frederick has gone to the bank to take Lieutenant Kirk's deposit. And we have received a letter from Mr Packham. He intends to call upon us at noon today. I am sure he will propose. Are you not delighted?'

'That would be gratifying, certainly,' said Louisa, unable to summon up quite as much satisfaction as Mary. Still, if the business were to be done, it were best done promptly.

When they retired to the parlour, Louisa was surprised to observe that much of the furniture had vanished.

'I am having it re-upholstered,' Mary explained. 'I weary of that dreadful orchid pattern. One finds it in half the parlours in town. There's a lovely new chinoiserie damask, just come in from the East Indies. I could not resist it.'

Such a step seemed extraordinarily profligate to Louisa, but it was not her place to comment on the domestic affairs of her hosts. A man in a handcart came and took away half the linens.

'I have been obliged to dismiss my charwoman and must send everything out to be washed until I can replace her,' said Mary. Unable to settle, Louisa rose and stepped to the window. The sky was as grey as unwashed sheets. Further down the street, a hatless figure in a dark greatcoat was approaching, weaving between the dawdlers, her brow knitted. Seeing Sarah Davenport's familiar outline, the way she strode briskly through the crowd, stirred Louisa's spirits, although she could not think that Sarah was in the neighbourhood to visit her. But Sarah approached and turned up the steps to the Levitts' house. A moment later the doorbell jangled.

'Mr Packham!' cried Mary Levitt, rising. 'And five minutes before his time. The man is willing.'

'I do not think—' Louisa began, as Sarah was announced.

'Miss Davenport? What business can she have with us?' Mary Levitt wondered aloud. 'You must tell her we are not at home.'

But Sarah had followed the footman in, without waiting to be called.

'Louisa, I have come...' Sarah broke off, her eyes flicking towards Mary. 'That is, I would speak with you on a private matter.'

'You have walked here from Fenchurch Street?' Louisa asked, her nerves unaccountably agitated.

'I have been to the City to visit my banker. I would not trouble the Lowthers for their carriage. I have not money to waste on hackneys.' Sarah's words tumbled after one another. Louisa could only suppose the long walk must have made her breathless. A strand of hair dropped onto Sarah's forehead and Louisa felt a strong urge to reach out and brush it back into place.

'I regret that you have had a wasted journey. We are just

going out. You might come back tomorrow,' said Mary, craning her neck to try and see through the window.

'I leave town tomorrow,' Sarah addressed Louisa. 'There is a particular matter I wish… That is… might I persuade you to delay your excursion?'

'Impossible,' said Mary Levitt. 'All is arranged. Why, Louisa, here is the carriage now.'

Louisa pretended not to notice her pointed look. Clopping hooves and the cry of a coachman told Louisa that a carriage was, indeed, drawing up. It could only be Mr Packham.

'You are not leaving so soon?' she asked Sarah, feeling as if a noose had been laid around her neck.

'Mrs Lowther blames London for her ailment and wishes to return home. We all go together. Perhaps you and I might walk to Fenchurch Street now? Everyone will wish to see you before they depart.'

'I cannot,' said Louisa, bowing her head miserably. She knew her duty. 'Please, you must leave.'

Sarah's brow creased in confusion.

'What errand is so important that you neglect your friends?'

'I'm sorry, but I really must. . . I beg you will give all at Fenchurch Street my love.'

'Love?' Sarah echoed with a bitterness that stung Louisa. At that moment, Mr Packham was announced. Mary greeted him warmly and bid him sit.

'You are at home to Mr Packham, but not to me?' Sarah observed tightly.

'We are,' Louisa admitted. What did it matter now if she lost Sarah's friendship? In a few moments, she would be engaged to Mr Packham.

'Then it seems I must bid you adieu.' Sarah's blue eyes rested on Louisa's for a long moment, and then, after brushing her gloved hand through her hair, she was gone. Louisa forced herself to sit and face Mr Packham, resisting an almost overwhelming impulse to go to the window for one last glimpse of Sarah Davenport.

Mr Packham was attired in his usual sombre garb, although his cravat appeared new and his errant lock of hair had been tamed by the application of generous amounts of pomade.

'Mrs Levitt, I hope you will permit me the indulgence of a private audience with Miss Silverton,' he said, after the usual salutations.

'Of course.' Mary rose speedily and gathered up her skirts. 'You would do well to take him without delay,' she said to Louisa in a low voice as she passed. 'I say this as a friend.' With a smile and a wink at Mr Packham, she left the room. Louisa took advantage of the distraction to glance towards the window. A shower had come, sudden and hard, and a flurry of rain blurred the windowpane. She could see nothing but an indistinct muddle of umbrellas and dark coats.

'Ahem, Miss Silverton,' Mr Packham began. Louisa felt curiously removed from the situation, as if she were watching the scene from above. She hoped that he would come to the point quickly. The sooner all was agreed, the sooner she could write to her father with the good news. She formed her lips into an encouraging smile. Mr Packham cleared his throat.

It was soon clear that his was to be no speedy proposal. Mr Packham outlined the rationale for his choice and the many arguments, back and forth, that he had made with himself before coming to such a step. He listed the legal requirements and other assurances that would be needed to set his mind at rest, as well as his expected future returns, which included a male heir in addition to a minimum of eight per cent on capital invested. It was all very reasonable, very practical. Why then, did her insides feel like they were shrivelling?

'I have only one, last question,' said Packham. 'I have heard a rumour, unfounded I am sure, that your father is pursued for debt. If you assure me there is nothing to it, I will take you at your word, Miss Silverton.'

Louisa wrung her hands together on her lap. She knew what her father would wish her to say. Mr Levitt too. But she found she could not do it. She could not lie.

'Alas, I cannot give any such assurance,' she said.

Mr Packham stood swiftly and looked about for his hat.

'I would never have made my proposal had I any misgivings regarding your father's fortune. You will not hold me to words spoken without knowledge of the true circumstances, I hope?'

'I will not,' said Louisa. She might have attempted to explain that the underlying business was sound, and the problem was one of liquidity only, but she was too repulsed by his craven manner to appease him. 'I release you from any obligation regarding myself.'

'Although, if it came to it, there are no witnesses. It would be my word against yours.'

Louisa lifted her chin.

'Mr Packham, do not distress yourself. You are as free a man now as you were when you entered this room. All I ask is that you show discretion in this matter. Rumours can do untold mischief.'

Yet Mr Packham remained in a high state of agitation, spinning his hat between his hands.

'I must say, Miss Silverton, the fact that there has been any kind of doubt, or rumour in the matter, would make me extremely hesitant to repeat... that is to speak on any future occasion concerning an alliance. You must not expect it. I bid you good day.'

He left in such haste that Louisa wondered if there was a fire somewhere in the house and the servants had neglected to inform her. Mary Levitt hurried into the parlour, eager to wish Louisa joy. Louisa was obliged to disappoint her. She had failed, and with knowledge of her father's situation reaching London, she would have no further opportunities. Because of that failure, her father would have no choice but to retrench and sell many of their assets — maybe even their house in New York. Added to that, her friendship with Sarah Davenport lay in ruins. It shocked her to acknowledge which of these situations distressed her the most.

Chapter Thirty-one

A week after she returned from London, Sarah's father invited her into his office. It was just after dinner, and Joseph made to follow them, but her father said he wished to speak only with Sarah, raising hopes that he wanted to confer on the Kenilborough settlement, about which he had been silent since they had last spoken.

Lord Kenilborough sank into a high-backed chair, upholstered in pale calfskin. It had belonged to Sarah's grandfather, a tall man who had been a general during the American War of Independence. It made the present Lord Kenilborough look like a sprite, albeit an aged and weary one.

'Yesterday, I received a letter that troubled me,' he said.

'I hope it is not another demand for money,' said Sarah, taking the letter.

'Thankfully, no. It is from a fellow called Williams.'

'Any relation to the gallant captain whose fate is of such concern to Ann?'

'The very man. He asks for permission to correspond with your sister.'

Sarah scanned the letter. It was brief and to the point, which she approved. Captain Williams stated his admiration for Ann, set out honestly his own financial position, which was that he had nothing but his captain's stipend, but he hoped to achieve advancement to colonel through his own efforts. Until that time, being unable to court Ann in person, he sought permission to correspond.

'What am I to do? Is this not a little precipitous? Ann cannot have met this captain more than a few times.'

'Captain Williams did not seem a man to make empty declarations,' said Sarah. 'And I know Ann is greatly concerned for his safety and is always seeking out news from Spain. The question remains, should you permit it?'

'I suppose we cannot give her any kind of dowry?'

'Servicing our debts takes all our money.' Sarah ran the heel of her hand across her brow. 'Like me, she has only a thousand pounds from our mother. Perhaps we should encourage Ann to take Captain Williams while she can. Poor though he is, he has a profession. She may do better than us, in the end.'

'Are things so bad?' Her father looked at her in some distress. 'Were my faults so grievous that not even your efforts can save us?'

Sarah went to the window. The sun had long since set and she looked out onto a park that was a jumble of dark shadows.

'All is not lost, as long as we have Kenilborough.' She wondered if she was reassuring herself, as much as her father.

'Promise me you will take care of Margaret after I am gone. I know you are not good friends with your stepmother, but you would never send her away, I hope?'

She turned to him and placed her hand on his shoulder. He

carried so little flesh she could feel his collarbone jutting out beneath his waistcoat and shirt.

'I would never leave the woman you married unsupported. You have my word she would be comfortably settled, if it is in my power.'

'And Joseph? Will you treat him as a brother?'

Her jaw tightened and she withdrew her hand.

'That man will never be a brother of mine.'

'You would cast him out?'

'I will not deceive you. I could never countenance him living at Kenilborough if I am mistress.'

'But Sarah…'

'You cannot move me on this point, Father.'

Lord Kenilborough loosened his neck cloth.

'What am I to do about Captain Williams?'

'Let me speak with Ann,' said Sarah. 'And then we shall decide.'

Chapter Thirty-two

The next morning, as they dressed together, Sarah stood behind her sister, who was brushing her hair whilst staring vacantly into her dressing table mirror. Sarah placed her hands upon her sister's shoulders.

'Tell me truthfully, Ann. What are your feelings towards Captain Williams?'

Ann looked at Sarah's reflection in the mirror.

'I like him better than anyone I have ever met,' she admitted. 'Excepting you, of course. I know we only met on a few occasions, but a day does not pass without me thinking of him. The idea that he is in danger distresses me unaccountably. Could such feelings be love, do you think?'

'I do not believe you can truly know your heart after such a short acquaintance.'

Ann set down her brush.

'You have made even swifter judgements regarding character. To be sure, it is usually when you feel a strong dislike. As you did with Joseph and our stepmother.'

Sarah held her sister's gaze in the mirror.

'You make a fair point. I will also admit that I respect your captain very much. But liking is different to being his wife.'

'I do not know what I would say, were he to ask me,' said Ann. 'I am sure it is unlikely, for someone as handsome and brave as he could do much better than I.'

Sarah kissed the top of Ann's head.

'If Captain Williams thought that, I would have to change my opinion and think him an extremely stupid fellow. I suppose the only way we can find out his true character is to permit you to correspond.'

'Oh, do you think father would allow it?' said Ann with such hope that Sarah couldn't help but smile.

'I am sure we can convince him,' she said.

Captain Williams' letter was an unwelcome reminder that Sarah still had her own marriage proposal to answer. When Lady Melgrove stopped by in her barouche with an invitation to an evening party, Sarah knew that she could delay no longer.

As the Kenilborough party entered the drawing room of Melgrove Park, Sarah felt Vere's eyes on her. He lost no time in drawing her aside to a window seat. Sarah squared her shoulders. She may dislike him, but the man deserved a swift and clear response.

'I see that I am to be disappointed,' Vere said tightly.

'I acknowledge your proposal was delicately made and the terms more than generous.'

'Yet you reject them?'

'I'm sure you will recover from any fleeting disappointment,' said Sarah. 'Let us not pretend there are any feelings involved in the matter.'

He sniffed in disapproval.

'I had supposed you to be more pragmatic.'

He rose and departed as swiftly as he had engaged her, leaving her alone by the window. Another woman might have felt aggrieved at being abandoned so abruptly, but Sarah felt only relief. Although her decision left her family still teetering on the brink of oblivion, her heart felt lighter than it had done in many weeks. She was free of obligation, permitted once more to think and feel as she wished. Free, her heart whispered, to think of Louisa. But there was little comfort there. She had been prepared to lay her heart bare in London, only to be dismissed, with very little civility, so that Louisa might receive Mr Packham. She supposed they would be engaged by now, although Eleanor had not yet reported any news of that kind.

Sarah was so busy reviewing her thoughts, she did not notice Henry Mulcaster approach.

'Ahem,' he coughed, making her start. He thrust a glass of wine at her, even though the one she had was still half full.

'I see you are prepared, as always,' he said, his muscular neck bulging above his white neck cloth. He set down the spare glass on the windowsill. After a brief hesitation, he put his own glass beside it and sat down next to her.

'You are a damned fine woman, Sarah,' he began.

'If you are about to propose, I beg you will not. The idea is preposterous.'

'Is it?'

'Most certainly.'

He stood up.

'Oh, well, you know best.' He picked up his glass, raised it to his lips, lowered it again untasted and then, with a muttered apology, he moved away. Although once more finding herself alone, Sarah elected to remain where she was. It seemed safer, at present, to avoid others altogether. But then the discussion across the room began to command her attention.

'The bank has failed, you say? How unfortunate for poor Miss Silverton,' Sarah's father was saying.

'I had it from my agent in town,' said Lord Melgrove. 'They closed the doors yesterday.'

Sarah immediately demanded to know of what they were speaking.

'It seems your friend's father was not quite the success we were led to believe. There was a run on the bank and there are rumours that his businesses in New York have gone under.'

'A most unfortunate affair,' said Lady Melgrove. 'I am relieved Vere had the good sense not to get entangled with that family.'

'You are to be congratulated on your escape,' said Lady Kenilborough. 'I never liked that girl. Pretending to be rich when she was nothing of the kind.'

'That is unfair,' cried Sarah. 'There is no pretence at all about Louisa.'

'One should not be surprised, with such relations. The Lowthers are such uncivil people. That awful ball — such a dreadful, crowded affair. If Sarah were not so friendly with Miss Lowther, we would not keep up the acquaintance.'

'I found Miss Silverton to be quite pretty,' said Lady Melgrove. 'And she dressed well. I hope she will find a husband. But she should not be so eager to marry for money — or, at least, she should not own it so openly. Some might consider it vulgar.'

'But marrying for a title is not?' Sarah cried, enraged by such an open slight upon Louisa. She looked askance at her step-mother. 'Or, indeed, marrying for both?'

'Why must you always be so quarrelsome?' protested Lady Kenilborough.

Sarah bit back a response. She cared little for her stepmother's opinion, but there was another who had called her so — one in whose judgement she had greater faith. One who was now in desperate trouble.

'Are you certain?' she asked Lord Melgrove.

'Oh yes,' said Vere, with a level of satisfaction that made her blood boil. 'It is quite certain. Silverton's Bank is broke. You can be sure its creditors will be baying at Miss Silverton's door as we speak.'

Chapter Thirty-three

'iss?' It was her maid, Leah. 'Miss, wake up. Something is amiss.'

Louisa blinked sleepily, unused to being roused so abruptly. She had been finding it difficult to sleep these past few days. Rumours about the bank had continued to circulate and she had requested that Mr Levitt show her the reserve, so that she might reassure everyone that all was well. Mr Levitt had been happy to oblige, saying only that they must wait for Mr Simmons, whose key was required alongside Mr Levitt's to open the vault. The previous day, Mr Simmons had been indisposed, but Louisa hoped that today everything might be settled.

'What's the matter?' she asked.

'The Levitts are gone.'

'Gone out? At this hour?'

'No, miss, they've gone away. Took all the valuables with them and anything else that could be carried.'

'That cannot be.' Louisa sat up.

'I wish it were not so, but the servants are speaking of nothing else.'

Louisa threw on a shawl. Mr Panks, the butler, was waiting outside her door, looking grave. In his hand was a sealed note, addressed to her. It contained something hard and heavy.

'This was in Mr Levitt's study,' he said solemnly, extending the note towards her. 'I hope you will acquaint me of anything within that relates to the servants. As you can imagine, there is considerable disquiet below stairs.'

Louisa took the note wordlessly. Inside was a letter and two keys.

My dear Louisa,

I regret leaving you in such a situation. A mixture of unwise investments on my part and Mary's inability to live within our means brought me to such a desperate condition that I was obliged to borrow from the bank. I fully intended to pay it all back, with interest, but recent rumours arising for our selling off bullion has led to rising requests for withdrawals, which our depleted reserves cannot meet. My own creditors pursue me so closely that I am obliged to leave town. I enclose the keys to the vault at Silverton's, so you may see for yourself that it is empty. You are better knowing the worst than to carry any vain hope.

I beg you will pass on my deepest regrets to Mr Silverton, whose patronage was an honour that should not have been bestowed on such a poor wretch. I am thankful you have such good people as the Lowthers to take care of you. Your safety, at

least, will not lay on my conscience. I advise you to flee London as soon as you have read this.
Yours, regretfully,
Fred Levitt

Louisa let fall the note with a cry. Mr Panks asked if he might be permitted to read it. Louisa fluttered her hand in acquiescence, for there could be no hiding the shame.

'This is troubling indeed,' he said stiffly. 'I must inform the servants at once. They will need to look for positions elsewhere.'

'Of course,' said Louisa. 'I will provide characters for any that need them.'

'I fear the Silverton name will do more harm than good if the bank has gone under,' said Mr Panks. 'You are aware that none of the servants have been paid this quarter?'

Louisa coloured.

'I will give them what is owed,' she said. 'Leah, please fetch my reticule.'

'Oh, no miss,' said Leah. 'Mr Levitt's debts are not yours.' She and Mr Panks exchanged dark looks.

'I have been well served by those in this house. I have a responsibility to make reparation,' Louisa insisted.

'I honour you, Miss Silverton,' said Mr Panks. 'I will be sure to speak well of you, despite what has happened with your bank.'

'The bank!' Louisa cried, roused into action. 'I must go at once.'

With Leah's assistance, she dressed quickly. The coach house was empty and it was surmised that the Levitts had taken the carriage to make their escape. Louisa's spirits were too agitated to wait for a hackney and so she and Leah walked the two miles to Birchin Lane, where Silverton's Bank was situated. As she rounded the corner, Louisa started back in horror. A mob bayed at the door, notes of credit and cheques clutched in their fists.

'I must explain.' Louisa stepped out into the road. Leah pulled her back.

'Oh, miss, do not think of it. They'll tear you to pieces.' The heavy black doors of the bank began to crack beneath the blows that pounded upon them. Louisa blanched as the doors collapsed and the mob seethed forward.

'Miss Silverton,' said a low voice at her shoulder. 'You must not be seen here.' She turned to see a grizzled man, tidily presented despite his advanced years and his slightly hunched back. She recognised him as Mr Smythe, the clerk who had served her when she had drawn down her allowance of a hundred guineas. He was followed by a line of porters, each carrying a stack of books.

'We have saved the ledgers. Once everything has calmed down, we can ascertain who is owed what.'

'What can be done?'

'Nothing at present. I have sent for the militia to guard the strong room.'

'I fear there is nothing to protect,' said Louisa with a heavy sigh.

'Then the rumours are true? In that case, Miss Silverton, I strongly advise you to leave town as soon as you can, for you will not be safe here.'

'But what of our customers? Have they lost everything?'

'We must see to the balance sheet, but I suspect we will be able to pay out no more than a few pence in the pound. Unless your father can remit funds from abroad?'

Louisa could only shake her head. With this blow, after so many others, would the Silverton company itself survive? With one last look at the bank, she asked Leah to take her back to Portland Square. The servants were already packed, waiting only for Louisa and her promise of payment. Once she had settled with them all, Louisa was left with just three guineas.

'What shall we do now, miss?' Leah asked as the last servant departed, leaving them utterly alone. It was a question to which, at that moment, Louisa had no answer.

Chapter Thirty-four

a doorbell chimed through the empty rooms of the Portland Square residence. Louisa told Leah that she would receive no visitors, unless it was Mr Smythe. It was two days since the collapse of the bank. The previous day, the clerk had come to Portland Square to report that the mob was gone, having destroyed everything except the strong room. Louisa had accompanied the clerk to Birchin Lane and, using the keys left by Mr Levitt, they confirmed for themselves that the vault was empty.

The ringer of the bell was not Mr Smythe, however, but the post-boy, who had found the servant's door locked and had taken the bold decision to try the main door. Among a pile of letters for Mr Levitt was one addressed to Louisa. The paper was marked with grease and smelled strongly of fish, but Louisa recognised the handwriting as her father's. She tore it open, her heart swelling with a desperate hope that, by some miracle, he had rescued the company and was coming to England.

My dearest Louisa,

I am taken up for debt. *The Jupiter* has foundered off the coast of Panama and another of our ships was seized by the British, along with its cargo. Dare I hope, daughter, that you have succeeded in the task I set you? That you can release me? For if you cannot, you must instruct Levitt to sell the bank and bring all proceeds to New York at once. I cannot overstate our peril, for there are more writs now issued than can ever be repaid by the sale of our American assets. You and Levitt represent my last, best hope.

Louisa let out a low groan. Leah rushed to her side but the blow was too much for Louisa and she sank to the floor. All was lost. Her father was in prison and she had no means to help him. She had never known what it was to be poor, and now she was practically penniless. Despite Leah's attentions, she was unable to eat, think or act for the remainder of the day.

The next morning Louisa woke and, though a depression of spirits made her long to stay abed, she forced herself to rise. She must act. There must be some way of getting to New York. She refused to believe all was lost. She knew the assets of the company better than anyone and was sure that something could yet be saved. Her toilette was barely complete when there was an insistent banging at the front door. Having no servants, Louisa went to the door herself, Leah following close behind.

It was Mr Cossington, the moneylender she had met at Kenilborough, together with his one-eyed giant and two other men.

'I've come for Levitt's belongings.' He pushed his way into the house without waiting to be invited. As Louisa started to protest, he waved a paper in her face. 'I've a writ, right here. I don't suppose yer know where he went? The bearstard's skipped tearn without payin' what he owes.'

'I do not,' said Louisa. She had no strength to resist as the men streamed through the house. Everything was removed. Chairs, tables, rugs. Even the velvet drapes were torn down and taken out to a pair of large wagons parked outside. Only Leah's quick thinking prevented the loss of Louisa's own possessions. Louisa's maid gathered up her employer's gowns, shoes and trinkets and thrust them into her chest, before locking it up and tucking the key into her bosom. When the cyclops attempted to take up the chest, Leah sat upon it and refused to move. Yet the battle was not completely won, for Mr Cossington insisted he had the right to take everything in the house. He ordered his cyclops to drag Leah from her perch.

Leah was fending off the brute when there was a commotion down below, followed by the sound of footsteps in the hallway, heavy and rapid. They began to ascend the stairs. Louisa let out a cry of dismay. What new trouble was this? Had the Bow Street Runners come to arrest her? She had no idea whether English laws would deem her culpable for the collapse of the bank. However, as the new arrivals closed on her position, Louisa recognised something familiar in the vigorous cadence of those footfalls. Her spirits soared even before she could quite comprehend why.

The door to her chamber was thrown open and Sarah Davenport strode in, the hem of her coat clogged with dirt, her boots leaving a trail of muddy imprints in her wake. Her groom, Thomas, followed close behind, equally bespattered. Louisa could not have imagined a more unexpected and yet heartening sight, unless her father could have been miraculously transported across the Atlantic.

'Mr Cossington, how unpleasant to see you again. I hope you are not seeking redress from a blameless person,' Sarah remarked.

'Hardly blameless, when she shares her name with that bank what's gone bust.'

'Even if Miss Silverton could be held accountable for her father's business, I cannot believe you are owed anything from that quarter. You do not strike me as the sort of fellow who keeps his money in a bank.'

'I've a writ, fair an' square.'

Sarah held out a gloved hand.

'Show it to me.'

Cossington thrust his paper at Sarah, who perused it quickly.

'This gives you rights to anything of Mr Levitt's. Nothing of Miss Silverton's. Leah, stay exactly where you are.'

'I intend to, Miss Sarah,' said Leah stoutly.

Cossington snatched back his writ and jerked his head toward the chest. 'How do I know there ain't nothing of Levitt's in there?'

'Admit defeat, man. Would Mr Levitt leave anything of value if it were small enough to be carried away?'

Cossington wiped his nose on the back of his hand.

'Mebbee yer right. But mebbee I'm owed something for keeping Miss Silverton's whereabouts secret. There's plenty of folk would like to speak with her, I'm sure.'

Louisa recalled the mob at the door of the bank and shuddered.

'You are owed nothing more than a sound thrashing,' said Sarah. 'Tell whomever you wish, for Miss Silverton is leaving. Come, Louisa. Thomas, bring Miss Silverton's chest. Leah, if you will allow us?'

With a dark look at the cyclops, Leah relinquished the chest to Sarah's groom. Louisa found herself bundled into a hackney carriage. Leah and Sarah joined her, whilst Thomas climbed up the outside with the chest.

'Where are we going?' Louisa asked, her pulse still thready and erratic from the shock of Cossington's visit.

'Charing Cross, to pick up the country coach. I am to take you back to Athelton.'

Her blood began to settle. After three days of feeling helpless and alone, it was a great relief to know she had such friends.

'You heard what happened?' Louisa wondered how the news could have travelled so fast.

'I was at Melgrove Park the night before last. I heard the news there.'

'How came you to London so quickly? Surely you did not ride all this way?'

'Never mind that. Your uncle will protect you until your father can sort out this unfortunate matter.'

'My father!' Louisa's throat closed up and tears pressed against the back of her eyes. She turned aside to hide her distress and felt Sarah's gloved hand press against her own. That gesture of concern made it impossible for Louisa to hold back her anguish and she broke into sobs.

'Miss Silverton's pa's in prison for debt,' Leah explained. 'And Miss hasn't more than a few guineas in her purse, not after she paid off Mr Levitt's household. I told her she shouldn't.'

'I felt honour… duty…' Louisa sniffled through her tears.

'You did right,' said Sarah approvingly.

But Louisa could only remember the mob at the door of the bank. 'All those poor people.' Her hand went to her mouth. 'Oh, Lieutenant Kirk — his prize money — all gone!'

'Louisa, you are not to blame.'

'Am I not?' she protested bitterly. Tears stung her eyes. 'After priding myself on understanding numbers and calculations better than anyone else, I have been taken for a fool.'

'Let me take you home, to Athelton.'

Only now did Louisa realise she had felt more at home at Athelton than she ever had in her father's house in New York. The idea of accepting her uncle's protection was tempting, but she shook her head.

'I cannot.' She sucked in a lungful of air and wiped the tears from her cheeks. After another settling breath, she looked up. There was nothing in Sarah's expression but concern. 'I must return to America, to help Papa.'

'I don't like to say it, miss, but how are we to get there on three guineas?' asked Leah.

Louisa chewed her lip. 'I have not thought of the means, only that I must do it.'

'If it comes to it, I have brought the money I owe you,' said Sarah. 'I was concerned the collapse of the bank might have placed you in immediate difficulties.'

'I will not take money that was meant as a gift for… you and your sister.'

Sarah leaned forward.

'Louisa, do you not see? It is your own liberality that now gives you the means to help your father. Had you not lent Ann that money, or if you had not helped me pay off Cossington, there would be no money in this purse. It is rightfully yours and you must take it.' Sarah pressed a heavy purse into Louisa's hand. 'Do not argue with me on this point, for a quartet of oxen could not be more stubborn.'

The cab drew up at Charing Cross.

'I must find the coach to Plymouth,' Louisa said.

'Will you not change your mind?' Sarah asked. 'Nobody will condemn you for accepting your uncle's protection.' She ran her hands down her thighs, thumbs first, as though squeezing water from the material of her skirts. 'Or, if you prefer, you would be most welcome at Kenilborough.'

However, Louisa's mind was made up.

'I shall follow your advice. I will use my own talents to help my father instead of looking to marriage as the answer. It is what I always longed to do, but never had the courage to insist on it.'

'Do I understand, then, that Mr Packham's interest did not survive the collapse of Silverton's?'

'It died before that.'

'Then the man is even more of a fool than he looked.'

'You are unfair, for it was nothing but good sense on his part. When he offered me his hand he asked if there was any truth in the rumours about my father debts. I could not lie to him.'

'Even though twenty thousand pounds would help you greatly — particularly at this moment?'

Louisa attempted a smile.

'I have discovered, after all, that some things are more important than money. A fine time for such a revelation, but that cannot be helped.'

Chapter Thirty-five

S arah sensed that Louisa was distressed to the point of imminent collapse and insisted on accompanying her to Plymouth.

'While Leah has shown admirable courage, I will not let you go alone to such a place. There may be some wait before we can find you a ship.'

They were fortunate, for the New England packet was due to leave on April 25th, which fell two days hence, although it took thirty guineas to secure the last remaining passenger berth. They were indebted to Lieutenant Kirk, who had happened to be about the docks when they had arrived, overseeing the provisioning of his ship. Poor Louisa had shrunk from approaching him, but once Sarah had explained all, he immediately offered his assistance. Sarah was impressed by such generosity of spirit from a man who had been wronged so grievously. She could tell by Louisa's tearful apologies and expressions of gratitude that she felt the same, but the Scotsman refused to accept Louisa's regrets; refused to accept she was in any way to blame. Without him, they would certainly have missed their chance. He knew about the packet and it was only his speedy intercession with the agent that secured Louisa's berth.

'We must find somewhere to stay for tonight and tomorrow,' said Sarah, seeing that Louisa was too distracted to make any decisions. 'But I must beg you to pay for my accommodation and a bed in the cellar for Thomas, for I gave you all the money I had. No, you must not try to give me any of it back, for it was only what you were owed.'

'You did not tell me how you got it.'

Sarah did not wish to concern Louisa by admitting that she had signed a note for a hundred and twenty pounds, brokered with a moneylender by their London banker. She had sworn never to take out such a dangerous and costly form of credit, but Louisa's need had been impossible to ignore. The only stipulation she made was that her banker should not deal with anyone named Cossington.

'How were you going to get home?' Louisa asked. 'You did not intend to walk all the way to Kenilborough, surely? It must be hundreds of miles.'

'I have a shilling or two, somewhere,' said Sarah patting her pockets fruitlessly. 'And a viscount's daughter can usually beg a lift, in exigent circumstances.'

It turned out that the inns in Plymouth were full of navy men, for half the fleet was anchored in the Sound. They were obliged to share a room at a grubby little inn along one of the back streets. When the innkeeper showed them to the small attic room with a bed scarce big enough for one person, let alone two sharing, Sarah felt something akin to panic. Louisa did not seem to notice, or consider the practicalities of their situation, sinking onto the bed with a deep sigh.

'I'm suddenly extraordinarily weary.'

Sarah called for a servant, giving instructions for a fire to be set in the hearth and for hot food and ale to be brought up.

'I thought you might prefer to eat privately,' she explained.

'Just what I would wish,' said Louisa.

The fire was soon crackling in the grate, sending out a pleasing warmth. The stew, although bland, was hot and there was plenty of it. Sarah, who had not eaten since a brief stop at an inn outside Exeter, devoured hers swiftly. Louisa pushed hers away.

'Are you going to eat that?' Sarah asked.

'I am not hungry.'

Sarah took the plate and finished it, eating more steadily now her initial hunger had been sated.

'What did you wish to tell me, when you came to Portland Square?' Louisa asked. It was such a surprising question, given their circumstances.

'Nothing of importance,' Sarah said swiftly. This was not the time to burden Louisa with any kind of declaration. Yet Louisa seemed to be expecting her to say something more.

'I wished to thank you,' she added. 'I showed my banker the accounts and projected profits for the quarry and they agreed to extend our repayment period until after the summer harvest. Had they not done so, I would have had no choice but to accept Vere Mulcaster's proposal after all.' This was the truth, although by no means the whole of it.

'You must have thought me intolerably rude,' said Louisa. 'But with my father's business in such straits, I had determined to accept Mr Packham. What a dreadful mess I have made of everything.'

Louisa's dark eyes began to swim with tears. How Sarah

longed to kiss those tears away, but it was no time for indulging her own selfish desires. She settled for squeezing Louisa's hand.

'Oh, Sarah, come with me,' Louisa cried with such desperation that Sarah's heart cracked, for what Louisa asked was impossible.

'I cannot,' she said brokenly. 'The future of Kenilborough depends on what happens over the next months. I cannot abandon it.'

Louisa dashed a hand to her eyes and nodded. 'Forgive me. I should never have asked. Forget that I did. It was a moment of weakness.'

'You are stronger than you know, Louisa. You will survive this.'

Louisa composed herself and then raised her hand to her mouth to stifle a yawn. She reached for her nightgown. 'I am beyond weary. Will you unlace me? I don't want to disturb Leah so late.'

'Of course,' Sarah said casually, although her fingers trembled as Louisa turned and lifted her hair so that Sarah could access the silk ties that cinched her dress in just below her bosom. The scent of rosewater lingered on her neck and made Sarah's breath catch in her throat. She fumbled ineffectually with the ties.

'I do not know why I am so clumsy,' she said with a cough. Her fingers brushed the warm skin at the nape of Louisa's neck and sent a sharp but delicious thrill jolting down to the pit of her stomach. At last the ties were free and Louisa slipped one arm from her dress, revealing a smooth, bare shoulder.

'I will give you your privacy,' Sarah stuttered, fleeing the room before her desires betrayed her completely. She stalked up and down the corridor for almost a half hour before she felt sufficiently composed to return to the room. When she did so, Louisa was in bed, fast asleep, her dark hair falling around her neck and shoulders. Sarah had left Kenilborough so swiftly she'd had no time to pack, so she undressed down to her chemise and drawers. When she slipped beneath the sheets, the bed was so small, she could not help but touch up against Louisa. She felt the warmth of Louisa's skin, separated from her own by just a few thin layers of linen. Just like the night after the ball. Then, Sarah had no thoughts of passion. Louisa had needed comfort and reassurance and Sarah had been glad to supply it. But tonight she yearned to take Louisa in her arms. Yet was not Louisa equally vulnerable at this moment? In need of succour and comfort, rather than a passionate embrace? Sarah did not trust herself to place so much as a hand on Louisa's sleeping form and lay awake beside her, stiff and unmoving, for the entire night.

Chapter Thirty-six

*L*ouisa paid the innkeeper and gave one of the stable boys a sixpence to carry her chest down to the quay, for word had come that her packet would depart on the next tide. It was a blustery day, and the surface of the sea was choppy, whipped up into frothy white peaks. Lieutenant Kirk stopped to say his goodbyes, for his ship was also due to leave.

'What is your opinion of Mr Kirk?' Sarah asked as they watched the lieutenant being rowed back to his ship by sailors wearing their best duck trousers. In return for his service, he had asked only to be remembered to Mr and Mrs Lowther, whose kindness in taking notice of a poor and lonely Scotsman he would never forget. He had not mentioned their daughter, but from his look Louisa had deduced that Eleanor was very much in his mind. The little boat struggled against the lively swell, dipping and rising as it made slow progress out into the bay.

'I think there can be few finer men in existence,' said Louisa. 'To have assisted me so generously, after all that has happened.'

'I believe Eleanor is of the same opinion. She has already

subscribed to the naval gazette so that she may follow the fortunes of the *Cadmus*. I am glad of it, for I shall look in it for any news of America. But I hope you will write to me yourself? I shall not rest until I know you are landed safe.'

Louisa promised she would do so. She couldn't help but notice that, since her desperate plea for Sarah to come with her, Sarah had reverted to her usual stiff and abrupt manner. It pained her, but she could only blame herself. What had prompted her to demand something so selfish?

'I, in turn, hope you will think sometimes of your own happiness, Sarah, not just your estate,' she said, clapping her hand against the top of her bonnet as a gust of wind threatened to dislodge it and send it spinning into the sea.

'The two go hand in hand, for I will never be happy until Kenilborough is out of debt.'

'If my stay in this country has taught me anything, it is unwise to rely on just one thing to be happy.'

'But I am nothing without Kenilborough,' Sarah insisted, the stiff breeze catching the hem of her greatcoat and sending it swirling about her booted feet. Above them seagulls circled, screeching in protest as they were swept upward.

'That is not true. You are a most loving sister and the very... the very best of friends.' Louisa's voice gave out. Sarah, with a decided motion, pulled a flat velvet box from a pocket within her greatcoat and thrust it towards Louisa.

'I cannot bear to think of you alone and penniless, so far from your friends. I know no one more capable in matters of business than you, but everyone must have capital. Let this be yours. You might pawn it, or, if things get very bad, you have my permission to sell it.'

Louisa opened the box. Inside lay the sapphire necklace that Ann had worn at the ball. Her heart swelled.

'I cannot take this.' She snapped the box shut and thrust it back towards Sarah. 'It was your mother's.'

'You must. If my mother knew what my feelings... that is to say, if she knew of your situation, she would wish you to have it. I do not know how much it will fetch — you will know the value of the gemstones better than I.'

Louisa's fingers curled around the box.

'I know only that this is a gift beyond price.' She leaned towards Sarah and kissed her tenderly on the lips, her eyes misted by tears of gratitude. So deeply stirred were her emotions that she barely felt Sarah disengage awkwardly and help her towards the quayside. Without quite knowing how, she was placed in a small launch, along with her chest. Sarah muttered something incomprehensible before turning and striding away, and Louisa realised only too late she had lost her last chance to say farewell. The launch took her aboard the packet, and a servant showed her to the tiny cabin that would be her home for the next month. The cry went up to raise anchor. Coming to herself, Louisa ran on deck and looked anxiously towards the shore.

There, on the quay, stood a hatless figure, the tails of her great-coat flapping in the wind. Louisa raised her hand and the figure, after a slight hesitation, did likewise. The capstan turned, the anchor weighed, and all too fast the shoreline retreated. As the gap widened between the ship and Sarah, Louisa felt something break inside her, and she had to fight a strong urge to run to the captain and beg he drop the launch and send her back. She wished she could fling herself into the arms of that stubborn, blunt, impossibly generous woman who made her feel so safe. She felt an aching need to cleave to Sarah and feel the warmth of her body and the soft, tender touch of her lips. If this was the impulse that had driven her mother to abandon her family, then Louisa at last began to understand it. But she had her duty, just as much as Sarah, and remained where she was. She watched the receding shoreline until they had rounded the headland and were heading into the choppy waters of the Atlantic.

Chapter Thirty-seven

Kenilborough, July, 1813

*S*arah looked out of her office window, tight lipped. The rain, incessant for the past month, had finally stopped, but the sun showed little sign of breaking through an obstinate blanket of grey cloud. Without sunlight to ripen it, their corn would rot in the fields, like their turnips.

''Twill come, Miss Sarah,' said Thomas sagely. 'Old Bess says we'll have no more rain 'til th'harvest moon is waning.'

'This is the same wise woman who told my father he would have a son to inherit the estate, after a passing glimpse of my mother's belly when I was yet unborn?'

Old Bess was an old woman, well known in the area and celebrated for reading tea leaves and entrails. As a rule, Sarah had no truck with such superstitions. Although, if someone were to suggest that a fortnight's sunshine could be guaranteed by the sacrifice of a few goats, she would be perfectly willing to oblige.

A week later the sun at last broke through the clouds. A brisk wind dried out the wheat and barley whose dull green kernels began to ripen into gold. Sarah was not yet prepared to credit Old Bess with second sight. A sudden storm might ruin everything. But the sun continued to shine and over the next month the corn ripened and the harvest could begin at last. Sarah was out before dawn and seldom returned before dark. Her days were spent overseeing the workers in the fields, chivvying any laggards who failed to pull their weight. At noon each day, she served the labourers with beer and pies, which she brought up from Kenilborough Hall using one of the gardeners' traps. Some days, the sun grew so fierce she was forced to borrow a straw hat from Mrs Morris to ward off sunstroke.

Yet, despite the distraction of the work, she could not shake off the feeling there was a void within her, as if some backstreet surgeon had removed a vital organ. A feeling that had been with her ever since Plymouth.

Halfway through the harvest, Sarah returned to Kenilborough to be greeted by Mr Hogg the instant she entered the kitchens.

'Any letters?' she asked, perching on the edge of the shoe-rack to pull off her dusty boots. She brushed down her split skirts, which were speckled with husks of wheat and barley. It had been months since she had received a brief note from Louisa to say she had landed safely in Marblehead and was on her way to visit her father in gaol, but, since then, nothing. Sarah herself had written several letters, longing to openly offer Louisa the devoted and unconstrained assistance of a lover. However, she found it impossible to write what she felt. In desperation, she had turned to the poets she had so long despised for inspiration but had found nothing to help her. The romantic language of poetry had only deepened the aching emptiness she had felt since Louisa's departure. She had set the books aside. What was to be gained by stoking the fires of heartache? She had lost her chance when she had failed to speak her heart in Plymouth.

'No letters, Miss Sarah,' said Hogg, 'but Captain Williams has arrived. The war in Spain is over. He is in the parlour with her ladyship and Miss Ann.'

Captain Williams' looks had been only enhanced by his exploits in Spain and France. His face was tanned and he had lost weight, which increased the impressive definition of his jaw. His uniform had not fared so well. The Spanish sun had leached colour from the shoulders, leaving the material as pale as wilting geraniums. The chest and arms boasted dark stains, about which it was probably best not to enquire. He greeted Sarah cheerfully.

'You will forgive my appearance,' he said. 'My dress uniform has been misplaced somewhere betwixt here and Bordeaux, but I could not bring myself to wait for it.'

Sarah assured the captain that his appearance gave those at Kenilborough nothing but pleasure. Lady Kenilborough failed to second Sarah's assertion but Captain Williams, who looked only at Ann, did not appear to notice. Ann was unable to speak, and her neck and cheeks were so flushed, she might be mistaken for a ripening strawberry. Taking pity on them, Sarah suggested Ann show Captain Williams the gardens, remarking that the hothouses contained much of interest at this time of year, while she went to speak with her father.

At the base of the Tudor tower, Sarah encountered the family lawyer coming down from the floor above. Mr Gregory rounded the corner of the narrow staircase with great caution, crabbing his substantial bulk sideways as he placed a buckled shoe on the next step. His glasses, tiny round frames no bigger than sixpences, teetered on the end of his bulbous nose and he carried a writing case beneath one arm and several rolls of papers under the other. Sarah hurried to assist him, but he would not permit her to relieve him of any of his burdens.

'These are legal documents, Miss Davenport, and subject to privilege. I must not let them out of my possession. When you see his lordship, you might advise him to drink less in the afternoon. These stairs present manifest peril, even for a sober man and his health should be our first consideration. In fact, I wonder if he shouldn't drink less altogether. Men make strange decisions when a bottle is involved. But I can only advise. I have no power to prevent my client doing what he wishes, however wrongheaded. Good day, Miss Davenport.'

Sarah found her father slumped in his chair, his fingers drumming restlessly against the base of a half-filled glass of sherry. Standing behind him was Joseph.

'I hear that fellow Williams is come,' said Lord Kenilborough with a dry cough. 'I suppose he is speaking with your sister?'

'We agreed they might correspond,' said Sarah. 'You must have known it may come to this.'

'I rather hoped they would come to their senses. That their initial infatuation might wane, knowing each other better.'

'You must refuse your consent,' said Joseph. 'Ann is pretty enough to marry extremely well. If she cannot catch an earl or a duke, then her husband should at least have money.' He glared at Sarah. 'Since Sarah refuses my help with the estate, our fortunes must be restored by other means. And we all know that any hopes of an advantageous marriage must rest with Ann.'

Sarah's father dabbed his brow with a cotton handkerchief.

'Joseph makes a good point. We have discussed Ann's prospects a good deal over the past months.'

'Have you indeed?'

'Do not look at me so crossly, Sarah. It is not unusual for noble families to improve their fortunes by marriage.' He broke into a wheezing cough.

'We need the money,' Joseph insisted. 'We cannot even provide a decent dinner. And our stables are an embarrassment.'

Sarah picked up a crystal jug from a nearby shelf. It still had a few fingers of water in it. She poured out a glass and gave it to her father, concerned by his straining throat and damp brow. Despite Joseph's aggravating presence, she spoke as mildly as she could.

'I will not allow Ann to be put up to auction so that Joseph might have another horse, or you and I might have an extra course in the evenings.'

'But you would permit your sister to live in poverty with a penniless soldier?' Joseph remarked with a snort.

'I would not. We must find them something to live on.'

'You have some money that you've been keeping to yourself?' Joseph turned to Lord Kenilborough. 'It is as I have said. Sarah is not honest with us.'

Her father looked up from his coughing and Sarah was shocked to see distrust writ across his features. These past months she had been too busy with the harvest to spend much time with her family. Had her stepbrother gained so much influence over her father that he would take Joseph's word over her own?

'You agreed to leave all management of our finances to me,' she reminded him. 'And with good reason. I have never lied to you. We have no capital to speak of, but perhaps we might sell our share in the quarry.'

Her father glanced at Joseph, who shook his head almost imperceptibly. Sarah's jaw tightened. She knew then it was imperative to get Ann away from Kenilborough before Joseph's malign influence over her father could take further hold. She clasped her father's hands in her own.

'Father, I must tell you that Ann's heart is given. She could never be happy with another man. As you love her, I beg you not to make her miserable.'

Lord Kenilborough's eyes grew moist and he nodded. 'Very well. If you can make a settlement, I will consent.'

Chapter Thirty-eight

The share in the quarry was sold for three thousand pounds. Added to the thousand pounds from Ann and Sarah's mother, it was enough for the lovers to marry. It was agreed that Ann and Captain Williams should be married out of Kenilborough, on the same day as harvest supper. A delighted and grateful Captain Williams prepared to set out for Pembrokeshire to seek his father's permission. Before he left, he asked to speak with Sarah about his friend Kirk. The *Cadmus* had been involved in a skirmish with two French vessels off the Dutch coast, and Lieutenant Kirk had lost his leg in the ensuing battle.

'I was hoping you might consider taking him on as your steward,' said Captain Williams. 'You could find no better fellow, and I hate to think of him cast ashore with nothing but a miserly naval pension.'

Sarah had not forgotten Lieutenant Kirk's generous assistance in Plymouth and wrote immediately to the naval hospital, extending an offer of employment. Three weeks later, Mr Kirk presented himself at Kenilborough. His face was pale, yet his grip was firm as he took her hand.

'If you offer me this position out of pity, or from gratitude for any service I might have given in the past, I must decline it,' he said brusquely. 'I will not accept under such terms.'

'I cannot afford charity,' Sarah returned with equal curtness. 'I need a man of energy, organisation and resourcefulness, all attributes I know you possess.' She looked at the crutch beneath his arm and the empty space below his left knee, where the bottom of his breeches had been folded over and pinned up.

'How will you get about?'

'Once the wound is fully healed, I shall have a wooden leg. Until then, I believe I can ride, if you can supply a steady mount.'

'You must have Jack until you can procure another horse,' said Sarah, although not without a twinge of regret. 'That shall be one of your first tasks, for which I can advance you no more than twelve pounds.' She rang the bell and ordered Tanner to take Mr Kirk's chest.

'Mr Kirk must be accommodated on the ground floor, so show him to the blue room, if you please.' She turned back to Mr Kirk. 'There is a cottage set aside for the steward, but it is let out. I cannot afford any of our property to lie idle. I trust you will make your own arrangements in due course, but until then you must stay at Kenilborough Hall as our guest.'

'When can you show me the books?'

'Today, if you are willing?'

Mr Kirk's dour expression lifted a fraction. 'If this is how you do business, I think we shall get along very well, Miss Davenport.'

Sarah set Mr Kirk to review the books and calculate the rents while she continued to oversee the harvest. Day by day, acre upon acre of swaying golden corn was cut down to stubble, chaff blooming up from the fields like sparks from a fire. Once dry, the sheaves were taken to the stack yards. With each wagonload safely delivered, Sarah felt a lifting of the axe that had been resting against her neck. The harvest was turning out better than she could ever have hoped. If she could negotiate a good price for the corn, they might even contemplate paying off a small portion of the loan that was secured against the family's possessions.

After thanking her workers for their efforts, she returned home, late in the evening, to find Mr Hogg waiting for her with a bundle of letters. She rifled through them.

'Nothing from America,' the butler said, 'but there is one that carries the seal of Hoare & Company.'

Sarah sighed. Hoare's Bank had long been demanding she present herself to discuss her arrears against their loan. Now the harvest was in, she could put it off no longer. She must go to London.

Chapter Thirty-nine

The premises of Hoare's Bank dated from just after the Great Fire. Within sight of Temple Bar, its frontage of red and grey bricks squeezed between the pale stucco of the newer houses and shops that were slowly transforming Fleet Street from an uneven hotchpotch of styles into harmonious Palladian grandeur. Its low-ceilinged shop floor was so crowded that Sarah was forced to stop on the threshold and look for a way through. Banking must be profitable, for some at least. Her jaw clenched as she thought of how Louisa and her father had been swindled by Mr Levitt.

Those memories must have been playing tricks for, at that moment, Sarah imagined she glimpsed Louisa among the crowd. She shook her head, disgusted with herself. It was not the first time she had conjured up that familiar figure. Any young woman with a full figure and dark hair could spark an eager hope in her breast, one that was always extinguished. Even so, Sarah raised herself on her toes to look. Good Lord, it really was Louisa. She was certain of it. Attired in black and wearing a veil, but the way her head dipped as she walked to reveal the pale skin at the nape of her neck was exactly like Louisa. As was the slight reticence in her step, the way her elbows pointed outwards as she clasped her hands in front of her waist. The crowd seethed and the young lady disappeared from view. Sarah let out a clenched cry of frustration.

'Miss Davenport?' A clerk with elaborate moustaches emerged from the throng. 'Mr Hillier is ready for you.'

But Sarah was pushing impatiently through the crowd, careless of the remonstrations of those she brushed aside.

'Louisa?'

The woman turned. Although her veil was densely woven, there could be no mistaking the well-remembered features that lay beneath, or those intelligent brown eyes.

'It is you!' Sarah cried.

An inarticulate noise emerged from behind the veil, barely distinguishable above the hubbub of the crowd.

'Mrs Mason, won't you come up?' said a skinny young clerk with pomaded hair who stood by Louisa's side.

'I, ah… thank you,' Louisa replied unsteadily. With only a brief, distressed glance back at Sarah, she followed the clerk towards the stairs, which Sarah knew led to private consulting rooms on the upper floors.

'You are married?' Sarah's shocked query addressed only Louisa's retreating shoulders. The crowd surged and a tall gentleman with a broad chest inserted himself between Sarah and her prey.

'Excuse me,' Sarah said in a sharp tone. 'Let me by.'

'If I could oblige, I would.' The man twisted in an effort to move, but he was hemmed in on either side.

'Miss Davenport.' The moustachioed clerk had somehow

contrived to reach her. 'Mr Hillier has but a quarter hour before his next appointment.'

'Confound it man, cannot you see I am busy?'

But by the time Sarah had squeezed around the large-chested gentleman, Louisa had disappeared. She had no choice but to follow the clerk into a parlour just off the foyer. It was a haven of quiet after the hurly-burly of the shop floor, empty aside from Mr Hillier, tapping his foot in one corner. Sarah attempted to compose her thoughts, but the knowledge that Louisa was returned to England made that impossible. How could it be? Why had she not written? And, more pressing than all other questions, how came she to be married?

Chapter Forty

er business completed, Louisa hurried to escape the oppressive confines of the bank, leaving behind the mass of sweating bodies and the overpowering smell of powder and pomade. Her mission had been a success — a loan for five hundred pounds agreed and signed over to her — but she was unable to celebrate for the thudding of her heart, which caused the delicate skin between her ribs to vibrate like a drum subjected to a brisk tattoo. She supposed a meeting with Sarah was bound to happen eventually, but she wished it had not been when she was so utterly unprepared.

Palm to her chest, she almost collided with a donkey carrying two paniers of kindling down the street. Her impetus took her to the opposite pavement, which was bathed in the late August sunlight. Still breathless, Louisa rested her back against the warm bricks, closed her eyes and lifted her veil to let the sun warm her face.

'In this district, young women who lean against walls are believed to be selling a particular service. One you may not be willing to render.'

Louisa's heart, which had just begun to calm, burst into another frantic gallop.

'Sarah.' She opened her eyes and blinked away the jumping motes that had formed behind her eyelids. Tall and slender as ever, Sarah's face and neck were darkly tanned, giving her a faintly exotic look, as if she were an adventurer returned from an intrepid voyage. Her cornflower blue eyes carried an intensity that made Louisa shiver. She observed that Sarah wore the same split skirts as she had the previous year, the navy blue so faded it was almost grey. Her boots, those she had displayed so proudly to Louisa after selling her apples, were now quite as worn and patched as those she had been wearing when they first met. It was an image etched in Louisa's memory: Sarah in close-fitting buckskin pantaloons, jumping effortlessly down from an apple tree.

'Have you nothing to say to me?'

Louisa knew she owed Sarah an explanation, but her spirit rose at the sharpness of Sarah's words.

'You accuse me of whoring,' she protested. 'Why not ask what price I charge for my services?'

Sarah leaned over Louisa, her palm pressed against the wall beside Louisa's left ear. Louisa's breath grew shallow and strained.

'I see you have returned to your original philosophy.' Sarah said disdainfully. 'Everything must have a price.'

Her face was close enough for Louisa to make out the downy hairs on her jawline as they caught the afternoon sunlight.

'Any woman of trade deserves to be paid for her services. Gifts given willingly are a different matter,' Louisa managed, before running out of breath. She did not know whether to be relieved or disappointed when Sarah eased herself away.

'It seems much has happened since we parted,' Sarah remarked. 'If you are willing to acquaint me with any of it, there is a coffee house nearby where we may speak.'

Louisa acceded with relief. She could not bear such frigidity, not from Sarah. She would explain herself and hope that Sarah would understand.

The coffee house was full of men; clerks and bankers dotted about with bewigged lawyers. At their entrance, everyone ceased talking to stare at them. Louisa quickly lowered her veil, not wanting to be recognised.

'I'm not married,' she informed Sarah as they took possession of one of the few vacant tables. For some reason, this seemed to her the most urgent communication. 'I go by Miss Mason now, my mother's maiden name.'

Sarah's shoulders, which had been stiff and tense, loosened a little.

'I must have misheard the clerk in all that hullabaloo. I suppose Miss and Mrs are easily mistaken.'

She called for coffee and Louisa requested a pot of Pekoe tea.

'You must think the worst of me,' Louisa began, but Sarah gestured her to stop.

'Louisa, I blame my shock for robbing me of my ability to see and think. Only now do I observe that you are in mourning. For your father?'

Louisa nodded. The air in the coffee shop was thick with tobacco smoke and her eyes began to sting.

'Tell me,' Sarah said with such gentleness that Louisa was almost overcome, for she was certain she did not deserve such compassion.

'I went to the prison, but too late. My father had hanged

himself. He had left me a note. He could not bear to start again at the beginning. To live in poverty — to be thought a failure.'

She was glad that Sarah said nothing, for at that moment words were useless. The tea arrived. Louisa took a sip to soothe her throat. Sarah waited, silent and steady, as Louisa composed herself.

'I blame myself. If I had gotten there sooner or, better still, if I had never left him to come to England — such a foolish, ill-fated scheme. It took me only a few weeks to sell our New York house and make various exchanges and sales against our licenses and property leases that cleared our immediate debts. Had Papa but waited, I could have released him. But he had no faith in me.'

Her voice had grown loud and tremulous and it attracted, once more, the attention of their fellow clientele. A bearded man in the corner was paying them particular attention. Sarah glared at every onlooker, as if she could, with the intensity of her gaze, banish them all from the room.

'Sarah, I would not confess this to anyone else, but I was angry. I adored my father but I resent him for thinking that money was all that mattered in the world, and for teaching me to believe the same.'

Expecting condemnation, Louisa was surprised when Sarah grasped her hands, which were resting on the table between them. She felt Sarah's strength flow into her like rich, sweet wine.

'It is quite natural to feel anger towards those we love,' Sarah told her. 'We are all imperfect creatures. My father — I love him dearly but sometimes he infuriates me. When my mother died, I was angry for so long, but it did pass. Will you take strength from the knowledge that you have friends who love you?'

'I do,' said Louisa, choked by her emotions. 'I will.'

Beneath Sarah's square jaw, the open neck of her shirt revealed a triangle of sun-darkened skin where the strong lines of her collarbones came together. Louisa sucked in her breath and averted her eyes. She was swimming in dangerous waters. It would be so easy to throw herself on Sarah's protection.

'Why did you not come to us?' Sarah asked gently.

'When my grief settled, I felt only shame. I should have been more like you, Sarah, and taken responsibility, but I did nothing while my father and Mr Levitt led us to ruin.' She pressed a fist to her breastbone. 'I knew they were wrong to take such risks. If I had understood how deeply their actions would affect the lives of others, I might have insisted they listen. But I saw only numbers.'

Louisa stopped, for her culpability still sickened her.

Sarah applied extra pressure to her hand, as if to signal that she was listening and that she offered no judgement.

'Having settled our debts, I determined to build anew, so I might make recompense to those, like poor Lieutenant Kirk, that we had wronged. I had only a few hundred dollars to my name and just a single cargo ship from a fleet of eight. But dealing so effectively with my father's affairs had given me belief. With the British blockades continuing, I felt I had more chance of success working out of London.'

'I applaud your intentions,' said Sarah. 'Yet we might have helped. I have been deeply concerned, not having heard from you for so long. I supposed my letters languish, unread, some-where in America?' Her expression was pained, and Louisa quickly reassured her.

'I have them all. I had them redirected from the sorting office to my premises on the South docks. They have been of great comfort to me. But I could not bear to see you, or my uncle, until I felt worthy of your... your friendship.'

'You need prove nothing to me.'

'But to myself, I do,' Louisa insisted tremulously. Despite her resolution, she felt herself weakening. Sarah released her hand and brushed some crumbs from the table, her expression unreadable.

'And how does your business progress?' she asked blandly and Louisa breathed a little easier. This was firmer ground.

'Promisingly. I am grateful to Mr Smythe, who has been untangling what assets he can from the bank. Selling on our loans, and so forth. Last month, another of my father's ships, long believed lost, turned up in Spain, badly damaged, but with cargo intact. With two ships, I can do much, even if I refuse to do business that involves slaves. How ashamed I am that our family was ever involved in such iniquities. However, I needed capital for repairs and so I was forced to pawn your necklace. Another reason I could not come to you. I vowed I should not, until I can return it. And I intend to, as soon as I can.'

Sarah swatted at a non-existent fly.

'What is a necklace but metal and stones? Who is this Mr Smythe? What reason can he have for helping a young woman so assiduously? Is he a handsome man? Charming, no doubt?'

Louisa found Sarah's poorly disguised jealousy immensely gratifying.

'I pay him a wage. What more reason would he need?' she asked, feigning innocence. The vein in Sarah's neck pushed out beneath her skin and then receded.

'There are many motives for people assisting others. Impractical, emotional reasons.'

'What would you know of those?' Louisa wondered aloud, a smile playing at the corner of her lips.

The bearded man in the corner began to whisper in the ear of his neighbour. Through her veil it was difficult to be certain, but Louisa thought he might have attended one of the dinners the Levitts had given when she had first come to London. The man rose and headed towards them.

'I must go,' Louisa said. Although she planned to make good all debts related to Silverton's Bank, any present writs or demands would choke her fledgling company before it had a chance to thrive. It was for that reason she was using her mother's name. She hurried towards the exit. Sarah threw a few coins onto the table and followed her from the shop. They stopped on the pavement and faced each other. The heat of the sun had baked the stones, and Louisa felt her face dampen with sweat. Sarah looked up and down the street, as if making some sort of resolution, then her eyes fixed upon Louisa.

'Will you permit me to convey your compliments to Ann? And to Eleanor? They will want to know you are safe.'

'I did not even think to ask.' Louisa was mortified. With the business taking up every waking hour, she had neglected Eleanor dreadfully. 'I will write to Eleanor as soon as I can. I hope she and your sister are well?'

'Eleanor is in good health, I believe, although I have seen little of her. Ann is to be married to Captain Williams.' Until that point, her words had been clipped and business-like, but speaking of her sister caused Sarah's countenance to soften. As it always had, Louisa realised.

'We must thank you, for it is all your doing,' Sarah continued earnestly.

Louisa's brow furrowed in confusion.

'How so?'

'I sold my stake in the quarry for Ann's dowry. I got three thousand pounds.'

Despite Sarah's obvious satisfaction, Louisa's heart sank. She could only think that, in relinquishing the profits from the quarry, Sarah had tied herself even more resolutely to Kenilborough's yoke.

'To think that I almost gave away the rights for a mere two hundred,' Sarah added with a rueful shake of her head.

Despite everything, that brought a faint smile to Louisa's lips.

'I do recall informing you that you were being foolish.'

'A perfectly accurate assessment, for which I bear you no resentment. They are to be married next month.' She reached out towards Louisa, but then seemed to think better of it. 'Will you come?' She spoke so low, her plea was almost drowned out by the rattling wheels of a passing Hackney.

The bearded man emerged from the coffee house and, although he gave her a hard stare, Louisa was relieved to see him walk away. Somewhere, a church bell chimed three o'clock. With a start, Louisa remembered she had an appointment at the docks at four.

'I… am not… That is, I cannot commit myself. My endeavours are at that delicate point where all is wagered and a wrong decision, or delay, or even a piece of bad luck will bring ruin.' She did not add that seeing Sarah had so shaken her resolve, she feared a visit to Kenilborough might shatter it to pieces.

'I understand that — perhaps better than anyone,' said Sarah. 'I beg you will consider the invitation an open one. You would delight many, if you would come.'

In a formal gesture, Sarah took Louisa's hand and pressed it to her lips, before turning and heading away.

Chapter Forty-one

*J*n Sarah's absence, Mr Kirk had started collecting the quarterly rents and negotiated an excellent price for the corn. Everything except what she kept back for the local market was sold at an attractive rate and shipped off in good time. Preparations for the wedding progressed well but Sarah could not think of the celebrations without wondering whether Louisa would attend. Had she made it clear to Louisa how welcome she would be? Of course, it might have been better had Sarah's first words not been to insinuate that Louisa was a prostitute. But seeing her leaning against the wall, eyes closed with sunlight playing across her face, had made Sarah shudder with such intense yearning that she had said the first thing that came to her mind. A failed attempt at wit to hide the strength of her feelings. What defect was it in Sarah's nature that provoked her to always say the wrong thing? Aside from Louisa's unwarranted shame, Sarah feared it would be difficult to pull her away from her pursuit of profit. Although certain that Louisa's intentions were honourable, it pained Sarah to observe that her first thought on returning to England was not for her friends, but to the making of money. Had nothing changed? Would money always remain Louisa's highest consideration?

Sarah realised there was another factor that might discourage Louisa from attending the wedding: her stepbrother, who was acting more and more as if he owned Kenilborough. In Sarah's absence, he had invited the Mulcasters to dine at Kenilborough, regardless of the expense. They were to come that evening. The only thing that made the idea bearable was that Ann had insisted the Lowthers were also sent an invitation.

'How long it has been since we were together,' said Eleanor, going straight to Sarah.

'Too long,' Sarah agreed as Eleanor's eyes darted eagerly around the room. Mr Kirk was seated by the fire and Sarah realised this would be the first time they had seen each other since London. Sarah lost no time in taking her friend to him. The Scotsman appeared ill at ease, responding to Eleanor's gentle salutations with terse politeness but failing to offer any conversation beyond general enquiries about her family. Sarah was relieved when Ann joined them, for it was all rather awkward.

The Mulcasters arrived and Vere made a point of ignoring Sarah and asking Ann if he might hand her into dinner, since Captain Williams was still in Pembrokeshire. Henry secured Sarah's hand, which left only Eleanor without an attendant. Mr Kirk pressed his lips together and examined his crutch minutely. A flush rose to Eleanor's cheeks. Joseph seized her hand.

'We cannot suffer poor Kirk hopping along beside you, Miss Lowther. It would be quite absurd, the pair of you together. A woman with your infirmities requires a strong arm. We may precede my sisters, now that my name is Davenport.'

Vere gave a dry cough and Joseph's face reddened. He stepped back.

'But I forget our noble guests.'

Sarah found herself seated between Henry Mulcaster and Mr Kirk, with Eleanor left to the attentions of Joseph. Soup was succeeded by a course of fresh trout with buttered greens. Roast pheasant followed and, although the household budget couldn't stretch to a haunch of venison, Mrs Morris had made a hot water crust pie filled with beef and oysters that had even Lord Melgrove smacking his lips.

'Sarah is quite enamoured by her pet Scotsman,' Joseph informed Eleanor as a baked custard was brought in. 'They spend an inordinate amount of time locked away in her poky little office.'

'Mr Kirk has been a great help to me,' said Sarah steadily.

'She has even lent the fellow her hunter.'

'That is generous.' Eleanor offered Sarah a faint smile. 'I know how fond you are of Jack. I thought you had sworn never to let another ride him?'

'Mr Kirk is an excellent horseman,' said Sarah, 'although I shall be glad to have Jack returned to me. Mr Kirk, how does the search progress?'

'I have a viewing in Spenwick on the morrow.'

'You are buying the fellow a horse?' Joseph leaned towards Eleanor conspiratorially. 'What, I wonder, could be the cause of such uncommon extravagance?'

'There is no mystery,' Sarah remarked. 'Mr Kirk must have a horse and he cannot have Jack.'

'I do not see why we should have Mr Kirk at all. Let the fellow go and save us the cost of his wages, as well as twelve guineas for the horse.'

Mr Kirk gripped the edge of the table, preparing to stand. Sarah placed a hand upon his arm.

'Mr Kirk is greatly valued,' she said. 'He will remain the estate's steward for as long as he is willing to undertake the work.'

After dinner, Sarah sought out Eleanor.

'Have you heard from Louisa?' she asked. 'When I saw her in London, she said she would write.'

'No,' Eleanor said tightly. 'It seems I am out of favour with my cousin, as with everyone else.'

'What can you mean?'

Eleanor's expression softened. 'Forgive me. Since I heard Louisa is returned but chooses not to live with us, I have been moping about like a petulant child. I am quite disgusted with myself.'

'Then I shall make it my business to cheer you up. With Mr Kirk here, I shall have more time to call on my friends.'

Eleanor only sighed.

'I see the prospect of my visiting is not as welcome as I hoped,' Sarah remarked. 'That is chastening. I admit I am a poor substitute for Louisa, but I shall rise to the challenge. Suppose I read you some of those poems you like so much? I have recently acquainted myself with parts of *Queen Mab*.'

'After despising it all these years, what can have led you to embrace romantic poetry?' Eleanor asked tremulously. Sarah blinked. In the presence of so many, it was impossible to be frank, but she could not bring herself to lie to Eleanor.

'The deepest affection for a person I esteem greatly,' she

confessed, before adding quickly, 'but I can only pledge to a half-hour of poetry per day — no more than that, I beg.'

Eleanor turned away.

'Do not make promises that you cannot keep. Kenilborough has such a strong hold on you. Now more than ever, I see.'

'Whatever do you mean?'

Eleanor would not explain herself, nor would she be drawn into further conversation. Such peculiar coolness on the part of her oldest friend was unsettling and Sarah was relieved when the gentlemen appeared. Eleanor looked up eagerly, but Mr Kirk was not among the first group, which was led by a distinctly flushed and unsteady Lord Melgrove. At his elbow, Henry provided a supporting arm as the earl weaved across the room.

'I take it the wine met with your approval, my lord?' Lady Kenilborough asked complacently.

'I have a delicate palate, madam. Today's offering was distinctly inferior to what we had when I last was here.'

'I beg you will pay no heed to my husband,' said Lady Melgrove smoothly. 'If he truly objected to your wine, he would not have drunk so much.'

'It would've been impolite to refuse,' her husband mumbled.

'It is a shame your good manners have not accompanied you into this drawing room,' his wife remarked frostily as Lord Melgrove sank into a chair.

'I had Hogg bring up the best we have,' said Lord Kenilborough fretfully.

'Do not blame my father,' said Sarah. 'I sold off a parcel of our most valuable bottles last year. Although I was assured that we still retained some exceptional vintages.'

'The port was excellent,' said Henry. 'You need not apologise, Sarah.'

'I did no such thing. I merely accept responsibility.'

Mr Kirk and Mr Lowther followed behind. Sarah rose to leave an empty chair by Eleanor. To her bewilderment, instead of taking the available seat, Mr Kirk chose to follow her instead.

'I had thought you would wish to speak with Eleanor,' she said with a frown, for she could not help but notice that Eleanor's eyes were glistening. 'You will not please her with such neglect.'

'I cannot... I could not...' Kirk gritted his teeth.

'Good heavens, man, what's wrong with you?'

His fingers went white as bone as they tightened around the stem of his crutch.

'I would not distress Miss Lowther by assuming any regard based on our previous friendship, now that I am as I am, as well as having barely a penny to my name.'

He glanced down at his stump.

'Of all the people in the world, you could find nobody more sympathetic to your situation than Eleanor,' Sarah said impatiently.

'I have no desire to be pitied.'

Sarah lowered her voice.

'Such pride does you no favours if it makes you treat your friends so callously. Trust me, I speak with some authority on the topic.'

Too annoyed with him to remain, she returned to Eleanor.

'Mr Kirk is out of sorts this evening,' she remarked.

'He seemed quite at ease during dinner. I have rarely seen him speak so freely as he did to you.'

'We spoke of the estate. He has an excellent mind and

impeccable judgement. Every day, I esteem him more highly.' Sarah sensed an opportunity to soothe her friend's wounded spirits. 'I hope Mr Kirk can be persuaded to remain in the country,' she added with a smile. 'I must beg you to assist me in that regard.' Although unpractised in the art of dropping hints, she believed on this occasion she had acquitted herself with some distinction. Her suggestion that Eleanor had it in her power to secure Mr Kirk for the neighbourhood must surely be welcome. Eleanor fiddled with her gloves.

'I have borne much cruelty in my life, Sarah, but I never expected it from you.'

She rose, her eyelids swollen with unshed tears, and burst from the room.

'What is the matter?' cried Mrs Lowther, rising from her chair. 'Is Ellie unwell?' When a speechless Sarah could give her no answer, she followed her daughter from the room.

'I congratulate you on your continued ability to offend those around you,' said Vere Mulcaster, appearing at Sarah's shoulder. 'Even Miss Lowther deserts you.'

'Is Miss Lowther ill?' Sarah turned to find Mr Kirk by her other shoulder. Mrs Lowther reappeared to ask that their carriage be called for.

'Eleanor is unwell. We must return home at once.'

The commotion roused Lord Melgrove, who had been gently snoring, his chin resting upon his ample chest.

'What, is the party done already?' He took out his pocket watch and examined it, an activity which involved much blinking and squinting. Yet even after stretching his arm to its fullest extent and closing his left eye, he was unable to ascertain the time.

'I think it would be best if we left also,' said Lady Melgrove, rising, 'lest my husband extend his excessive civility in the direction of Lord Kenilborough's brandy.'

'You cannot think of going,' Lady Kenilborough protested. 'The loss of the Lowthers cannot signify. Ann was to play for us. Lord Vere, I'm sure you would not wish to miss it?'

'I am well acquainted with Miss Ann's proficiency,' said Vere nonchalantly. 'I require no further proofs.'

'If you do not care for music, then I am sure Ann will be pleased to converse with you instead. Or Sarah, should that somehow please you better.' Evidently, Lady Kenilborough was growing desperate.

'Miss Davenport's conversation has given me little pleasure of late.'

'You will not let Sarah's manners frighten you away?'

Vere grimaced and gave a short bow and within a short space of time, their guests were gone.

Chapter Forty-two

Try as she might, Sarah could not fathom the reason behind Eleanor's curious outburst. The next morning, she sought out Ann in the hope that her sister could provide some explanation. Ann was in the drawing room, practising at the harp.

'I suppose I must have unwittingly said something offensive,' Sarah mused.

'We must concede the possibility, however improbable,' Ann remarked with a perfectly straight face.

'I cannot think what it could be. I did my best to cheer her. I even offered to read poetry.'

'There cannot have been a more noble sacrifice in all of history.'

'I sang the praises of Mr Kirk. Who would not wish to hear admiration for the object of their affections?'

Ann stilled the harp strings between her palms.

'Compliments from a rival are not always welcome.'

'A rival? Ann, you cannot think… Good heavens! You cannot believe there is anything between me and Mr Kirk?'

'I do not. But after the great kindness you have shown him, Eleanor may imagine differently.'

'Eleanor would never be so foolish.'

Ann began to play a gentle, soothing melody.

'Rationality and love are poor bedfellows.'

Sarah was unconvinced. However, if Ann was right, then Eleanor was to be pitied indeed. She would get to the bottom of the matter. Her friendship with Eleanor was too important to be lost to ridiculous misunderstandings. She saddled Jack and rode at once to Athelton, cutting across empty fields, giving Jack his head as he galloped over the shorn stems of wheat and barley. She seldom allowed him such sport and he responded willingly, his ears pricked as he bounded eagerly over gates and fences, bringing her to Athelton by breakfast time.

It took the servants longer than usual to answer the bell, and Sarah wondered if Eleanor's resentment would result in her being refused. However, she was admitted to the breakfast parlour without delay. Eleanor rose to greet her. Mrs Lowther, who was also present, attempted to leave the room without being noticed, an endeavour hampered by her backing into a side table and dislodging a large Chinese vase. Sarah and Eleanor affected not to notice the loud crash as it hit the floor, nor the broken shards that skittered across the black and white tiles. After emitting a stifled squeak of dismay, Mrs Lowther exited the room successfully, leaving them alone. Eleanor hurried towards Sarah at the same time as Sarah strode forward, the soles of her boots crunching on fragments of broken vase as they came together. Eleanor reached out with both hands.

'Sarah, I am glad you are come. My manner last night was inexcusable. I will not permit jealousy to come between us. I value our friendship above all other attachments.'

'Eleanor, I believe there has been a grave misunderstanding,' Sarah began, as Eleanor took up her hands and pressed them to her lips.

'I wish you all happiness in the world,' her friend whispered with a tearful smile.

'Eleanor, you must know there is only one object of Mr Kirk's affections, and that is you?'

Eleanor swallowed and looked doubtfully up at Sarah.

'I wish it were so, but his behaviour could not be mistaken. To you, he paid every attention that I, in my foolishness, hoped he might address to me. I do not blame either of you. It is only natural he should admire you.'

'Natural? My intemperate nature is no match for a disposition as sweet as yours. I assure you that Mr Kirk has paid me no attentions beyond his duties as my steward.'

'If that is true, then why was he so cold — so distant?'

'He thinks himself unworthy. It is damnable pride and I will not allow it, even if I have to haul him here myself.'

'I would not marry anyone who has to be dragged to my door,' Eleanor protested. 'I have some self-respect.'

'Oh, I express myself badly, as I often do. Only, I beg you, do not give up hope.'

Eleanor looked up hesitantly.

'Then — you and Mr Kirk — you are not engaged?'

'We are not. My hopes and thoughts lie in an entirely different direction.'

Eleanor broke into sobs and buried her head in Sarah's chest. 'I should never have doubted you,' she said, 'but Mr Kirk was so changed. And when you spoke of reading poetry…'

'I do not know which is worse. To be thought guilty of

usurping Mr Kirk's affections or to stand accused of admiring such self-indulgent ramblings.'

Eleanor sniffled, but at least she was smiling.

'Can you forgive me?' she asked. Sarah set her hands firmly on her friend's shoulders.

'Eleanor, you have never done anything that needs my forgiveness. Banish these unhappy tears. Kirk will see sense, I assure you. I am quite angry with the fellow.'

'In that case, I pity him indeed,' said Eleanor. 'Although not as much as my poor mother. That vase was a particular favourite.'

Chapter Forty-three

he wedding day arrived, with clear skies and glorious sunshine. It had been Ann's suggestion to combine the wedding with the harvest supper to save money, although Ann insisted it was because the harvest celebration had always been her favourite day of the year.

The ceremony took place in the small chapel at Kenilborough. Captain Williams had been reunited with his dress uniform and Mr Kirk had brought his navy-blue coat out of retirement to act as his friend's groomsman. They made a fine pair, Sarah thought, as she followed her sister and her father down the aisle; the gallant captain and his medals alongside the lieutenant whose ebony peg-leg spoke of the noble sacrifice he had made for his country.

Sarah wore a new gown of pearl grey silk, embroidered with delicate blue cornflowers. Eleanor and Ann had saved money from their own allowances to buy it for her, along with a pair of new satin gloves. Sarah was grateful for the gesture. Although careless of her own appearance, she did not wish to embarrass her sister on her special day. And she could not deny that today there was another reason she wished to look her best. Aside from the Davenports and Captain Williams' family, only the Lowthers had been invited to attend the ceremony. Sarah looked eagerly towards where they were sitting, but there was no sign of Louisa. Would she come?

'Miss Ann is the prettiest bride the county has seen in years,' said Louisa's neighbour, as they stood among the crowd outside the chapel, waiting for the bride and groom to emerge.

'She looks very fine indeed,' Louisa said, although her eyes were fixed on Sarah as the chapel door opened. There she was, at Ann's side, her face alight with pleasure as she looked at her sister. She wore a perfectly fitted dress of pearl grey silk which emphasised her fine shoulders and displayed the smooth curve of her modest bosom to great advantage. The sight did nothing to quell the breathlessness Louisa had incurred in running from her coach, which had pulled up only moments before. She knew others would never consider Sarah as pretty as Ann. Her features were not so delicate, her skin was darkened by exposure to the sun, and her arms lacked the soft pliancy that was universally venerated, but Sarah's appearance only emphasised everything that Louisa admired: her strength of character, her selflessness. Louisa knew the danger in which she placed herself by coming, but she had been unable to resist the chance of seeing Sarah again.

She waved at Ann as the bride and groom headed for the lawn. Ann smiled at her and waved back, pointing her out to Captain Williams. He offered only a cold nod of acknowledgement. Louisa swallowed. After what had happened with the bank, she could not expect to be welcomed with universal delight.

'Louisa!' She was suddenly surrounded and embraced, first by a tearful Eleanor, and then by Mrs Lowther, who had somehow contrived to spill tea, or perhaps coffee, on the bodice of what appeared to be a new silk gown. Even Uncle Lowther, looking very fine in a purple coat, said he was pleased to see her and asked how she did, looking at her as if he actually expected a response.

Hordes of well-wishers followed the bridal party out onto the freshly cut south lawn. Ladies and gentlemen, among whom Louisa recognised the Mulcasters, mingled in their finery with labourers and their families in their Sunday best. A gazebo had been laid out with chairs and long tables arranged to form three sides of an open square. Beyond it, more tables had been laid out on the lawn, covered in pressed white tablecloths. They groaned under the weight of large hams and rounds of cheese, and platters piled high with veal-and-ham pies and beef patties. Loaves of bread had been cut into thick slices, giving off a yeasty scent. Beside them, crocks of melting butter glistened in the sunlight. A hog roast, fresh from the spit and still steaming, was being carved by Mr Hogg, coatless, with black sleeve protectors covering his arms. Further along, Brock was tapping a large keg of ale, watched eagerly by a group of young farm men.

The ladies and gentlemen headed for the gazebo, while everyone else laid siege to the tables on the lawn. Louisa hung back, uncertain where she belonged.

'Louisa.' Sarah's low voice in her ear made her skin tingle. She could hardly trust herself to turn. When she did, all she could think was how the cornflowers embroidered on Sarah's dress emphasized the colour of her eyes. At that moment, she knew that seeing Sarah was not enough. She needed more. She longed to hold Sarah, to feel her smooth brown skin beneath her fingers, to possess her and to yield in return.

She felt Sarah's hand press gently against the small of her back. 'We have saved you a seat.'

'You knew I would come?'

'I very much hoped you would.'

Sarah guided Louisa towards a seat between herself and Eleanor. Next to Eleanor sat Mr Kirk. Louisa blushed to see him, but Mr Kirk rose to shake her hand.

'A great pleasure to see you again, Miss Silverton,' he said. 'I know how glad Miss Lowther is that you are come.'

'I need not add my own pleasure in seeing you here,' Sarah murmured. 'Will you be staying with us, or at Athelton?'

'I... I have ordered a post-chaise to collect me from here early tomorrow, since I must be back in London by Friday. I hope you do not think me presumptuous?' Louisa flushed.

Sarah gestured towards the vast south wing. 'I am sure we can fit you in somewhere,' she said dryly. She leaned in. 'Although I hope I can entice you to stay longer.'

Louisa's mouth became so dry she was forced to take a sip of water from a nearby glass.

'I cannot.' She steeled her resolve. There was a difference between giving herself, which she was perfectly willing to do, and losing herself, which she could not countenance. She could not afford to neglect her business for more than a few days. 'There is a ship up for auction on Friday that I intend to bid on. It presents a rare opportunity if only I can grasp it.'

'You are already expanding? That is quick work.'

'My father always said starting a new venture was like sailing a high sea. It is imperative to move forward, even if that means pressing on sail. You must stay before the wind, or else founder. I am at exactly such a point, for I have a cargo of corn lined up, ready to be dispatched to Spain, and another of iron for the return journey. But I must have a ship which means I must be back in time for that auction.'

'I do not think I have ever seen you so certain of yourself,' Sarah remarked. 'It is a pleasure to observe.'

'It delights me to be making use of my abilities,' Louisa admitted.

'I wonder what other talents you have, that might be uncovered in the right circumstances,' Sarah murmured. She took a slow bite out of a slice of chicken. At that moment, Captain Williams' young niece and nephew began to chase each other under the tables, preventing Louisa from wondering whether it was possible to envy a piece of cold meat. The antics of the children caused much amusement, although Lady Kenilborough scolded them as they ran past her chair.

'Your stepmother is not enjoying the celebrations,' Louisa remarked.

'She hoped Ann would marry one of the Mulcaster boys. It is universally acknowledged that Ann was our family's only chance to make an advantageous match.'

Louisa's lips twitched in amusement as she sipped from a glass of golden Tokay.

'Did you never inform her of Vere Mulcaster's proposal?'

'I decided the consequences of making such a communication would not be worth the fleeting amusement. As for Henry, I cannot think he was in earnest.'

Louisa almost choked on the sweet wine.

'Henry also proposed? I hope you let him down with something less than your customary bluntness.'

'I told him the idea was quite ridiculous. Or preposterous. One or the other.'

Louisa broke into a laugh. Sarah was wholly unaware of how and why she was so attractive to others. It was utterly endearing.

'Miss Sarah, I hope you are well.' A man in duck breeches and a collarless shirt approached and raised his hat.

'Burrows — glad to see you,' said Sarah, rising to shake the man by his hand. 'Your hard work in the north field was much appreciated. I hope your leg has suffered no ill effects?'

''Tis all better now, thankee.'

'Your children — I hope they are come too?'

'Aye, Miss Sarah. Our Sammy's bin looking forward to 'is beef pie all week. An' our Joe has brung 'is penny whistle.'

'Delighted to hear it.'

Burrows was followed by more tenants and labourers, who took their turns to congratulate Sarah upon the harvest before paying their respects to Lord Kenilborough and tipping their hats to the bride and groom. Lord Kenilborough had removed his coat and his brocaded waistcoat was unbuttoned. His face was grey, and carried a bright sheen of moisture.

'How is your father?' Louisa asked, concerned by his wasted appearance.

'He has been troubled by a cough these past few days. I suggested he retire, but he insists it is his duty to acknowledge our people.'

'An argument he knows you cannot resist.' Louisa said, not without some regret, as she lost Sarah to the attentions of her labourers.

Chapter Forty-four

Once she had spoken to all her tenants and labourers, Sarah returned to Louisa's side. The knowledge that she was to stay under their roof filled Sarah with quivering desire, but she was uncertain, still, of Louisa's wishes. Dare she hope Louisa's presence meant she wanted more from Sarah than just friendship?

As the sun dipped behind the stables the air cooled and the sound of a fiddle and the high notes of penny whistles rose from the far corner of the lawn, to be greeted by loud cheers. There was a general movement in that direction. Sarah was relieved when her father retired to the house, together with his discontented wife. Joseph had gone off with the Mulcasters, his absence regretted by nobody. Captain Williams took Ann and all the Williamses towards the dancing. That left Sarah and Louisa with Eleanor and Mr Kirk.

'Sarah, do you remember when we were children?' said Eleanor wistfully. 'How I loved to dance. But I was so clumsy and odd-looking that no-one would dance with me, except for you.'

'I never had a partner I liked more,' Sarah insisted.

Mr Kirk rose and presented his hand to Eleanor. 'There can be no-one more awkward and clumsy than I. Would you do me the honour to stand up with me?'

'We shall be awkward together,' said Eleanor, eyes shining. They headed towards the music, arm in arm. Sarah turned to Louisa, her eyebrows lifting.

'Would you…?' she began.

'I suppose it is quite out of the question…?' Louisa wondered, at the same time.

'At harvest supper, nobody cares for formalities.' The promise of a dance with Louisa made Sarah feel as if her blood had turned to champagne, popping and tingling through her veins. 'Children and women may dance together. Even men have been known to make a pair, once they have drunk enough ale.'

Louisa's brown eyes twinkled.

'I do not need the courage of drink to dance with you,' she said with a smile that sent Sarah's heart soaring.

'I always knew you were a woman of rare spirit.'

A circle of dancers had formed around a large brazier. Although the sun had long since disappeared beneath the horizon, the sky retained a pale, pearly blue hue, broken only by the faint pinprick of the North Star. Kenilborough Hall rose as a dark silhouette behind the living flames of a row of braziers. Louisa felt she had never seen anything so beautiful. As she and Sarah approached, the circle of revellers split open to admit them. With one hand in Sarah's, Louisa's other hand was taken by the rough palm of a labourer who welcomed her with a nod and a gap-toothed smile. The circle reformed, and they were absorbed into the dance.

Most of the dances began with everyone skipping or clapping together in a circle or square, before breaking off to swing or promenade one's partner. At first, Sarah held Louisa at a distance, but as night drew in and the dances slowed, Sarah began to draw closer. First their elbows linked, and then Sarah cast an arm around her shoulder or her waist. Louisa welcomed every contact, but it was the way that Sarah gazed at her so intensely that filled her with delicious anticipation. When a dance called for the swapping of partners, she felt bereft, as she was sent in one direction around the circle, while Sarah went the other.

''Tis a treat to see Miss Sarah so happy.' Louisa's new partner was Mr Burrows. 'She works so hard, 'tis meet she has such a true friend to help her forget her cares.'

Louisa thanked him, touched by the warmth of his approbation, before he passed her on to her next partner, who was Captain Williams.

'Miss Silverton,' he said stiffly, as he took her hand. 'Or is it Miss Mason now?'

The sight of his red coat, together with his cold demeanour, left Louisa unable to respond. Yet in an odd way, his resentment on behalf of his friend assured her that she was plotting the right course. Only the knowledge that she was striving to make reparations made it possible to bear his disdain. She peered along the line to see how many more partners she must endure before she was reunited with Sarah. Not so many, yet it seemed an age before Sarah's strong hand grasped hers once more.

'Captain Williams is a good man at heart. He will learn to understand you,' Sarah reassured her.

'I do not blame him. I have only recently learned to understand myself,' Louisa remarked with a small smile.

Sarah pulled Louisa into her body. Louisa's blood flared like the flames that leapt up from the nearby brazier. Their faces were almost touching. Tiny beads of sweat formed above Sarah's lips. What might it be, to taste such sweet saltiness? The music stopped and most of the couples broke away to applaud the musicians, but Sarah held Louisa against her for a moment longer, as if reluctant to release her. Their chests were heaving from the dance and Louisa felt Sarah's breath against her forehead, and the press of her bosom against her own, swelling and receding with every gasp. Her ears began to ring, and all other sounds and sensations disappeared, save the twin beating of their hearts, almost, but not quite in time. The heat from their bodies mingled, as if they were merging into a single being.

'Since we have you only for one night, we must make the most of your time here,' Sarah murmured.

'The carriage is here,' someone cried.

'They're off — the Captain and Miss Ann.'

"'Tis Mrs Williams now.'

'Miss Sarah, your sister's going. Hurry, or you will miss her.'

With a low sigh, Sarah pulled away, but she kept hold of Louisa's hand as they followed the crowd to the east driveway, as if she could not bear to let go. Which was exactly how Louisa felt. They waved at the happy couple as they set off in a postchaise garlanded with white phlox.

'They are going to the Lakes and then to Scotland,' Sarah said. 'I think Captain Williams has had enough of the continent.'

'I envy them,' said Louisa. 'To escape all cares and duties, even for a short while, and think only of themselves.'

'Tonight, I envy no-one.' Sarah ran her thumb over the back of Louisa's hand, and Louisa's pulse quickened.

Carriages were called for the ladies and gentlemen, and everyone else slowly dispersed. Sarah led Louisa into the house via the Tudor tower. Dozens of candles had been laid out in candlesticks on a small table. Sarah seized two of them and escorted Louisa to her chamber.

'That is my room,' said Sarah, quite distinctly, as they passed a pale blue door. Louisa could think of no reason for such a communication other than as an invitation. Her own chamber was three doors further down the corridor. Sarah gave Louisa one of the candlesticks.

'I must thank Morris and the servants for all their hard work and bid my father goodnight. Half an hour should suffice, no more.'

'Half an hour?' Louisa groaned. It seemed such a long time.

In the flickering candlelight, Sarah's eyes looked almost black, her pupils swollen and smoky. She leaned towards Louisa, who thought — hoped — that Sarah was about to kiss her lips. At the last moment, Sarah diverted to plant a kiss on Louisa's forehead.

'Half an hour,' she repeated huskily and departed.

Louisa checked the time on the mantel clock. Quarter to midnight. She undressed quickly. She had packed her favourite nightgown, made of soft new linen. She looked again at the clock. Ten to midnight. She had never known time to pass so slowly. She shivered and draped an Indian shawl around her shoulders. She forced herself to wait a few more minutes until, unable to bear it any longer, she took up her candle and slipped down the corridor to Sarah's chamber, noting that the door had been left ajar.

'Sarah?' There was no answer. Lifting the candle, she established the chamber was empty. There was a four-poster bed, whose damask coverlet had been turned back to expose a triangle of pure white cotton. Louisa ran her hand along the soft sheets, and then knelt on the mattress. Firm, but not uncomfortably so. She set down her candle and rested her head against the bolster. Sarah's scent lingered strongly. It was a scent of turned earth, cut grass and wildflowers, with just a hint of horse mingled in. Louisa inhaled deeply and waited.

And waited.

She had no idea of the time, but she was certain it had been more than half an hour. Had she mistaken everything? The longer she waited, the more she distrusted her interpretation of Sarah's words and hints, but she could not bring herself to leave. Tiredness pulled at her eyelids and she slipped under the covers. She would rest for a moment. Just until Sarah came.

'Louisa.' Her name was spoken loud and harsh and it took Louisa some moments to realise where she was. In Sarah's bedroom. In Sarah's bed, wearing nothing but a thin linen nightgown. Sarah sat before her, still fully clothed, a plain blue shawl around her shoulders.

'That was a long half…' Louisa began, before noticing Sarah's face was contorted and her skin blotched. Dark circles bloomed beneath her eyes.

'What is it? What has happened?'

'My father,' said Sarah brokenly. 'He was coughing. There was blood. Oh, Louisa, there was so much blood! We called the surgeon, who says there is a tumour and we must prepare for the worst.'

'Oh, Sarah.'

'He was distressed. Begged me to forgive him. Insisted that he had been a poor father.' Sarah struggled for breath. 'I vowed it wasn't true. It wasn't, Louisa, I swear it. I told him he was never cruel and always let me act according to my own principles and wishes. Even... even when he did not agree with them.' Her distress was obvious, and it pained Louisa beyond measure. 'It is I who failed him,' Sarah insisted, flinging her arms upwards. 'Always so ill-tempered and impatient. How could I not have seen how ill he was?'

Louisa had never imagined Sarah could be so vulnerable, so unmoored as she was at that moment.

'There can be no more dutiful, loving daughter than you,' she insisted gently. 'You have kept him safe, all these years.'

'He seemed like a child, so fearful, so lost.'

'Always, I think, you have been the true parent,' said Louisa. 'Let me take some of this burden from you. Permit yourself to grieve — to weep.'

Sarah's shoulders heaved and shuddered. She sank to her knees and buried her head in Louisa's lap. Louisa pressed her lips to the crown of Sarah's head and wrapped her arms around her.

There was a knock at the door. Louisa felt Sarah pull away.

'What time is it?' Sarah asked.

'I'm not sure, but it is light,' Louisa replied, blinking. She must have fallen asleep sitting up and her shoulders were stiff and sore. The knock at the door was repeated, a little louder.

'Miss Sarah?'

It was Tanner, one of the footmen, come to inform Sarah that the surgeon wished to speak with her. Also, Louisa's post-chaise had arrived.

'Send it away,' Louisa said. She would not leave Sarah, not now.

'What of your shipping company — the auction?' Sarah asked.

'I care for none of it, when you are in distress!'

Sarah stared at her for a long moment. Although her eyes were red veined, there was no other outward sign of the broken woman who had fallen into Louisa's lap just a few hours ago. Her posture was stiff and formal, her shoulders high, her back straight. Louisa couldn't imagine the effort it had taken to gather herself to appear so composed in front of the servant. Paying no heed to Louisa's wishes, Sarah ordered Tanner have the post-chaise wait at the south entrance.

'You must not think of staying here,' she said as the footman departed.

'I beg you, do not send me away,' Louisa pleaded. 'Can't you see that I would do anything to help you, whatever the cost? Can't you see that I love you?'

She stepped towards Sarah, desperate to rekindle the tender connection they had so recently shared. As she reached out, Sarah stiffened, as if any touch between them would be fatal.

271

Louisa's blood seemed to thicken and slow in her veins like cheese clotting. She felt a dreadful premonition of what was to come. Her declaration hung in the air, unanswered. When Sarah at last spoke, her voice was harsh.

'But you do not help, Louisa. You only make me weak. While I have been indulging myself in tears and recriminations, my father has grown worse. I cannot give him the care he needs if you remain here. You had better dress. I will send Meadows and Tanner to escort you to your carriage.'

Chapter Forty-five

*L*ouisa barely felt the juddering and clattering of the post-chaise as it took her away from Kenilborough. The coachman had given her a blanket to wrap around her shoulders, but it proved woefully insufficient to dispel the chill in her bones caused by Sarah's abrupt dismissal. She had been prepared to give herself to Sarah, body and soul, only to be callously rejected. Her eyes stung with hot tears, her chest felt hollow. Was it always to be this way with Sarah? She remembered Joseph Davenport informing her, when they had first met, that Sarah would take up acquaintances and then cast them off. It was not the first time that Sarah had withdrawn suddenly and with no warning. Sarah's harsh words made her wonder whether fickleness was, after all, the heart of her character. Louisa shook her head. She refused to believe that. Refused to accept that Joseph was a better judge of character than herself, or Eleanor.

And yet, how to explain such indifference in response to Louisa offering up her heart? It could only mean one thing. For Sarah, duty would always come first. Duty to her family, and to the estate would always come before the dictates of her heart.

Or perhaps she regretted showing weakness in front of Louisa. But there must be more to it than that. After some moments of deep contemplation, Louisa was forced to admit a painful truth. Sarah could not truly love Louisa, to spurn her so cruelly. It was as Louisa had always suspected; she was unlovable. Just as her father had returned her facsimile banknotes, over which she had laboured so hard and so long, Sarah had refused to accept Louisa's offering of love. Overwhelmed by wretchedness, Louisa shrank into the deepest recesses of the seat, her growing distress only exacerbated by the jolting motion of the carriage.

For the next week, Sarah watched over her father every night. In the morning, she was invariably met at the chamber door by Lady Kenilborough who sat with him during the day. Sarah had to acknowledge that her stepmother was never late in taking over the care of her husband, and never shirked this duty.

'How is he?' asked Lady Kenilborough.

'Not good.'

Sarah felt a touch of a hand against the crook of her arm as her stepmother walked past her to take up station by her husband, so fleeting she thought she might have imagined it. But she had not. In this matter, if no other, she and Lady Kenilborough were of one mind.

Some impulse drove her to walk across the inner courtyard and into the main entranceway with its marble floor and high ceiling. The morning sunlight slanted through the east-facing windows and bounced off the veined marble, dazzling her. She turned her back to the windows and looked up at the beautiful paintings by Thornhill. For once, they brought her little pleasure. Her beloved Kenilborough felt like a stranger, her lonely footsteps accompanied only by their own echoes. She realised that her affection for the house was inseparable from her love of the people within it. With Ann gone and her father dying, what was the point in her working so tirelessly to preserve what, after all, was only stone and mortar?

And what of Louisa? She had permitted herself to dream that one day Louisa's steps might walk here, beside her own. But she had destroyed that dream. She recalled Louisa, waiting for her in her room that night, wearing only a silk shawl draped over an almost sheer linen nightgown. It was evident that she had come of her own free will, ready to give herself.

To know, at last, that Louisa was prepared to give up everything for her sake was almost impossible to comprehend. Such a priceless gift, freely given, had touched Sarah deeply. Although she had longed for that gift with all her heart, she had been unable to accept it. Louisa had found strength and value in the work she was doing. The Louisa who had attended Ann's wedding had been so confident and sure of herself. So aglow with purpose. To permit her to give up the business would be to diminish her. No matter her feelings, Sarah refused to let Louisa make such a sacrifice. Dismissing her had been the right thing to do; indeed, that was so evident that Sarah thought Louisa might even welcome the excuse to return to town in time for the auction. How wrong she had been. The pain in Louisa's face had almost undone her. It had taken every last inch of Sarah's resolve not to take back her harsh words and beg Louisa to stay.

Whatever Louisa might have felt for her — and oh, how tenderly, how bravely Louisa had expressed those feelings — Sarah's brusque dismissal must have destroyed them forever. She had behaved like some blundering gardener taking his scythe to the weeds, and in so doing beheaded a rare, exquisite flower. If only she could have found some other way to persuade Louisa to leave, something less brutal. But diplomacy had never been among Sarah's virtues. Her defects of nature had betrayed them both. She did not regret sending Louisa away, but she bitterly lamented the manner in which she had achieved it. Louisa's anguished expression as she had left was branded across Sarah's memory, an image that tormented her dreams and most of her waking hours. It was a just punishment.

The tapping of wood against stone, interspersed with the softer tread of a booted foot, announced the approach of Mr Kirk along the cloisters.

'Miss Davenport,' he said gravely. 'I hope you have better news of your father?'

'I think we are good enough friends now that you may call me Sarah.'

'Thank you,' he said, taking up her hand. 'In return, you must call me Robert.'

'Well, Robert, my father grows worse, I'm afraid. Have you any news?'

Letters had been sent to Scotland, but without much hope of reply, for Ann and her new husband had left no itinerary, planning to travel where their fancy took them, making it impossible to know where to direct the letters.

'Not yet.'

'Was there something you needed to speak with me about?' she prompted. 'Some estate matter?'

'Everything is in hand.' He scraped the flat of his hand around his chin. 'But there is something you should know. I was in Spenwick yesterday and Mr Faversham stepped out of his office to inform me that his agent in London, the one who supplied you with that credit note, has sold the debt onwards.'

For a moment, Sarah wondered what he was talking about. Then she remembered the note for a hundred and twenty pounds she had signed so she could pay back Louisa. Payment had been due weeks ago, but she had quite forgotten about it.

'Well, what of it?'

'The debt was sold to a fellow named Cossington.'

Sarah started back. 'Can that be possible?'

'Sarah, may I ask why you took such a dangerous step? Why not look to your friends? I am sure Mr Lowther would have loaned you the money.'

'I have long vowed never to ask my friends for money.'

'You once rebuked me for my pride. Must I remind you of your own lesson?'

'You try our friendship, Robert.'

'What is the value of friendship, unless we can speak truths to each other?'

'Well said. Yet you cannot know that, years ago, my father took money from his friends, Mr Lowther among them. He neglected to inform me of this until I had taken some pains to see off certain creditors — moneylenders in the main, for I wished to get out from under their thumbs as soon as I could. I was mortified to discover that I had discharged such dubious men of business in preference to our acquaintances. I was able to pay back our friends, by taking out a loan against our household possessions. But after such an abuse of their trust, I could never approach our friends again.'

Except Louisa, she reminded herself. Only from Louisa could she bear to accept help. And now she had spurned even her.

'I think they know that you are not your father, Sarah.'

'I am in no mood to discuss my father's shortcomings. Not today.'

'Of course. Forgive me.'

'Miss Sarah?' In the doorway stood Meadows, her head bowed.

'What is it, Meadows?' Sarah asked, dread crawling through her veins.

'Her ladyship sent me.'

'My father. Is he...?' Sarah could not bring herself to complete the question.

'I'm so sorry, Miss Sarah.'

She could have sworn the room darkened. Sarah retained just enough command of herself to ask Meadows if she would be so good as to inform the rest of the household. As the maid departed, Sarah felt as if her world was crumbling around her. Only Robert's presence and strong arm bearing her weight prevented her collapsing with it.

Chapter Forty-six

T he drapes of Kenilborough were closed. The manservants tied black ribbons to their sleeves and the maids did the same with their caps. Lady Kenilborough could not bring herself to prepare the body and so it was Sarah who washed down her father's emaciated frame and dressed it. He had never been an imposing man, but the sight of his skeletal remains, so bent and shrivelled, was so pitiable that Sarah was relieved Ann was not there to see it.

Their friends and acquaintances paid their respects. Mr Lowther removed his hat and pressed Sarah's hand with silent gravity. Mrs Lowther, with a whisper that reverberated only around the chamber and those that immediately surrounded it, bemoaned the terrible shame of losing so eminent a personage, even if that personage had a regrettably casual approach to financial affairs. It must be a comfort to those who loved him to believe that he was now reunited with his first wife, who everybody knew was an angel, unlike somebody else — someone of whom Mrs Lowther would not speak ill at such a time, even though it was common knowledge Lady Kenilborough had laid out more than fifteen pounds for her mourning attire.

Eleanor came every day to sit with Sarah, providing more comfort by her quiet presence than all the words of condolence attempted by others. She offered to write to Louisa, but Sarah begged she would not. She did not want Louisa to feel obliged to neglect her business to pay her respects. The locals came in their droves to view the body. Eleanor listened patiently to their remembrances and comforted those who wept, for which Sarah was grateful, as it saved her the effort of doing so herself. She had no patience with such public displays of emotion.

Lord Kenilborough lay in state for a week before being buried in the family tomb alongside his ancestors. His wife declined to take part in the funeral rites, her grief too raw to be displayed. Joseph, who had been absent during most of Lord Kenilborough's illness, reappeared in time to attend the funeral. He wore a new mourning suit and his expression appeared, to Sarah at least, to be one of poorly disguised glee. His aura of barely repressed excitement was still in evidence the morning after the funeral when, at breakfast, he informed Sarah that they were expecting a visitor.

'Who presumes to visit us at such a time?' Sarah asked indifferently.

'Mr Gregory of course. He must read the will.'

'Cannot it wait?' asked Lady Kenilborough with a glance at Sarah. That morning was the first time she had left her bed-chamber since her husband's death. 'Would it not appear vulgar to rush into financial matters at such a time?'

'Nothing vulgar about money. Best we all know where we stand,' said Joseph. Sarah could only suppose her father had agreed to bequeath him some of the more valuable family heirlooms — those few that had not been sold, or perhaps committed her to providing Joseph with a yearly income from the estate. Unable to remain another second in the room, she flung down her napkin and departed, her breakfast untouched.

Mr Gregory was shown into the large drawing room. Sarah listened impassively as he read the will. The reason for Joseph's glee soon became clear. Her father had signed no deed of settlement and so could dispose of the estate however he wished. She had been right about one thing. Her father had not separated the land from the rest of his possessions. Everything, in its entirety, was left to his adopted heir, Joseph Davenport. Sarah was left with nothing but a thousand pounds from her mother, which could be released only when she married or reached the age of twenty-five. Until then, any interest that accrued from it formed part of the Kenilborough estate and so was controlled by Joseph.

'There is a petition addressed directly to you, Mr Davenport,' said the lawyer, eyeing Joseph severely over the top of his glasses. 'You are asked to make good on the verbal promise to your father to provide a home for your mother and your sisters for as long as they remain single. It is non-binding, but I'm sure you would wish to follow the late Lord Kenilborough's wishes.'

'He needn't lecture me from the grave,' said Joseph. 'My mother will be given everything she needs to support her noble position. Sarah will get no less than she deserves.'

Mr Gregory bowed. He gathered up the papers and tucked them beneath his arm. He walked ponderously towards the door, stopping as he reached Sarah.

'I fear this must be a dreadful shock, on top of what you have already suffered. I argued strongly against it with his lordship, but others had more influence.'

Sarah recalled their meeting on the stairs, a few months ago. He had tried to warn her. As had Louisa. Even Vere Mulcaster had tried to make her see sense. Sarah had ignored them all. It was a weakness, she realised, to rely too much on one's own resources rather than accept help and advice where it was given. Instead, she had allowed Joseph's malign influence to gain a hold. Her father had never had the strength to oppose the will of others.

Mr Gregory glanced forlornly towards Joseph and Lady Kenilborough, who were engaged in a short, whispered exchange.

'No, Mother,' said Joseph, walking away from her. 'My will is firm on this point. I will not be moved.' He went over to the large sash window to survey, with obvious satisfaction, the lands that were now his.

Sarah thanked Mr Gregory for his service and he took his leave. She felt a hand on her elbow. It was her stepmother.

'Please believe me, this is not what I wish.' Holding a handkerchief to her face, Lady Kenilborough swept from the room. The door closed heavily behind her, the only noise in the otherwise silent house.

'You are to leave Kenilborough within the hour,' said Joseph, not deigning to turn to look at her.

'Leave?' Sarah repeated uncomprehendingly.

'I have ordered one of the maids to pack up your clothes and personal effects.' He took out his fob watch and examined it. 'That should be done by now. I have taken the liberty of locking up the room you have called your study. I will not have you stealing money or papers.'

'Stealing?' Sarah's mind was as sluggish as cold treacle. Joseph turned and walked towards her, his heavy tread causing the floorboards to creak in protest. He came on until he was standing so close to her that she could smell the coffee and stale tobacco on his breath.

'And do not think of taking Jack. He is part of the Kenilborough estate. I shall sell him as soon as I can. To the army. If there is to be another war, the cavalry will need cannon fodder. I hope that does not distress you?'

His mocking tone roused her at last. She rounded on him.

'I am glad he is to be sold. Any fate would be better than leaving him in your hands.'

Chapter Forty-seven

arah's trunk had been placed on the south driveway, in front of her beloved Tudor tower, her greatcoat draped over the top. She sat down on it and pressed her palm to her forehead. The anger she felt at her shabby treatment gave way to a profound sense of sadness. She glanced up at the house. The leaded windows of the old tower seemed to return her gaze, peering unhappily between thick fronds of spreading ivy. Dear Kenilborough, her only home, and that of her family for centuries before her. But it was so much more than that. How could she have thought, even for a moment, that it was nothing more than bricks and mortar? It was a symbol of prosperity and stability for everyone in the county. Here, tenants could air their concerns and seek redress for any wrongs. It was a place where girls took up positions as maids to earn a pot of money before getting married, and where young men with ambition could learn new trades. That would soon be over. Joseph's gambling would surely lead to ruin within a twelvemonth. The house would be sold — doubtless to a merchant or rich financier. The Packhams and Levitts of this world, who could never comprehend the obligations that came with an estate such as Kenilborough.

There was movement from the western end of the drive. Sarah rose to her feet as, one by one, the servants rounded the corner of the house and came towards her. There was Thomas, her groom, and Mrs Morris with the kitchen girls. Mrs Irvine, the housekeeper, led a line of chambermaids with a red-eyed Meadows at the rear. Tanner and Brock came out of the Tudor tower, their coats brushed and their wigs freshly powdered, accompanied by the petite Mademoiselle Renarde in her freshly pressed pinafore. Even the gardeners were walking towards her, brushing their dirty hands down the front of their breeches, together with Forrester in his tweeds. Bringing up the rear was Mr Hogg, immaculate in his dark suit. Sarah's heart swelled with strong emotion. A pony and trap clip-clopped around the corner of the library before performing a slow turn and pulling up in front of her. The servants formed themselves into a line with Sarah at one end and the trap at the other.

'Tanner, take Miss Sarah's trunk to the trap,' said Mr Hogg. 'I hope you will forgive us the liberty, Miss Sarah, but we thought you might need some form of transport, what with having your trunk to consider. And we all wished to say goodbye.'

'It is no liberty, Hogg,' Sarah said huskily. She walked up the line, shaking every hand. At the end was Mrs Morris, dabbing her eyes with the hem of her grease-stained apron.

'I shall miss you, Mrs Morris.'

'And I you, Miss Sarah.' She put her arms around Sarah's waist and squeezed.

'Mrs Morris, remember yourself,' Hogg said. The cook pulled back.

'Beg pardon, Miss Sarah. Don't know what I was thinking.'

'Do not apologise, Mrs Morris, for I am sure I was thinking the same thing myself.' Sarah planted a kiss on Morris's glistening cheek and turned quickly to the trap before she could lose what little composure she had left. She squinted up at the driver.

'Is that William Burrows?'

The driver tugged at the peak of his cap.

'Yes, Miss Sarah. I was told you might be needin' some 'elp. Where'm I tekkin' you?'

That was an excellent question. Where was she to go, now that Kenilborough was no longer her home? The truth blossomed within her. There was only one other place where she might find a true home.

'I shall go to London.' *To Louisa.*

'I'll tek you to Hollaston,' Burrows said with a brisk nod. 'My Joe's off to London tonight with some hops. If you don't mind goin' with him, it'll save you payin' fer mail.' He reached into the pocket of his trousers and pulled out five crumpled notes which he thrust towards her.

'I couldn't possibly accept.'

'Beg pardon, Miss Sarah, but you've forgot last year you forfeited my rent. When I had the broken leg. Anyone else would have cast me out, but you let me stay.'

'I have not forgotten,' said Sarah. 'And it won't do, for we agreed you could break the rent that year. I will not go back on my word.'

'You wouldn't deny a man a chance to pay what's owin'?' Burrows scratched his head. 'Why, that's like askin' me to steal from my neighbour. I thought you understood us, Miss Sarah, more'n his lordship ever did. 'Tain't just lords an' ladies who got their dignity.'

Sarah knew she was defeated. She accepted his offering and tucked the crumpled notes into a pocket in her skirts before jumping into the back of the trap. It was half-filled with hay. Tanner had placed her trunk just behind the driver's seat and so she perched upon that, back-to-back with Burrows. Thomas clambered up behind her, a rough hessian bag slung across his shoulders.

'You are not coming with me,' Sarah exclaimed. 'I cannot pay you, nor even promise a roof over your head.'

'Allus wanted to travel,' said Thomas stubbornly. 'An' I'd rather take my chances with you, Miss Sarah, than with them in there.' He jerked his head towards the house. The trap jolted forward. Mrs Morris and the other servants followed them all the way round the house and on to the driveway, waving and shouting their good wishes. Sarah supposed there must be grit in the air, for her eyes felt itchy and in need of wiping.

William Burrows was in a talkative mood, peppering her with questions and observations. Sarah felt ill-disposed for conversation and was grateful when Thomas took it upon himself to respond on her behalf. She shifted her greatcoat and felt something heavy in the pocket. She pulled out a small, linen-wrapped parcel, tied with brown string. Inside was the ruby pendant necklace her stepmother had so often worn, together with a note in Lady Kenilborough's hand.

Sarah,

I do not deny I did everything I could to secure Joseph's fortune. But it was never my intention for you to be treated so unjustly. You and my son could never be happy under the same roof, but if I had any influence in the matter, you would have a yearly income. A hundred pounds, as much as you permitted me as pin money, would have been fitting. Joseph would not hear of it. Neither did he heed me when I asked him not to cast you out so abruptly, with no concern for your grief. In lieu of such considerations, I give you this necklace. I do not expect you to keep it. I know you have always despised it, but the stone is of considerable value and its sale should relieve you of any immediate distress until such time as you are reunited with your sister. If an excess of pride makes you unwilling to accept any offering of mine, then let me assure you that it was a gift from your father. He would wish you to have it now.

Margaret, Dowager Viscountess of Kenilborough

Sarah fingered the large ruby. Her stepmother was quite right. She had always hated it. It was so ostentatious and garish. The note was very much of a piece with their relationship — no pretence at affection, no apology for what had passed. But the gift was a selfless and honourable gesture, she could not deny that.

'Who be these strangers, loitering on the bridge with Mr Parker?' said Burrows, rousing Sarah from her stupor. Standing in the middle of the bridge into Hollaston was a great brute with an eyepatch and a weaselly looking fellow with a pale, domed head. With them was Mr Parker, the parish constable. They were clearly waiting for someone. With a sickening jolt, Sarah realised that Joseph must have schemed with Cossington to have her taken up for debt. Burrows pulled the trap to a stop.

'Shall we turn back?' Thomas suggested.

'No,' said Sarah, stepping down from the trap. 'I will not run from my obligations.'

She strode towards the approaching men.

'Mr Cossington,' she said in brisk, clear tones. 'You have saved me the trouble of seeking you out. Most considerate of you to come to Kenilborough, when I was on my way to London expressly to pay off my debt.'

'But… I…' he spluttered. 'Yer surely haven't got the money?'

'I have this.' She proffered the pendant. 'It must be worth at least a hundred pounds.'

Cossington seized hold of the pendant and examined it with a professional air. 'A hunnerd, p'rhaps,' he said, 'but yer bill is for a hunnerd and twenty.'

She dug around in her pockets. With the five pounds from Burrows and everything in her purse, she had just enough. The moneylender made no move to take it.

'We were to take you up,' he protested. 'I brung the constable.'

'I am afraid I will have to deny myself that pleasure.'

Mr Parker wiped his brow with the back of his hand.

'I am glad not to be needed.'

'Let's not be hasty.' Cossington smoothed his wispy hair over his head in his habitual gesture. 'With interest, yer still short twelve pound.' He flashed his teeth.

'You would take me in for twelve pounds?' Sarah did not hide her contempt.

'I'd take yer in for sixpence, Miss Davenport, just for the pleasure of pricking that pride of yern. Constable, clap her in irons.'

'I don't think there's any need to make a fuss,' said Mr Parker.

A crowd had gathered, drawn by rumours that Miss Sarah Davenport was about to be arrested. As Thomas placed himself between Sarah and the constable, the crowd parted. To Sarah's utter amazement, Mrs Lowther burst through the gap, her bonnet and shawl awry and her cheeks blossoming.

'Let us through.' She slapped away a hand with a closed parasol. 'I have never been so poked and prodded in all my days. Quite intolerable. Let us through, I say. We have business here.'

She was followed by Mr Lowther, who looked particularly grave, and Eleanor, arm in arm with Mr Kirk.

'Sarah, there you are,' said Mrs Lowther. 'We have found you at last. We have been on quite a chase, I can tell you.'

'Yer too late,' Cossington protested. 'She's bin arrested.'

'What is owing?' Mr Lowther reached for his pocketbook.

'Twelve pound. It's too late. Yer'll have to go to the magistrate.' Cossington's voice rose to a high pitch. 'I'll have the Honourable Miss Sarah in prison, I will!'

'Twelve pounds?' Eleanor's eyes settled upon Sarah's with a dismay that was heart-breaking. 'You would rather this than ask your friends for twelve pounds?'

'When you put it like that, it does seem a little foolish,' Sarah admitted.

'Foolish! Oh, Sarah — how could you?'

'I would be most obliged, Mr Lowther, if you would lend me the money,' Sarah said, trying to retain what dignity she could in the face of Eleanor's perfectly justified remonstrance. To say nothing of the crowd that was gawping in delight at the spectacle.

'No!' cried Eleanor. Everyone turned to her in shock. Even the crowd went quiet. 'We will not lend Sarah anything.'

'Ellie!' gasped her mother.

'Well then,' said Mr Cossington, rubbing his hands together gleefully. 'Let us proceed, Constable.'

'Sarah will accept our money as a gift or she shall have nothing,' Eleanor said tremulously. 'We are not business acquaintances, to speak of loans and interest.' Her declaration seemed to take all her strength. Once she was done, she broke into heaving sobs and buried her face in Mr Kirk's breast. The Scotsman looked at Sarah and tilted his head towards Mr Lowther. Sarah cleared her throat, uncertain she could trust her voice, for she was feeling a strong mix of emotions.

'Mr Lowther, I would be grateful for your assistance, under any terms.'

Mr Lowther drew out his pocketbook, and the crowd let out a disappointed sigh and began to disperse, for it was clear that the entertainment was over.

Chapter Forty-eight

Rather than talk in the middle of the road, Mr Lowther suggested they go to the local inn and take lunch in a private room. He insisted Sarah ride the rest of the way in his carriage. She took a seat next to Mr Kirk, opposite the others, while Thomas and Burrows followed in the trap with Sarah's trunk.

'How did you find me?' asked Sarah.

'We came to tell you Ellie's news. That she and Robert are to be married,' explained Mrs Lowther. 'We could get nothing out of your stepmother and that… that dreadful man. I refuse to call him by the name he has stolen. He does not deserve it. I went to the kitchens and soon had the truth of it from Mrs Morris. Ellie insisted we come and find you right away. She chivvied the coachman so much that I was quite jolted about. I dare not walk past a mirror. I must look an absolute fright.'

'I disagree. There was never a more welcome sight in all my life than when you broke through the crowd,' Sarah assured her. 'To see you all there, coming to my aid. I cannot tell you how much it meant.'

She tried to catch Eleanor's eye, but her friend's head was bowed and her gloved fingers were intertwined on her lap.

At the inn, Mr Lowther ordered luncheon. The events of the morning had chased away Sarah's appetite and she asked to speak with Eleanor alone. Eleanor consented silently and they stepped out into the courtyard.

'Eleanor,' said Sarah. 'I have been monstrously selfish. I did not consider how my sudden disappearance would distress you.'

'To think you might have been taken to the Marshalsea, or another of those dreadful places. Sarah, do you not know how dearly we love you?'

'Of course I know it. And I am delighted that you and Robert are to be married.'

Eleanor paced across the courtyard, absently stepping around a heap of fresh horse dung.

'Where were you going? Why not come to us — your friends who have always cherished you?'

She stopped and looked at Sarah imploringly. Sarah pressed her palm to her forehead. She was not in the habit of revealing her feelings, but Eleanor deserved to know the truth.

'I was going to Louisa.'

'Louisa?' Eleanor coloured.

'Eleanor, you know I love you as much as my own sister. But my feelings for Louisa, they're… different.' She ground to a halt, fumbling for the right words. She looked pleadingly towards Eleanor, hoping that her friend would understand.

Eleanor was silent for a long moment.

'Different?' she said hesitantly. 'In the same way my feelings for Robert are different from our friendship?'

'Yes,' cried Sarah. 'Can you understand, Eleanor? Louisa has quite captured my heart. She has such courage, such integrity.'

'And she is very pretty,' Eleanor added, and Sarah was relieved to see her smile.

'She sees who I truly am and she is not afraid to tell me when I am being foolish, or proud.'

'Unlike the rest of us,' Eleanor said with a dry cough.

'You appear to be learning.'

Overheated, Sarah removed her greatcoat and slung it over her arm. Eleanor stepped towards her and placed her hand on the cloth with a thoughtful expression.

'Does Louisa return your feelings?'

Sarah kicked at a lump of sawdust, her hands on her hips.

'I don't know. She may have done once, but I treated her dreadfully after Ann's wedding.'

'Louisa must know you well enough to be used to that,' Eleanor remarked. Sarah looked at her in anguish.

'You are quite right. It is hopeless. What have I to offer, except pride and selfishness?'

'You have more to offer than anyone I know,' Eleanor insisted. 'Above all, you do not shirk a battle. Not for anything worth the fight.'

Sarah stared at her oldest and dearest friend, who knew her so well and always knew what to say.

'But this being in love, Eleanor, it is so confounding. However hard I try, I cannot grasp how to manage it.'

Eleanor's smile, which had been slowly broadening, melted into laughter.

'Oh, Sarah, what are you going to do?'

Sarah shifted her coat onto her shoulder.

'The only thing I can. I must go to London and beg her forgiveness.'

Chapter Forty-nine

*L*ouisa counted the last quarter of maize onto the three-masted barque *Harvest Moon*, the largest ship in her small fleet. Captain Jones, a Bostonian who had also decided to ply his trade away from American waters, was to sail on the late tide, bound for Spain.

'If you see the *Jamestown* on your travels, I beg you will signal her to make haste. I will have strong words with Captain Matthews if he is not here by Saturday,' she said.

'I'll be sure and pass the message on,' Captain Jones said briskly, beckoning his mate. 'There'll be a strong blow tonight, and I'll be happier if we can get out into the estuary before it comes on.'

Louisa disembarked via the gangplank and headed for a nondescript door in the side of a brick warehouse, marked with a brass plate engraved 'Mason's Import and Export'. It led into a tiny office with two desks and a small stove in the corner. The hunched figure of Mr Smythe looked up briefly from his desk, before continuing to enter numbers in his ledger. A small window next to the door gave them a view of the wharves and another at the rear overlooked the floor of the warehouse. Bales of cottons, silks and other textiles recently unloaded from the *Harvest Moon* lay in tall stacks, ready to be collected by her buyers. If only the *Jamestown*, the ship she had bought at auction, could make it to London safely with its cargo of iron she would be well on her way to remaking the Silverton fortune. Numbers had always been her friend and, after the heartache of Kenilborough, Louisa had retreated into their embrace. Accounts and calculations were not fickle or jealous, they were solid and substantial, and never had she been more in need of their comfort as she had these past weeks. She had done her best to banish Sarah from her mind. Only once had she been forced into remembering when, a week ago, there had been a notice in the *Times* announcing Lord Kenilborough's death. Louisa had cast the paper aside and busied herself in preparing a detailed quote for a shipment of prime lumber. It had taken twice as long as it should, but in the end, the numbers worked their usual magic and soothed away Louisa's agitation.

Mr Smythe attracted Louisa's attention by means of a polite cough. They spent the next few hours going over bills of shipping and customs forms. As always, such prosaic activities were a comfort to her. With lists of numbers, there were no motives to fathom, no emotions to battle. The weather began to turn, just as Captain Jones had promised. Louisa told Mr Smythe he might leave early before the weather got any worse, but he said he wished to remain until he had completed his work. She put a pot of coffee on the stove and threw in a couple of logs. Wind howled around the wharves and rain lashed against the outer window like flung pebbles. Louisa pitied anyone out in such conditions. The bitter aroma of coffee filled the office. Her first sip banished any drowsiness and the second had her stalking up and down the room like a cat. Since the office was only a few paces long, she soon grew dizzy from turning about so often. She looked out of the window to see if the *Harvest Moon* had left, but it was dark out and the window so fogged with condensation she could see nothing.

An urgent rap at the door made her jump. Who could be visiting at this late hour, and in such weather?'

She opened the door to a hatless figure, her dark hair and face glistening from the rain, the shoulders of her greatcoat thoroughly soaked. Louisa's heart lurched.

'Sarah?' she gasped. 'How did you find me?' A more urgent question arose within Louisa's breast: what purpose brought Sarah Davenport to her door? That question, however, remained unspoken as Sarah shook water from the cuffs of her coat.

'An excellent question. I was about to give up all hope of finding you amongst these ill-favoured alleys. We have been turned around so many times, I hardly know where we are.'

Her face was pale and pinched with cold. Thomas stood behind her with a trunk on his shoulder, water dripping from the end of his nose. Rain continued to slash against the window. Louisa could hardly turn them away in such foul weather and so, with some misgivings, she beckoned them inside. Speech proved impossible, but she managed to gesture towards the coffee pot. Thomas dropped the trunk and reached for the pot with an eagerness that was quite unlike the usual cool politeness of a servant. He poured a mug, and then recalled himself sufficiently to offer it to his mistress. Sarah, however, was oblivious, engaged in staring at the floor, then at the ceiling. Anywhere except at Louisa, it seemed. Louisa dared not pour another cup for herself; her heart was palpitating enough already.

'How came you here?' she asked at last. Sarah looked to Mr Smythe in a desperate, unspoken plea. He took the hint and quickly packed up his desk. Sarah then transferred her attention to her groom.

'Thomas, I wonder...' she said, in hesitant tones, so unlike her usual self.

'Where am I to go, Miss Sarah?' Thomas asked wearily.

'Do you not have accommodations?' Louisa asked. After a heavy pause, Sarah's shoulders heaved, her feet shifted. She still wore the same boots she had purchased with money from selling her apples in London. One of those apples, Louisa recalled, had been hurled at her head the first time they met. That should have been warning enough, really. But then Sarah spoke.

'We are entirely in your hands, Louisa, for I have not a penny upon me nor a stitch to wear beyond what is in my trunk.'

It was impossible to know what to make of such a statement. Why was Sarah not still at Kenilborough? And why would she come here, to Louisa, after all that had happened between them? Whatever had occurred, Louisa could not countenance poor Thomas being cast back out into the rain. He, at least, did not deserve such a fate.

'Mr Smythe, would you be so good as to show Thomas to my house,' she said. 'Thomas, you must tell Leah I gave express instructions for you to dry yourself by the kitchen fire.'

Thomas nodded gratefully.

'Thankee, miss.'

As soon as they had gone, Sarah ran a hand through her damp hair and shook the droplets from her fingers.

'Louisa, if I could make amends for the way I spoke to you, I would do it in an instant.'

Louisa fiddled with the lid of the coffee pot.

'Can it be? An apology, from Sarah Davenport?'

'There was never one more heartfelt. Or necessary. But I know that mere words are not enough.' When at last she raised her eyes to Louisa, her expression was desolate. Louisa felt a tug at her heart, an urge to forgive her, but fought against it.

'You wounded me,' she said stiffly. 'More than I ever thought possible.'

'I know it,' Sarah returned. 'I don't deserve your forgiveness but find myself unable to live without it.' She spread her arms. 'So here I am, entirely at your mercy.'

'I will be satisfied by nothing less than a complete explanation,' Louisa said querulously. Sarah opened her mouth as if to speak, but Louisa's own need to unburden herself suddenly proved so pressing that she stilled Sarah with a stiff motion of her hand. 'You will not conceal your motives or your feelings. You will not hide behind pride, or duty, or unwanted delicacy over what you imagine to be my needs. You will speak from your heart, or not at all!' she said, her voice rising with passion.

Sarah's shoulders sagged.

'You shall have it. Upon my word, Louisa, you deserve nothing less. But there is so much to say, and I have been three days on the road. I do not believe I can stand up another moment.'

She swayed and fell forward into Louisa's body. She was surprisingly heavy and her clothes so sodden the front of Louisa's own dress was soon wet with transferred moisture.

'Sorry,' Sarah mumbled, attempting to right herself. 'God, but I'm so sorry. I have made such a mess of everything.'

Shocked by the unexpected vision of the Honourable Sarah Davenport crumbling in front of her, Louisa decided that explanations could wait.

'Let's get you home and into a hot bath,' she said.

Chapter Fifty

*L*ouisa's lodgings were so small that the copper bath was located in the kitchen. Leah had lined it with linen strips and filled it with bucket after bucket of steaming water. Louisa was so agitated that she had offered to help, a proposal that was greeted with a decided and surprised negative. At last Leah shut the kitchen door behind her and reported that Miss Davenport had sent her away. Louisa could still hardly believe that Sarah was on the other side of that closed door, responsible for the gentle splashes and swirling of water that could be heard. Her heart had not yet settled from the shock of Sarah's appearance and she paced up and down the hallway, her nerves a-flutter, heedless of Leah's questioning looks.

Unable to bear it any longer, she took up an armful of linen cloths and burst into the kitchen on the pretext of bringing something for Sarah to dry herself with, even though she had seen Leah carry in plenty of towels. The tall end of the bath was nearest the door and she could see the back of Sarah's bare shoulders above the copper, her skin gleaming, the muscles gently rippling as she squeezed water from her dark hair. Louisa caught a glimpse of the sinews of her neck before she let the hair fall back in gleaming ropes.

'Might you bring me some clean clothes?' Sarah asked without turning. Steam rolled up from the edges of the bath. Louisa swallowed. She could barely trust herself to speak.

'Certainly. Which should I fetch?'

There was a startled splash as the soap dropped from Sarah's hands.

'Oh, it is you? I thought it was Leah.'

Sarah's head swivelled halfway round, her arms hugging her body, and Louisa felt a perverse pleasure in realising that, for once, Sarah might be the more discomposed of the two of them. There was certainly a pink flush rapidly ascending Sarah's neck, although possibly that was due to nothing more than the heat of the bathwater.

Louisa set down the linens.

'I could not help myself. I had to see that you were really here, for I still cannot believe it. Do you have everything that you require? Should I ask Leah to bring more water?'

Sarah's head disappeared behind the thick copper as she lowered herself into the steaming water. 'Everything is perfect.'

She gave out a sigh of deep contentment. It must have been infectious, for Louisa felt a shifting in the pit of her stomach and a warmth between her thighs that was extremely pleasurable. Sarah sat up again and began to soap under her arms.

'I must have mud and dirt in every crease and wrinkle,' she said, rubbing up a lather.

'I, er, could get Leah to help you wash,' Louisa said weakly. So much for composure!

'No need. I am used to managing such things myself. If you are going to stay, you should take a chair.'

Louisa wondered if she would ever be able to breathe properly again. The only chair was at the other side of the room. In deference to Sarah's privacy, she kept her eyes resolutely averted as she retrieved the chair and took it back behind the high end of the bath. Even so, she could not help but catch a glimpse out of the corner of her eye of a bent knee, emerging from the sudsy water and the thrilling dip and swell of Sarah's breasts above the linen-draped rim of the bath. It took every ounce of Louisa's resolve not to turn her head. The chair landed with a bit of a thud and she sat down with a gasp and attempted to retrieve her poise.

Sarah began to soap and then rinse her hair, an undertaking that gave Louisa enough time to recover herself. Why should she feel so discomposed? It was Sarah, after all, who owed her an explanation.

'Are you ready to explain yourself?' she blurted out. Sarah froze, a sponge pressed against her shoulder.

'Cannot it wait, just a little longer?' she pleaded, her voice strained with fatigue. Louisa felt instantly ashamed of her own impatience. However much she wanted to hear what Sarah had to say, it was unfair to force any kind of confession while Sarah was at such a disadvantage. She murmured her assent and they sat in silence until Sarah had finished her ablutions.

At last, Sarah asked for a drying cloth and reminded Louisa that she needed clean clothes. Louisa could have called Leah, but she did not wish to share Sarah with anybody, not even her maid, and so she went herself. Opening Sarah's trunk, which Thomas had deposited in the hallway, the first thing she came across was Sarah's faded blue riding skirts. And then the green twill gown — the 'old favourite'. Louisa ran her hands over them, memories resurfacing. At the bottom of the trunk was the pearl grey silk that Sarah had worn for Ann's wedding. Louisa lay it carefully over her forearm and picked up a patched chemise and a pair of drawers. Touching Sarah's undergarments did nothing to quell the fever in her blood, but she steeled herself. However deep her physical attraction to Sarah, she would not give way. Not until they understood one another. She returned to the bathroom. Sarah was standing next to the bath swathed in a large linen cloth, her shoulders bare and glistening, her feet and ankles peeping out below. She looked like a statue of some Roman goddess in a toga, only all too real and most definitely flesh. Trembling, Louisa laid the silk dress on the back of the chair with the undergarments on top. Beside them, she placed a flat velvet box that she had fetched from her own room, and then left Leah to help Sarah dress.

Louisa began to make her own toilette. In general, she wasted little time deciding what to wear, but this evening she could not settle upon a choice, picking up and discarding half a dozen options before settling upon a deep purple velvet with silver threads beneath its high waist. In the absence of her maid, she attempted to pile her hair into an elegant swirl but her hands were trembling so much she made a poor job of it. Giving up, she ran a brush through her dark tresses and let them fall where they may, before descending to her small parlour to await her guest. Sarah came in not long after. Louisa thought she had never looked so well, not even at the wedding. Her skin retained its glow from the heat of the bath and her eyes seemed more vividly blue than ever, augmented by the necklace of sapphires she wore around her neck. As Louisa gazed upon her, Sarah's satin-gloved hand went to her throat and her fingers rested on the necklace, a self-conscious gesture that was most unlike her.

'It seems odd to wear it again, after so long,' she said with a half-smile.

'It must be fate, for I retrieved it from the pawnshop only yesterday,' said Louisa. 'I was going to send it to Kenilborough, but you have saved me the trouble of doing so.'

The necklace was such a strong reminder of their history, of Sarah's selflessness, that Louisa felt some of her remaining hurt and anger drift away.

'I hope this means your business is doing well?' Sarah asked.

'It is.'

'I am glad of it.' Sarah's relief was clear. 'It was why I sent you away. I couldn't allow you to sacrifice all this for me.'

'You did more than send me away. You broke my heart,' Louisa said bitterly. She saw the words hit home but couldn't bring herself to regret them. Sarah spread her hands in contrition.

'I have never regretted anything more completely. To be the cause of such pain, after the infinite kindness you showed me, was unforgivable. And yet here I am, desperately hoping you will.'

The Sarah Davenport that stood abjectly before her reminded Louisa of the broken woman who wept in her arms the night of the wedding. It was a Sarah she suspected few would ever see and her heart, already softened, gave way.

'If I had my time again, I would act with more consideration for your feelings,' Sarah added morosely.

But perhaps, after all, there had been no other way. If Sarah had been any less harsh, Louisa would never have left

Kenilborough. Some other trader would have bought the *Jamestown* at auction and her hopes of rebuilding her fortunes would have foundered. Could she really expect Sarah to be anything other than herself? She had never been fickle — Louisa could see that now. Instead, she had been selfless. Her apparent cruelty had been an act of honour and friendship of the highest kind.

'Even with your father on his deathbed, you thought only of me.' It was a startling revelation and Louisa's heart swelled. Sarah pressed the heel of her hand against her forehead, a gesture Louisa remembered well.

'I just wish I had expressed myself better, instead of trampling over your feelings.'

'That is quite a specialty of yours,' Louisa observed, but her bitterness had vanished. Now that she understood, all that remained was love. And desire. The only question was whether Sarah felt the same.

Sarah plucked at the high-waisted dress. 'You chose my new gown,' she remarked. 'It really should be kept for special occasions.'

Louisa reached out and took Sarah's hands in her own, barely trusting her voice.

'As far as I am concerned, there can be no occasion more special than this. I will forever remember the day you finally let yourself ask for my help. My house can never be Kenilborough, but you must consider it as your home. Were you family, you could not be more welcome.'

'Once I had no responsibilities, I wished only to be with you,' Sarah returned. 'But I cannot permit...' she began, breaking away. 'I must...' She paused. Louisa waited as Sarah paced up and down like a groom waiting for his bride. At last she came to a stop and her blue eyes locked onto Louisa's.

'I cannot let you share your house — to grant me such kindness, without us coming to a complete understanding. I must tell you, as I have wanted to do for so long, how much I love you.'

And, at that moment, Louisa's world was made whole. She would have spoken, but Sarah hurried onwards.

'Not only do I admire your intelligence, your candour and your resilience, but I ache to hold you in my arms. To kiss your lips and your skin. To breathe your scent. To...'

Before she knew what she was doing, Louisa pressed her lips against Sarah's with such passion she could no longer breathe. Sarah responded with an urgency that thrilled her. When at last they broke off, Sarah looked at Louisa in amused confusion.

'What do we do now?'

Louisa kissed her again, desperate for another taste of Sarah's soft, warm lips.

'Whatever we want,' she whispered, her voice husky with desire.

Sometime later, Louisa woke, her limbs entangled with Sarah's, their foreheads touching. Javelins of golden light streamed in through a gap between the drapes of the nearest window. It must have been late morning, perhaps even noon.

'Are you awake?' she whispered.

'Mm-mm,' Sarah murmured in return, her arms tightening around Louisa's body.

'That was...' Louisa hesitated, trying to find the right words.

'Lovely?'

'Yes. Quite lovely. It is a shame it took us so long to understand one another.'

Sarah planted a kiss on Louisa's forehead.

'It was not I who left the country and then neglected to inform anyone of my return.'

'And it was not I who sent you away when I needed you the most,' Louisa replied, prodding Sarah's shoulder. She turned onto her back, one arm pillowing her head. 'How long have you loved me?' she asked. She felt the tips of Sarah's fingers gently brush a strand of hair from her cheek.

'I admired you the very first time I saw you, beneath the apple tree. You looked so perplexed and yet so curious. It was excessively charming.'

'I always wondered whether you hit me with that apple on purpose.'

'It was not consciously done. But I must have been distracted, for my aim is not usually so poor. After that, I soon learned to love you for your spirit and your intelligence. You cannot know how many times I wished to tell you. But it seemed I could not — not until I was free of Kenilborough.'

'Did I not admonish you for putting duty before all?' Louisa teased.

'You were right. And to think I had the audacity to lecture *you* about love.'

'I deserved it. To have ever preferred money over this.' She lifted her head and kissed Sarah affectionately on the lips. Sarah raised herself onto an elbow.

'Tell me — when did you begin to have such feelings? Hurling apples at your head, I'm sure, did not make for a good impression.'

'You underestimate how splendid your legs appear in pantaloons. It is an image that has often filled my dreams.'

Sarah nodded sagely.

'Ah, so it was not my character that first attracted you? That I quite believe.'

'I saw your qualities and felt your charm early in our relationship. But I was brought up in a house without love. I did not understand or value what I felt.'

'It was not until the ball at Athelton that I began to acknowledge the true nature of my feelings,' Sarah admitted.

'For me it was Plymouth.'

Sarah closed her eyes. 'It broke my heart to watch you sail off on that packet,' she murmured. 'I almost jumped off the quay to swim out to you.'

Louisa laughed.

'I had a similar notion, although mine involved a boat.'

'Practical, as ever,' Sarah remarked appreciatively.

'But in London, you were not so certain?' Louisa queried, as Sarah's face hovered above hers.

'If anything, my feelings had grown more powerful in your absence. It took every ounce of strength not to kiss you, outside the bank. You look extremely attractive in black. Although there is not a colour I do not love you in.'

Louisa lifted the white cotton sheet, which was all that was covering Sarah's modesty.

'Whereas I prefer to see you thus,' she said. 'And vow to take every opportunity to do so in future.'

She cast off the sheet and kissed Sarah again with a fierce but tender passion and they did not stray from the bed for the remainder of the day.

Chapter Fifty-one

*S*arah insisted Louisa put her to work.

'You know I prefer to be busy.'

Louisa was grateful to have such a strong, active partner in the business. There was plenty to do in negotiating contracts, writing invoices and disbursing payment to their employees, all work with which Sarah was familiar. Knowing that Sarah was a shrewd judge of character, Louisa entrusted her with hiring staff as the company expanded. They purchased more ships at auction, the continued blockades of American ports causing other traders to founder. With Sarah assisting Mr Smythe in running the business, Louisa was free to concentrate on more strategic concerns and they began to buy and sell, in addition to shipping. She travelled to Cadiz and Toulouse to establish subsidiary offices there and, as soon as peace was announced between Britain and America, they established a trade route to Boston, where Louisa took every opportunity to negotiate for the resumption of the canal project. She explained to Sarah that, if they could get the canal completed at last, her shares, long considered valueless, would be worth a fortune.

For almost a year, they had time for nothing but work. In any case, Louisa's small house with its single bedroom and tiny parlour was hardly suitable for entertaining. Poor Thomas slept in the attic, since Leah had long since taken possession of the kitchen. With no servants' staircase, they were forever bumping into one another. Louisa thought that Sarah, used to the airy chambers of Kenilborough, took it with as much grace as could be expected.

The only holiday they took from work was to attend Eleanor's wedding. Sarah admitted to some unease at the prospect of returning to Athelton, it being so close to Kenilborough.

'I thought you missed it dreadfully,' said Louisa. 'Or were those regretful remarks concerning spring planting a ruse so that I would take you with me to Cadiz?'

'I recall you were thankful for my presence during the voyage. At night, in particular.'

'It is true that you earned some credit,' said Louisa with a smile. She had thought it impossible to love Sarah more than when she had finally declared herself, but their joy in each other only grew as they lived and worked together. Their lives were not without discord, for neither were afraid to speak their mind. However, they were quick to resolve their disputes and their trust in each other had deepened as they became partners in business, as much as in life.

'I do not trust myself to keep my temper if I should encounter Joseph, acting the lord of the manor,' said Sarah, returning to the subject at hand. 'That my father should be replaced by such a man. I dread to see what ruination he has brought upon the place, or hear the recriminations of our people, forced to labour for such a wicked, dissipated fellow.'

'But you will go?'

'I would not let down Eleanor for the world. Besides, I look forward to the general astonishment that will be aroused by my appearing in yet another new dress.'

They had recently shipped a large order of Spanish silks, from which Louisa negotiated samples for personal use. Thomas, who had proven adept at making friends among the denizens of Rotherhithe, found a seamstress who made them two dresses of sprigged muslins in the latest style, set off by Spencer jackets made from the lush Spanish silks. Louisa's was gold and studded with polished black beads while Sarah's was a rich, deep blue, embroidered in gold thread. Louisa felt the jackets were a mirror to their relationship — each distinct and unique but working together in harmony.

In the end, there was no need to pass through Kenilborough's lands after all, for Eleanor wrote to say they were to be married aboard the *Cadmus*, now docked at Plymouth. She had insisted she would much prefer a simple ceremony among Robert's friends than being stared at by everyone in the county. Robert's former captain performed the wedding himself, and Louisa took great pleasure in Eleanor's blushing delight. Sarah offered heartfelt congratulations and warm kisses to the bride. Even more pleasing, from Louisa's view, was that she was able to give Mr Kirk five hundred pounds as a wedding gift.

'Let you be the first of the customers of Silverton's Bank to receive what is due to them,' she said.

Mr Kirk thanked her, as did Captain Williams, who was there with Ann. He even shook her hand and apologised for any offence his previous resentment had caused. Louisa assured him she would never blame him for being loyal to his friend.

'Have you any news of Kenilborough?' Sarah asked Eleanor, once all was done.

'Everyone regrets your absence,' Eleanor reported. 'I cannot say how many people have stopped to tell me they wish Miss Sarah was here and to ask to be remembered to you. Your stepbrother is much disliked. He has increased rents and Robert tells me they were late with the planting. Joseph has dismissed two stewards already, and at present there is no-one managing things at all. He spends more time gaming in London than he does on the estate. But I have some news that I hope will please you. My father has bought Jack. I mean to give him to Robert as a wedding gift.'

'Bless you,' said Sarah, and Louisa could tell that she was deeply moved. 'To know that Jack has a good home is such a comfort.'

Everyone enjoyed the celebrations, although Louisa sensed a pensiveness behind Sarah's smiles.

'What's wrong?' she asked Sarah, as they sat down for the wedding breakfast. 'Something is itching at you, I can tell.'

'Nothing of consequence. You know that Captain Williams has been called up again. There is to be another Spanish campaign. Ann will need every comfort we can give her.'

'I suspect that seeing Eleanor and Ann has made you homesick for Kenilborough?'

'A little.' Sarah covered Louisa's hand in hers. 'Dearest Louisa, do not think for an instant that I do not cherish our time together. You have made me happier than I ever deserved. But Kenilborough is a part of me; I cannot help but feel its loss from my life.'

Chapter Fifty-two

*L*ater that year, there took place the famous battle of Waterloo. Captain Williams was one of the many thousands involved in that bloody exchange. Against all expectations, his valour did not get him killed but instead found him promoted, without the need to pay for the privilege, to the rank of colonel. He was afterwards posted to the tropical climes of the East Indies where Ann gave birth to a boy and then a girl in quick succession. Sarah regretted their absence, but with the trade and shipping company taking up all her time, she had to content herself with reading Ann's letters and writing back in return. Louisa was busier than ever, working late into the nights. They saw so little of each other that Sarah grew concerned Louisa was becoming ensnared, like her father, in the addictive lure of making profit for profit's sake. There was surely no need for such assiduousness, for the canal scheme had come to fruition. Together with the income from the shipping business, Louisa had at last been able to make restitution to all those who had lost money in her father's bank. But when Sarah suggested that Louisa take a less active role in the company, so they might spend more time together, Louisa smiled in a particular way and shook her head, insisting there was more work to do.

The summer following the Battle of Waterloo was a devastating one for farmers, as the skies remained dark all summer. Crops failed and landowners up and down the country were ruined in their droves. Kenilborough suffered more than most, for Joseph Davenport had never been the sort of man to set aside provisions against future misfortune. So blind was he to his own culpability, he sought to save himself by increasing his rents at the very time his tenants, suffering under the same climactic calamity, could never satisfy such unreasonable demands. Local feelings ran so high that it surprised nobody when Joseph Davenport was attacked by a mob and felled by a stone to the head. That was enough to kill him, which at least saved him the ignominy of being taken to a debtors' prison, for there were several writs out in his name, including one from his particular friend Mr Cossington.

Sarah did not know whether to rejoice or despair at the news. No one could argue that Joseph did not deserve his fate and she was not such a hypocrite as to mourn his loss. But it was painful to see the notices in the newspapers when her beloved Kenilborough was put up for sale to pay off its secured debts. Even more painful to read, a week later, that an offer had been made and accepted.

'They do not say who has bought it,' Sarah said in frustration as Louisa, casually, dropped a sheaf of papers in front of her. 'What is this? It looks like a formal contract of some kind.'

'The deeds to Kenilborough.'

'But they are in my name!' Sarah exclaimed, scanning the

documents. She turned to Louisa in utter disbelief. 'You have done this?'

Louisa rested her palms on Sarah's cheeks and planted a kiss on her forehead.

'My darling, you have permitted me to follow my inclinations and achieve all that I have dreamed of and more. Let me do the same for you. Before you thank me, I must warn you there is a mortgage attached. After paying off the investors in Silverton's Bank, I had not sufficient funds to buy it outright. Hoare's took the shipping company as collateral. But I know you, and I am quite certain you will be clear of debt before we are five-and-thirty.'

'This is what you have been working for? When I have chastised you for reverting to your old habits?'

'You have nothing to fear. I know now to value money only for the good it can do. And there is nothing I wish more than to see you back at Kenilborough.'

Epilogue

*A*nd so, three years after she had been so ignominiously banished, Sarah returned home. Lady Kenilborough was not forgotten. Out of duty to her father, and in acknowledgement that Lady Kenilborough was not wholly wicked, Sarah and Louisa provided her with an annuity of two hundred pounds per year, together with a respectable house in London. Living in the capital was sure to suit the dowager viscountess better than Kenilborough and had the advantage that stepmother and stepdaughter would not be forced to live together, a situation that could bring no pleasure to either party.

As Sarah and her friend were seen entering Kenilborough's park, side by side in a new barouche, there was great rejoicing. Everybody in the neighbourhood agreed that having Miss Sarah Davenport back in charge was only right and proper. Sarah's happiness was complete when Colonel Williams was posted back to England and she was reunited with her sister. Ann's children, Robert and Sarah, were soon firm favourites with their Kenilborough aunts. In due course, when wills came to be written, they were given equal portions, for neither Louisa nor

Sarah would countenance favouring a male heir over a female and, although both agreed that money alone was not the route to happiness, it certainly never hurt.

Acknowledgements

A Lady to Treasure has had a long road to publication, and I am grateful to the many people who have helped Sarah and Louisa on their journey. During early negotiations with another publisher I received a lot of editorial feedback on the novel. Although we were unable to agree contractual terms, I remain grateful to those unnamed individuals whose advice improved the book immeasurably. At various points in development, my wonderful beta readers Jess Lawrence, Michele Hutchison, Suzanne Moss and Katherine Blakeman provided invaluable insight and gave me confidence I was on the right path. I am grateful to Alice and Lisa at Bellows Press for their collaborative ethos, and for agreeing to continue our collaboration with *A Lady to Treasure*. Special shout out to my editor, Lisa Findley, for correcting my most egregious errors and for loving the book every bit as much as I do.

Finally, I'd like to thank my wife, Sharon, and my parents, Richard and Sylvia Ratcliffe, who are generally happy (or at least willing) to be roped in as additional proofreaders. Your support and love are what keeps this writer going.